The Lives
of Ghosts

MEGAN TAYLOR

Weathervane Press

Weathervane Press

Published in 2012 by Weathervane Press

www.weathervanepress.co.uk

ISBN 978 0 9562193 6 7

Cover image © Robcoquyt Dreamstime.com

Printed by Lightning Source

For Nigel Pickard

There were ghosts at the loch house long before we arrived with ours. Marie told me about them towards the end of the journey. After nine hours behind the wheel and all that silence, her voice didn't sound right. It was hollow and tinny and seemed to scrape at the air trapped between us. Air that had smelt of melting rubber for the entire four hundred mile drive.

"There have always been stories about the place," she said. "Sightings of shadowy figures and sudden lights. Strange noises in the night. For a while, we even thought about including them in the brochure. Some people like that kind of thing."

My new stepmother appeared to be talking for the sake of it, probably chatting to ward off the panic as the reality of what she was doing finally started to set in. Her eyes flicked at me in the rear-view mirror, a dark, wet flash and then away, and her shoulders hunched until she was practically cowering in her seat, clinging to that wheel. She certainly wasn't thinking straight to say the things she said.

"According to local legend, there are four or five, at least. A grey lady, of course – there's always a grey lady, and some old scraggy wise-woman type, perhaps a witch, from long ago. And a fisherman, lost out on the loch – actually, I bet there are a few of those, but this one left his widow too, still waiting at the house. She killed herself when he didn't come back. Hung herself, I think."

While Marie spoke, I turned away, away from her and from the junk piled alongside me in the cramped back seat. There was so much, her unfamiliar clothes and books and a few of my things, my metallic pens and bead-kit. My ancient Girl's World head wedged against my thigh. I was sick of looking at it all, as I was sick, already, of listening to Marie. The last thing I needed then was her thin, mindless chatter, her stumbling voice, so different from my mother's. I leant against the car window. Outside, there was only blue sky and yellow-lit grass. The blue was endless and very still, but beneath it, the grass moved in deep, slow swathes and ripples. It made me think of cat fur, of Mr Whiskers, left behind.

When I felt Marie's gaze again, quick, but cloying, I didn't turn. In the distance, across the grass, there was a black speckling of birds like a spreading rash. Crows, I decided. If I squinted, I could see that they were moving, but only just. Bobbing across that tide of grass. Pecking, I supposed.

"We used to be terrified, when we were kids," Marie went on. "Jamie, that's my brother – *was* my brother, he'd spend the whole summer playing tricks on me, jumping out of wardrobes. Putting ketchup on the sheets. Though really, I think that he was just as scared as I was."

Inside my head, I began to hum. Wondering why she thought I might be interested in her brother, in her family at all. Through the window, I watched the black specks crawl and separate and rise. 'A murder of crows', I remembered. Dad had told me that. Despite the day's shine, the glass was icy-cold against my forehead, but I kept my face there. I pressed harder, and felt the jolt of the car's wheels inside my teeth.

"Oh," Marie went on, just as brightly. Just as stupidly. "There was supposed to be a child-ghost too. Another drowning, I think. A young girl, apparently. About the same age as you –"

She stopped, hearing herself at last. She didn't gasp, but she might as well have. The thick air sucked in around her and I felt the chill from the window creep down my neck, and up again, beneath my hair. Goosebumps unfurled along my skinny arms. I kept my palms pushed flat against the pane, my small jaw gritted.

"Damn," she said. "Oh, Damn and Christ, Libby . . ."

Her voice had fallen, it was low and whispery now, dangerously soft; I hoped that she wouldn't start crying again. If she started to cry, if she so much as sniffed, I thought I might scream – although it wasn't her ghost stories that bothered me. She should have known that.

Despite the 'Misty' annuals buried in my suitcase (two dog-eared volumes of comic-strips featuring ghoulish teachers and cavernous portals and creeping, severed hands), the last three weeks had wiped away any belief I had in the supernatural. The world had become too solid for such fantasies, too harsh and real and hurting. There were no longer any mysteries, just cold, sharp facts.

And besides, I'd seen photos of the loch house and it didn't look haunted. It didn't even look real. It was too square and white, with a row of evenly spaced windows tucked beneath the roof and a bright red door. It was too obvious, like a kid's drawing – not that I'd have ever drawn a house that way.

In the front of the car, Marie was managing not to cry. Or sniff, even. I pulled myself away from the distant birds and the grass and the blue, to stare at the greasier stripes of hair sticking to her crown, and at her shoulder blades bunched-tight beneath her cheap, bobbled cardigan. Mouse-brown hair. Porridge-coloured wool.

At the cattery, Mr Whiskers had put his claws into that wool after she had dragged him from his carrier. He'd unhooked stray threads into baggy loops, and then drawn strings of blood across her fingers. But when they closed the cage, Marie had wept as if he was her cat, while I just walked away. I didn't put my hands to the mesh, I didn't touch him goodbye. As I reached the door, I had heard her blubbering behind me, and then a jangling crash as she dropped the contents of her handbag on to the tiled floor. No doubt fruitlessly searching for a tissue.

"That witch ghost," I said, and my voice remained totally my own, clear and precise as I leant towards that ratty hair. "Did she keep cats?"

Marie turned her face; she opened her mouth, but didn't speak. She shook her head instead and I found some satisfaction in that, as I did in the warm flutter of her sigh a moment later. A wave of helplessness that rolled out of her, despite herself. I let it lap over me. In the mirror, her eyes glittered. They were almost black.

The silence resumed between us as we drove on, although now there was a kind of ringing to the quiet, and I felt an ache beginning, in my skull. The rubber smell deepened, becoming something scorched, and outside, the trees reappeared, the furthest ones a spray of feathers and splinters, embedded in the blue. They were only just beginning to yellow at their edges, but it wouldn't be long until they changed, their softness vanishing altogether.

I was twelve years old. And I was ancient. I pictured my head drifting with dust instead of thoughts. I wanted that. But the turns in the winding road were distracting; they nagged at me, they kept me there. I realised that more than anything else, I was longing to be still.

The car, which had been grating uphill for a while, reached the summit all at once. The sparse trees and swirling grass fell away and for a moment, there was only that blue. The sky held us –

And then the valley opened and there was so much to see, I could only snatch at it in pieces. I glimpsed overgrown fields and the broken lines of dry-stone walls. Several shaggy pines towered over a great pyre of blackened logs, while gentler trees and bushes queued towards the water's edge. Down there, the shivering foliage grew gauzy beside a white crockery tumble of shattered-looking rocks. And in the midst of everything, the massive silver of the loch.

7

I winced and closed my eyes against the flash, but felt the burn even through my lids. The car descended rapidly. The road had become surprisingly smooth, as if we were slipping down some vast, soft throat, and when I opened my eyes again, the land felt thicker, closer.

I found myself grabbing for my window, cranking at the handle. As I wound down the glass, the scent of water was so strong that I could taste it; it filled my mouth with glistening stones. We rounded another bend and there before us, was the loch house, looking just like its picture, except that there was a car parked at an awkward angle outside, and people too, a man and a woman, their bags strewn about the drive.

"Damn it," said Marie. "They were supposed to leave last night."

The wide, rusted gate stood open and we bumped through it over a cattle grid, invisible beneath a carpet of mud and fallen leaves. The house grew larger. This close, its whitewash was not so dazzling. Age had soured it in places. Long greenish water-stains ran in giant fingers from the guttering and the door's vibrant paint was peeling, flaking away in ragged strips.

The man scarcely registered our arrival. He appeared busy with his fishing rod, but then instead of packing it up properly, he drew back one arm and simply threw it, spearing the yawning mouth of his Datsun's boot. Only the woman tilted her head towards us, narrowing her eyes. She stood with her arms folded while the breeze played with her blue-black hair, lifting it from her scalp in coiling springs, matting it like fleece.

Marie pulled over.

She cut the engine, but then simply sat there, in the emptiness, head bowed, clutching her keys.

"Damn, damn, damn," she muttered, before finally sagging against the door.

Her handbag bundled out first, the strap becoming tangled with her broad, clodhopping feet. She wore such heavy, sensible shoes, with thick soles and tightly knotted laces, but they didn't stop her tripping up. Briefly, I met the black haired woman's hazel eyes. I felt her cool, sharp smile play across my own pursed lips. But then Marie hovered between us and although I couldn't catch a single word she said, the tremor in her voice rattled all the way back to where I sat, among her luggage.

I gazed past them to the loch. I couldn't help it; it pulled at me, although it wasn't silver anymore, but a perfect petrol blue. Still

8

gleaming. With an effort, I turned and saw that the windows of the loch house were shining with the same slick light. The red front door was closed and judging from the visitors' bags and their open boot, I thought that the house must be empty – and yet that blue at the windows made it appear full. Full to brimming.

Then the red door slammed open and my heart swung with it, but in the next instant, I was rolling my eyes. There was a girl in the doorway, that was all. A girl with the same broad, brooding face as the black-haired woman. Her daughter, I supposed. She was older than me, fourteen at least.

She wore a turquoise beret and a denim jacket, a smear of lip-gloss so generous that I could see its glimmer from the car. The red door fell slowly shut behind her, but she left the house with wide, bouncing strides without once glancing back. Of course she'd be impatient to be gone. After all, what was there to keep her? Barely anything at all…

As she approached Marie's car, she stared right in. An impressive grey gum bubble expanded from her shimmering mouth and then snapped back, frog-like, against her face. Behind it, her expression was more bored than curious and when her eyes found mine, she slung out a long, slow, curling look, as if I was scum. She'd probably been practising that look all week (what with so little else to do), but where once I might have eyeballed her straight back, or barked "Yeah – what?" now I caught myself ducking away.

My hand rose involuntarily to brush my eyes, my lips. My features felt overblown, big and bare and babyish against my thin, scrubbed face. I was aware too of the tangles nesting at my neck. My dirty-blond hair was un-brushed, untamed, already growing free of its usual rigorous bob. I felt momentarily ashamed, ill-made. As if I was no better than Marie.

Except that I could never be like her. Not in a thousand years, *not in a million.*

I pushed open my door and climbed out in one smooth motion, though there was a chill to the air that I hadn't expected and the loch smell was even stronger down here. Danker. There were pungent undercurrents of slimy weeds and rotting leaves and old dead fish. The girl kept walking. She took no notice of me, but slipped into the back seat of her car, holding her turquoise beret to her head.

Meanwhile Marie went on speaking; she looked very young beside the black haired woman's harsh-set jaw and folded arms, almost as young as the beret girl. And while Marie squeaked, her hand

9

travelled slowly across her cement-coloured stomach. Her fingers crept and circled; they fiddled with her cardigan buttons before slipping back into an absent caress. She couldn't have felt much, there wasn't much there – a slight thickening perhaps, that was all. But then she wouldn't really have started to show yet, not properly; I knew that. I knew a lot of things I wasn't meant to. When Marie's other hand joined the first, I turned away, disgusted.

The girl cut across their gabbling: "For God`s sake Mum, can't we just go?"

I focused on the loch while their doors slammed and their engine caught. The water was like something alien now, an impossible metal plate that went on and on. Even the wind seemed tentative around it, ruffling it into small, silken spirals. It hardly made a sound.

The crump of the cattle grid was louder. I glanced back to see the Datsun bumping over it, and then Marie, returning to stand at my side. Black exhaust smoke trailed towards us, but the girl didn't turn. Through the rear window, the turquoise circle of her hat grew smaller and smaller. As I watched it disappear, something tugged, and then tore bitterly inside me. An unexpected part of me was rising up, crying out.

Come back, please. Come back…

"Well," Marie said. "Well, then. Here we are."

She reached out, but I stepped backwards, dodging her hand. I couldn't look at her, and even the loch was changing, shifting. I caught the darkness beneath that shining surface, its secret cold – and I realised I was scared. Scared of this place and of Marie's touch, and of crying when I hadn't cried yet, not once since I'd lost my parents. Not a single tear in those last three terrible weeks.

Not now, I thought. Please.

Not here, not now, with her, and I weaved out of her reach, hating her and her loch house, hating the loch itself for the way that it flashed and flickered and grabbed at me. I turned and strode off, but I felt it all closing in – the blue sky, the water, *Marie*. Even the distant birds were back, a blackness breaking overhead.

Swiping at my face, I tried to focus, to at least keep going, but when I reached the red door, I found it stuck, the loch house barred to me. Frustrated, I tugged at the small iron handle and then slapped at the patchy wood, at that coiling paint. I could sense Marie's cautious approach and I was about to draw back, but it was then that the door relented –

Opening with such a smooth, surprising ease, I stumbled. Feeling hoodwinked, disorientated. It was as if the shadows waiting in the hallway had been playing a game with me. Some kind of trick. And in a jumbled rush, I remembered what Marie had said.

A child ghost, I remembered.

A young girl, the same as me.

Even after twenty-five years, that moment remains. Those first seconds when the loch house held me. I can still feel my bewilderment. The sudden, soft clay darkness of the hall...

But I am being ridiculous. It was so long ago.

I shake my head and press my fingers deeper into the suitcase, absurdly grateful for the brief warmth as I smooth and flatten my packed clothes. I tuck in a pair of balled-up stockings, crammed too hastily down one side. But despite the layers of wool and cotton, and the flat's steady heat, my hands remain stiff with cold, perhaps anticipating Scotland already. I gaze down at my trimmed nails and ring-less fingers, at the veins running in fine blue cords beneath my skin, and I find myself thinking: *old lady hands*, which is also ridiculous when I'm not even thirty-eight. Still the right side of forty. In so many ways, I haven't begun.

And yet: *Twenty-five years since the loch house.*

Twenty-five years since the car crash that killed my parents. Since my stepmother, Marie –

A quarter of a century.

That's how long it has taken to even consider returning, although Dr Gilchrist told me that I should, all that time ago, attempting to explain about facts and truth. About the gulf of space, the haunted grey, between them.

That's what I'm travelling towards now, I think, that *grey*. And I picture the loch house as if it's on a T.V. screen, flickering behind a veil of static; that's where I'm going. If it's possible to actually reach it, through the rain inside my head.

But already, that's enough.

That's enough speculating and imagining, and more than enough of Dr Gilchrist too. I push the lid of the case firmly closed. I tug at the zip. But it seals with a noise like something tearing open, the sound grating against the room's ticking quiet. And it's only a matter of minutes, I realise, until the cab arrives.

Leaving the case on the bed, I walk into the kitchen. It's warmer there, almost humid, the brightest room in the flat. Sunlight rests in large pale panels across the tiles. I walk straight through them to the fridge, to the half-full bottle of wine, although I know I shouldn't. I ease out the jammed-back cork and stare at the faint, peachy half-smile smearing the rim. Yesterday's lipstick. *How crass*, I think, as if that mark might belong to somebody else, an uninvited visitor, a stranger in the night. I don't have much time; nonetheless, I fetch one of the good glasses from the draining board. I hold it up to the light and check for fingerprints before pouring.

Lemony sunshine, lemony wine.

As always, the glint and soft glugs evoke soothing memories of my mother. I think of her airy laugh and her clinking ice, and "Just a little one," I reason, as she might have. Just enough to take the edge off, to calm these thoughts. Surely that can't do much harm?

But then my mobile trills, and I jump. The glass knocks against my teeth and I swallow hard, fumbling the phone across the counter with my spare hand, before finally managing to grapple it to my face. *Richard*, I think, but of course it isn't Richard. Richard's far away, with his family. It's the cab driver. He's here already, waiting outside.

The gleaming windows make me blink. For a few seconds, my vision quivers with a warmth that I don't allow to spill.

"Give me a minute," I say. "I'll be right there."

Except after he's rung off, I don't gather up my things straightaway. Instead I drink steadily, until I've finished the glass. I drink with concentration, feeling the starchy chill slipping through me, reaching deep within me and then rising, to fill my face, my forehead. I welcome the shudder that it brings, and how that shudder falls away.

You can do this, I tell myself. You *need* to do this. It's the only way.

And then, as if I'm any ordinary traveller, I check I have my purse, my keys, my phone. I wheel my case out from the bedroom. I trail one old-lady-hand across the neat gold dimmer switch in its neat gold frame. *Goodbye little flat*, I think, and I'm coping. I really am –

Until I'm out in the hallway at the top of the stairs, pulling the heavy door closed and that other door, that red loch house door, returns to me once more. The feel of it, rough and resistant against my skinny fingers. And all over again, I'm watching Marie's hand explore her buttons; I see her just-swelling belly, swathed in wool.

I feel a dragging from my own stomach. But I don't touch it. I dare not touch it.

Exhaustion washes over me. I close my eyes. Rest my head on the panelled wood.

13

"Liberty?"

I turn, forced back.

Mrs Palmer is standing in her doorway opposite, a small, knotted bin-bag clasped at her side. She isn't a tall woman or a wide woman, but there is something about her presence, or perhaps simply the intensity of her floral blouses, that gives her bulk. A thin smile hovers through her inoffensive lipstick. The most neutral shade of rose.

It's the first time that I've seen my neighbour, that she has spoken to me, for about three months. Our last communication was the note she slipped under my door after Richard and I came stumbling in too late one night. I think of her precise handwriting, that gentle lilac ink – *If you're unable to return home at a decent hour, could you please consider other residents when using the communal stairs...*

But, "Off on your holidays?" she says now, seemingly friendly, nodding at my case.

I open my mouth to reply. I hear something click.

I stare beyond Mrs Palmer, to her wallpaper. Pink stripes, pink borders edged with silver leaves and a whole gallery of pictures of young kids, many of them babies, in matching frames. *Fifteen godchildren*, she once told me, although I hadn't asked.

Her eyes flick from my case back to my face, while her flat's acrid air freshener scent crawls between us. Fake fruit and petals, and beneath it, the smell of something roasting. She's waiting.

And I think of the story that I prepared after I'd first called the taxi firm, when I'd started to panic. When, on top of everything else, I'd imagined a driver full of questions and opinions and gruff, blustering chatter. In my head, I'd scrabbled for words, an explanation. Apart from Richard's answer-phone, I haven't spoken to anyone for days.

I'm going to Scotland to visit an old friend. Haven't seen her for years. We used to holiday together when we were children...

I'd rehearsed it compulsively, dreading the crack in my voice that would give me away. But of course, it's absurd now, useless, and: "Scotland," is all I finally reply. And even that word sticks like old tissues, wadded in my throat.

"Away for a while, are you?"

Naturally, I can't answer that one either. I picture my flat, closed behind me, the sparse, tidy rooms. How long will I be gone? I've tried not to wonder – *don't think*, that's been the plan. *Just go.*

I shrug at her, as if I'm twelve, still. "I've a cab outside," I say.

Her rose lips flutter. "You'd best be off then, hadn't you?"

14

"Yes, I'm going." My voice is petulant. But then to my surprise, I actually find my feet. I'm truly leaving.

As if it was nothing, or simply something normal, maybe *hormonal*, my fatigue has lifted, and I practically bound down the steps, away from Mrs Palmer and her pink stripes and her frames. Her disapproval burns a thin line into the back of my neck, but I don't care. Wondering exactly how much she might have heard on that complained-of night mere months ago, I allow my case to knock loudly, rudely, against the polished wood. I make it ricochet off the skirting boards, and for a few dumb, rebellious seconds, I'm almost happy. Relishing every clatter.

Regardless of my old, cold hands and everything that's happened with Richard lately, that night returns intently – those lurching shadows and how he touched me as we slipped and struggled up these steps. How for a little while, we forgot ourselves – and over all other memories, it's this that I cling to now. How I staggered with his kisses, and how we almost didn't make it to my flat... And by the time I've reached the cool, white hall, my body feels almost my own again, and then, perhaps more than my own. Fizzing with secrets.

Surely it will be all right this time? With this journey, I'm going to make it right.

After all, what happened at the loch house wasn't my fault. *None of it's my fault.* I'm not to blame –

There is no way I'm still *that* child.

On our first, full day at the loch house, I woke in that strange bed, in that strange, pale room and at the beginning, I felt nothing. Nothing at all. The ceiling drifted as if unhinged, and I gazed from one corner to the next, not really understanding where I was, but not really caring. I traced a quiver of cobwebs to the dull brass curtain pole. A pewter rain-light pressed against the glass.

I could hear the rain too, drumming away with its small, suede fingers, but the sound only deepened my detachment. I was nobody; I was nowhere. It wasn't until I turned my head and found the damp patch on my pillow that it all came hurtling back. Then everything was different. Everything reeled. It was like when a medicine ball had hit me smack in the face, in the playground at school. At the same time, it was like falling.

For several minutes, I had to lie as still as I could, breathing shallowly. It was the only way through. *Don't fight it – you can't fight it*, that was one of the first lessons I'd had to learn. Those last three weeks since the accident had been so full of learning that at times I imagined I could hear my skull ringing with it. A faint, discordant jangle, like crockery, swept into a pan.

And of course, I'd dreamt of my parents. As most nights, I dreamt of them – and with that wet patch, so the dream, and the truth of it all, came vividly back.

In my sleep, it was their last night all over again. I'd recreated those final, shining minutes before I lost them. When I wasn't even sitting at their side.

The Drama Club play was ending. I stood on stage with the other kids, against a faded village backdrop, the auditorium air as sweet and musty as the inside of my wooden pencil case, make-up caked across my face. I'd been trying not to rub at that waxy layer all evening, but now that the audience had started to applaud, I hardly felt it. Through the stage lights' haze, I'd finally managed to spot my parents and I wanted to cheer myself I felt so happy.

I didn't understand how I could have missed them before; they were only two rows away, sitting near the front. And they were sitting together. In my dream, I'd felt the surprise of it all over again. The rush of relief that for this night at least, Dad hadn't brought Marie.

And they were both grinning, their clapping hands a blur, their smiling eyes gilded as if the lights were tuned on them.

Now that I'd found them, I could see my parents in startling detail and I concentrated, as I surely hadn't in real life. When my mother rose – she was the first to rise – I glimpsed her black coat, stroked flat over the back of her orange plastic chair. I watched her gloves fall from her lap in a soft, blue tumble. They were her favourite gloves, but she didn't pause to retrieve them; she simply went on clapping. And then Dad was up too, standing beside her.

Despite everything that had happened between them, the shouting and screaming and the sudden icy silences. Despite the smashed plates and the weeping, and the cold, stark truth that they were now officially 'Divorced', they remained a stunning pair. Other parents in the audience glanced up at them not once, but twice, the way that strangers in the street would frequently turn, and then gaze after them. It was usual for women, especially, to stare.

In his own rougher, strong-featured way, Dad was almost as good looking as my ex-model mother. A tall, broad, handsome man with his tanned skin and his crisp cotton, always well dressed, and often laughing. He had a distinct, old-fashioned style. Cufflinks winked at his wrists like tiny stars... In my dream, they flashed as he lifted one large fist in a gesture of only partly mocking solidarity. I understood his meaning right away.

The world is ours, Liberty! Ours for the taking!

But as I stepped forward with the others for the final bow, the stage lights flared brighter too, rising in a wall of white, and as keenly as I'd studied my parents a moment before, I now lost sight of them completely. And I couldn't lose them – *not yet. Please.*

In my dream of course, a part of me knew. A part of me was already seething, already longing.

But it shouldn't happen until later, not until much later, on their dark drive home.

It wasn't fair; they were meant to come to see me first. They'd said goodbye –

It had been such a small and innocent goodbye at the time – but now, it was vital. They'd sneaked backstage before they left, taking turns to kiss and congratulate me, all three of us laughing. That was the way it had happened, wasn't it? I needed that to happen. It was the image that I'd been clinging to, replaying, for the last three weeks: the

17

way in which they had walked away *together* that night, giggling as they weaved between stray props and milling children. At one point, squeezing so close that their hips had brushed. They were practically arm-in-arm, practically *re-united*.

In my fantasy version of events, my dream-self broke away from the other dream children, as I never would have dared to in real life. I strode right out to the edge of the boards, but as the glare faded and face-by-face, the shadowy audience returned, I found only a gap where my mother and Dad had been. Even in my sleep, I couldn't hold on to them. Their orange seats were empty. Already, they were gone.

All over again, I felt it – that gasping shock, that vicious cut as if it was me who had been torn apart. Not simply hit by a weight or dropped from some height, but skewered open. Broken. Ripped in two.

I had to sit up carefully in that bare, white loch house room. My small, waking body felt as loosely connected, as untrustworthy, as my memories. I shivered, despite my bulky quilt. I gazed across the grainy yellow rug to the dusty wardrobe and then back to the window. To the pearls running down the panes. I tried to sit quietly. I waited and I listened and I waited.

I was straining for a distraction, or for the return of that emptiness, for anything to interrupt the ache, but at first there was only that rainfall, trembling on and on against the glass, and it wasn't enough.

But then came an abrupt clash of pans from the kitchen, the sound rapidly followed by the bang of jumping cupboards. And then there was Marie herself, calling, whining, from the bottom of the stairs.

"Libby? Hey, Libby… Are you awake yet, love?"

That hesitant, fumbling voice again, like the scratch and nudge of a stray dog at my door. I tensed before it, bristling.

"It's nearly ten o'clock. Libby? Time to get up. I'm making breakfast."

'Libby' – how I hated my name in her mouth.

Although Dad would sometimes call me 'Libs', my mother had never called me anything but 'Liberty', and when *she* had shouted for me, her tone was never tentative; she'd make my name expand to fill the house.

"Liberty! Liberty!"

18

My mother had relished the word. She adored saying it simply for saying it; she wasn't simply calling me, but declaring a revolution every time.

There was a muted scuffle from the floor below, and then several loud, hollow knocks as Marie's big, flat shoes ascended the worn wooden steps. Twisting the quilt between my fists, I yelled out "Coming!" and waited for her to bundle back down the narrow stairs.

Wearily, I forced my own thin pink feet on to the yellow floor. I pushed back the covers. I stared.

I stared from the sheet to my legs, and then to my hips, to the peach-coloured nightdress rucked in fleshy rings around my waist. And still, it took me a moment to realise that my bed wasn't just cold, but wet too. The mattress was soaked dark where I'd been lying and my thighs were flushed and sticky as well as goose-bumped.

Nervously, I touched them; I prodded them and my first thoughts were of meat. I thought of clammy meat, damp meat. Puffy packages bound up, but leaking, at the back of the fridge. I held my fingers high in a kind of wonder before my face. I drew them closer, and then recoiled at the unmistakable, acerbic tang of urine.

What –

It hardly seemed possible.

I hadn't wet the bed since I was a tiny kid, three, possibly four years old. I closed my eyes against the shame, but then aware that my fingers remained hanging, shaking, in the air, right there beside my nose, almost brushing my lips, I snatched my hand to my side. But the smell remained, as thoroughly enveloping as the raindrops' constant patter. And I don't know how long I might have sat there, surrounded, trying not to breathe that odour in, or listen, or even think – except then I pictured something blue through my darkness. A gentle shimmer.

I saw my mother's best blue gloves, still falling with the dust motes between two orange plastic chairs.

My eyes snapped open and I threw my quilt aside. I clawed at that white sheet, at that grey stain; I almost ripped the cotton as I yanked it from the bed.

I knew what I had to do; I'd hide it. I would wash the sheet in secret and somehow I'd dry it in secret too. There was no need for Marie to know. After all, I couldn't risk her sympathy, her *understanding*; it was the thing that I hated perhaps more than anything. Her whimpering and mewling. The way in which her eyes glossed over with the pretence of being kind.

19

Downstairs, in her Scottish kitchen, I found Marie at the stove, rather predictably making porridge, wrapped up in her own sludgy oatmeal-coloured wool. As she bent over the gas ring, I allowed myself a quick, bright fantasy in which that cardigan darted up, brought to new life in an explosion of flames.

"Morning Libby!" Marie inclined her head, but went on stirring. "Did you sleep well?"

I didn't reply, but slammed into the scored oak table and practically fell into a chair. Already the smell of her warming milk was sticking sickeningly to the roof of my mouth. I stared down at the chalky spot where the red lino was peeling away, to the old stone floor pressing up from underneath. The air seemed to thicken with each scrape of her spoon and the room felt cave-like, the light opaque with the rain. I glanced back to Marie. Her hair was tied clumsily, fraying loops caught in an elastic band. I watched her. Cooking for me.

Her movements were heavy and awkward, as they always were, as she shifted between her pan and the gaping sink, as she reached up to a shelf and claimed two dusty bowls. The china was part of a set, each item dull-white, flecked with blue, the same as her soap in the bathroom upstairs. Cheap and hardwearing. Bland.

Although she was supposedly artistic in her way, Marie didn't seem to understand about beauty, or grace, or anything like that. Not like my mother. And certainly not like Dad. For the thousandth time, I wondered how Marie had ever come to work for him, let alone become anything more.

With narrowed eyes, I watched her.

I watched as she slopped the porridge between the bowls. I watched the slow, wet-cement way in which it fell, the strings and clumps. I watched as she ducked between the lower cupboards, wooden cupboards with ill-fitting doors, their paintwork faded to a dingy pink that might once have matched the floor. I waited while she crouched there, shuffling through cans and jars, finally emerging with a battered tin of golden syrup. When she eased off the lid with the end of her spoon, her brow puckered.

I watched Marie and I watched her, picking away at her like yesterday's birds, that great dark scattering, peck-peck-pecking in a distant field. She grew even more bumbling beneath my scrutiny, and I imagined my beady eyes as a crow's eyes, very black and hardly blinking. With satisfaction, I took in the nervous flick of her head and

20

the pinch of her shoulders. The grey, dishevelled pigeon feathers hanging from her spine.

I saw how the long, oily drip of syrup cut a fine line through the steam as she drew a spiral into each full bowl and how, when she'd finished, she licked the spoon, sucking at that cloying sweetness as if she couldn't help herself; she needed it. *A desperate woman.* Even after she'd set the spoon aside, an amber smudge remained, glistening and repellent, on her chin.

And how, I wondered, all over again, could Dad have ever thought he loved her?

"*Why her?*"

It was a question I had often heard my mother voice. Out of all the pretty, young, willing girls who passed through Dad's studio, all those ethereal, ambitious creatures with perfect ribs and perfect eyes, who twisted so obediently into his perfect model-poses (who nonetheless weren't a patch on my own perfect mother), he had chosen Marie. Plain and stammering Marie, a second-hand camera slung like a noose around her neck.

"Why *her?*"

The question was staggering – and ongoing. After all, I hadn't a clue what I was doing with her, right then and there. Stuck in that strange, spooky house, so far from anything I knew,

Surely, after the funeral, *someone* else must have offered to take me? My Aunt Judith perhaps, who was certainly used to motherhood, having four hulking boys of her own? Or the American grandfather, my mother's Pa, who I'd only met for the first time on the morning of the cremation, but who had spoken to me with such kindness... What about my old best friend, Alice, and her family? Or Jemma, whose Pierrot-themed bedroom I was staying in, that final night.

Briefly, I allowed myself to recall how it had been at Jemma's house, before the police came. I thought about her sister's vast collection of Jackie magazines and how we'd eaten Monster Munch until our tongues shrivelled and our fingertips turned orange. Why couldn't I have stayed with Jemma and her crisps and her tinny tape deck, forever?

Why had Marie been so insistent when (aside perhaps from that new Grandfather), I probably knew her the least out of anyone? Why, when I hated her the most?

"*Why her?*"

What did she *want?*

Marie shuffled across the kitchen to set her food before me. Steadily, as if the dish might actually contain something worth considering, I took in the smeared oats and sallow milk, and the syrup, which wasn't drawn in circles as I'd imagined, but in a lopsided, leering smiley-face. One shining eye gazed back at me, more bulging than the other.

"I'm not eating that," I said, and as I pushed my chair away from the table, a wooden leg caught in the ragged lino. I heard its short shriek and then a thud, but I didn't pause to pick it up. I didn't even glance over my shoulder. Head down, no longer watching, I bowled out of the room.

I kept going. I went out, right out, through the rain. I left the loch house. I strode, as if called, down to the water.

I didn't stop to change my shoes, although she'd unpacked my wellies and they were right there, set neatly side-by-side on the cool, cracked tiles in the hall. I didn't bother with my hood either, and I didn't tell her I was going. The red front door was being battered mercilessly from without. Through the hall's shadows, I thought I could actually see the wood quaking against the frame, while the house rose, dry behind me – but I took no notice. I seized hold of the clammy latch and the heavy handle; I yanked and I walked out.

Immediately, the rain contained me, icy and vicious; it stung the back of my neck and soaked my hair. The sound of it was startling, a loud, layered hissing, a thousand snide whispers that built into a roar, and there was a sharpness to the air too. A powerful smell, like iron filings. The day was shredded, blinding; I had to keep my head bowed, my eyes focused only on my sodden shoes and on the next small patch of pummelled earth. Long before I reached the loch, the ground was alive with water. The stony path was engulfed, churning and breaking, melting with babbling rivulets of mud. Fist-sized rocks swept by as if they were no more than paper boats. On either side of the crumbling path, the grass pressed flat. Everywhere I looked I saw her greasy rat-tail hair.

But somehow I made it to the loch without skidding or stumbling. Sooner than I had imagined, the beach was there, opening around me. A beach made of pale rocks like the ones that had sailed there with me, a great, smashed harbour, jagged, and difficult to cross. Stones gave way beneath my flimsy soles, clinking and rolling and falling apart, but despite the greying downpour, they gleamed. A sallow, embedded shine, the glimmer of teeth.

22

When the water rushed and tumbled more thickly between them, black and silver and growing deeper, I stopped. With my hands gripping my hips inside the soaked pockets of my jeans, and my shoulders braced, I lifted my chin and I looked out.

The whole world was drowning.

The loch was everywhere. It had no edges and no end, but simply rolled outwards and onwards and up, swallowing the sky. Clouds and water ran together in a dense and seamless mist, creating a strange, rippling landscape of smoke and mirrors. A fallen tree, stretching blackly out from the beach into the spray, looked as unreal as its fractured reflection.

I opened my arms wide to the water. I wanted the rain to flow through me, to clean me out. I hadn't bathed before dressing and going downstairs, just scrubbed at myself in the cramped, chilly bathroom, hastily wiping my raw thighs, using only Marie's cheap soap and the lukewarm, rust-tinged tap-water and my shaking, useless hands. Now I wanted purity and emptiness; I longed to wash everything away.

Fill me up, I thought. *Fill me up*.

And I let the sounds flood my ears. There was a deeper crackling here, like applause, as the rain flared against the tight skin of the loch, stippling it with its own glittering goose bumps. I thought of hands clapping, of my parents rising, and about the wet patch I'd found, not on my mattress, but soaking the pillow beside my face. And I realised that I must have been crying after all – *for how long, for how many nights?* Weeping treacherously in my sleep.

Fill. Me. Up.

My feet sank until they became planted, rooted, in the cold, snaking pools. I don't know how long I stood there, gawping, with the rain – *only the rain* streaming from my eyes, but fleetingly, I almost found what I was longing for. For a moment, there was only this place, this loch, and nothing else, and what there was here was hardly real. Surrounded by melting hills and dancing water, I was caught in the base of a great, gleaming bowl. I tipped my head back further; stretched my mouth wide, and while my throat filled steadily with ice and silver beads, my head grew briefly blank, and bright, and still.

Marie was in the hall when I returned, but she wasn't waiting for me. She was hefting a box from the bottom of the stairs. Briefly, her face appeared moon-lit, her smile garish before I pressed closed the door.

"Oh. There you are."

As if I'd just popped out to a corner shop. As if there was a shop anywhere remotely nearby. Or even a corner.

"Guess what?" she said.

My trainers squeaked when I shifted. They were full of rain and I knew how my toes would look inside my clinging socks, white and fish-nibbled. But I didn't bend to release them.

Marie rattled her box. "I've dug out some of our old stuff," she said. "From when we were kids. It's mostly junk, I think. But there might, you know. There might be something you could use."

"Use?" I said.

I was dripping. Great, slow gobbets of rain, which fell with a strange elastic weight from my hair and cuffs and hems. The hall floor hadn't been carpeted or buried in lino and each splash flowered as it landed on the stone. I watched those flowers spread. I watched them meet.

"Stuff," Marie said. "Y'know. To play with?"

"Toys?" I said.

"Well, perhaps it's not all toys. Look..."

She stopped rummaging as if she'd found something, but then her grey hands simply lifted. They hovered.

"Oh, Libby," she said and her voice was smaller. "I don't know. I'm sorry. It's just that..."

I dripped. I waited.

"It's the telly," she said. "It's broken, Libby. I don't know what we're going to do."

It wasn't until much later, some time towards the end of the afternoon of that endless first day, that I delved into Marie's box. I sat with it, where she'd left it, in the hall, while the rain went on knocking at the red front door, behind my back.

I'd been inside for several hours, but I still felt waterlogged. Un-brushed and un-towelled, my hair had slowly dried to a stiff straw tangle. The cold rose in shuddering waves from the stone floor and kneeling against its gritty powder, with my bare legs tucked beneath me, I tried to focus on those chills. To welcome them, even. But it wasn't the same as with the rain outside; this cold didn't empty me, or blank me out. Not even momentarily.

Nevertheless, I went on sitting there, in semi-darkness. The hall light was on, but it wasn't much, a naked forty-watt bulb that couldn't touch the shadows clinging to the high, distant corners or the ones that spread in mossy patches here and there across the walls. I'd changed hastily, thoughtlessly, into dry clothes, a thin cotton cardigan, fraying at the cuffs, and an old woollen school skirt, navy and itchy and already too small. My ever-stylish mother would never have approved, but then, she wasn't there to see me – *was she?*

My bitterness sprang up too easily, flick-knife-quick and ugly, lying only just beneath the surface. There were too many thoughts inside my head. My face ached and I gazed down at my knees, peering out from beneath my skirt. They looked surprisingly round and rosy, nudging and healthy and newborn-bald. They were different animals from the rest of me. I considered giving them felt-tip faces; I did that sometimes. I'd draw faces on my hands too, and on my elbows, dividing my body up into so many different Libertys, some sweet and happy and eye-lash-fluttering, others sad, or monstrous. Instead, I turned and began to search absently through the box.

It contained nothing unexpected. Nothing of interest. That's what I thought, at first. It was just an outdated collection of childish things, chewed-looking colouring pencils and an ancient, scratched set of Russian dolls. Playing cards and an old pack of fuzzy felt, a knotted sewing kit. Her brother's Matchbox cars.

It was difficult to imagine Marie messing with any of it, to think of Marie, being little, with a brother at her side. I tried briefly, but all that I could picture were cardboard cutouts, a bigger one and a smaller one, and they weren't even coloured, but monochrome. Marie was only ten years older than I was, yet I couldn't believe that she had ever been a child – but then, despite everything, a part of me was still struggling to believe in her at all. In that moment, even the inescapable physical fact of her, hovering a few feet away through the open kitchen door, couldn't entirely convince me.

At the edge of my vision, I was aware of her, unloading pans and plates and mugs from the cupboards. She seemed determined to rinse everything, one piece at a time, in the cavernous sink. She moved robotically, in rhythm with the washing machine, which was churning over my wet clothes, along with my stealthily stuffed in sheets. She was constant in the same way that the rattling rain was constant, and the machine's hum and her streaming tap. The sound of all that running water brought the taste of metal back to my mouth, sharp and sweet. That longing –

Hastily, I grabbed her box and dragged it roughly against my little, hairless, too-pink knees. It made such a harsh grating sound against the tiles that I winced and glanced up, expecting to find Marie jumping or flinching too, but she simply went on with her washing and her emptying. She didn't even cock her head. Unlike this morning, with the porridge, she had no idea that I was watching her. As if I was the one now, who wasn't real.

Despite the cold, I felt my eyes warm as they narrowed. I reached deeper into the box.

It too smelt of metal, of rust and must and long-lost things. I rooted inside. There were so many cars – taxis and fire engines, Beetles and racers, a couple of solid red London buses and several motorbikes. The skin on my knuckles caught on a miniature set of clicking wheels, but I kept searching. And it didn't take long to find what I needed.

A sleek, black sports car. A chipped white van.

They were almost perfect.

I held them aloft, admiring their plastic windows and their little working, opening doors. They had tiny headlights and number plates, tiny steering wheels and seats. There were no drivers or passengers – never mind. I'd have to pretend them, but then, hadn't I already been doing that, in my treacherous sleep?

I snapped the small doors closed, *clack, clack,* and then, with one toy in each hand and one eye on Marie, I began to drive them back and forth across the stone.

The sound that those miniature tyres made was louder than I'd hoped, but it took several minutes for Marie to turn, for Marie to see me. That was ok. I was patient, and almost instantly mesmerised by the motion of my own hands, by those rolling cars... Black and white. Black. And. White...

In the pause after the washing machine had finished spinning, she heard us. I watched her head snap up, but as soon as she began to turn, I looked away, joining in instead, humming an imaginary engine's growl to accompany the clatter of miniature wheels. I felt her coming closer.

I kept playing, kept murmuring, "*brrrrrmm...*" as if I was a much, much younger kid. A toddler. Or a little boy with a dirt-smeared face, her dead brother, perhaps. If he was actually dead and he hadn't just disowned her, like the rest of her family had when she'd married Dad. If her brother wasn't simply missing, which didn't count at all.

Her shadow joined the others at the edges of the hall.

"L- Libby?"

Slowly at first, I brought the cars together. I whispered with the collision, my words as soft as breathing.

"Crash," I muttered. "Smash."

26

The washing machine and tap were quiet now. There was only the sound of the cars between us, and that rain, drumming on against the door, like the gallop of small heartbeats. *Mouse-beats*, I thought as I went on driving the cars together, then drawing them apart, my hands moving a little faster, a little more forcibly, every time.

"Libby," she said again.

I could smell the washing-up bubbles on her fingers, and beneath that the thickening, earthier scent of her sweat. I imagined stains spreading across her blouse beneath that matted wool. But still, I wouldn't look at her, but only at those cars. I watched them crash, again and again.

It was a terrible thing, a marvellous thing. And almost out of my control already – they were driving themselves. Destroying themselves.

"Smash," I mumbled. "Shatter."

But they didn't break.

They would not break, or even dent, although the tip of my chewed, left thumb, catching repeatedly between them, grew suddenly hot. A fine line of blood opened and then blossomed along the rim of my nail, but I kept going. I kept crashing those toy cars together. Quicker. Harder. I felt a growing power, building both inside me and from without. The shadows in the hallway gathered closer, urging me on – while Marie fluttered. Her panic spiralling.

"Libby, what are you doing? Libby. Listen to me. You stop that now, Libby! Please."

And I realised that I was laughing a little; I was breathless and giggling, unless it was the darkness that was giggling, or the rain, with its tapping and hissing and juddering outside, or the trembling chill from the floor. I felt dizzy and airy, a part of everything. As if the cars were me and the cold was me. And the house was me, triumphant –

Marie grabbed my arms.

She reached down and snatched hold of my wrists with her soapy fists and yanked me up to face her with a strength I never knew she had.

"You stop that!" she screamed. "You stop that right now!"

And she shook me, and shook me. Her fingers bit into me. She shook me so hard that the toys fell from my hands. There was a crack as the black sports car hit the floor.

Her face was rash-red. Her eyes wide and appalled and openly wet, and gazing back at them, I felt a renewed surge of energy, a fizzing, irresistible new strength as it dawned on me how many ways there might be to hurt her. And although I could feel her rage, her outrage, like a heat, and although she wouldn't let go of me (she went on rocking me, and my clenched wrists were aching, my head bobbing as if I was her doll), I understood. Marie was trapped here. She was just as trapped as I was.

I was her inheritance. And there was no way out.

Even now, I still conjure up the crash. I suppose that I've been doing it for years, on and off. Of course, it's a private thing these days. A quiet thing. And it hardly hurts anymore. It's simply another habit, like the wine.

So, surrounded by the tinny heat and plastic cushion covers of my slow moving mini-cab, I'm not surprised to find myself imagining it once again. Their last dark minutes.

17th August 1983, *'At approximately 9.30pm…'*

Our Summer Drama Club's fairytale performance had been over for half an hour when my mother's bullet-sleek, black sports car folded like a paper fan against the stubby, harmless-looking face of a delivery van. I was told that my parents were killed outright. Almost certainly instantly. It was a head-on collision; they wouldn't have suffered – they *couldn't* have suffered.

"Wouldn't have known what hit them."

I was meant to feel grateful for that, at least.

Except that the perceived facts of things, as Dr Gilchrist so frequently reminded me, sometimes stand quite separately from the supposed truth. The truth here, for example, is that nobody can really understand exactly how much my parents might have felt, just what they might have realised, before the end. No one can honestly comprehend the depth of their pain, or just how long those final (precious? agonising?) moments *truly* lasted. For all any of us know, instead of everything contracting, their dying might have caused the universe to slow and expand, to swell around them.

And even the practical details, those so-called 'facts', aren't cast in stone. After all, nobody could state with any certainty that the crash happened at 9.30. The van's driver, a Mr Edward Stean (who, according to the papers, was known to his friends without irony as "Steady Eddie") was also killed, and there were, it seems, no other vehicles on that particular stretch of lamp-lit concrete that night, no witnesses. The reported time has remained 'approximate', as those platitudes too were simply guesses. Statements of hope and consolation for those of us left so stupidly behind…

29

But then, as far as I can remember, those early news stories were riddled with inaccuracies. Hardly any referred to Marie. Somehow, among all the broken glass and blood and faded glamour, the Second Wife, newly-wed, newly widowed, plain Marie, was forgotten, along with my parents' divorce and the fact that my mother hadn't actually modelled in years. But then, I'm not entirely sure that they remembered me either.

The tabloid's images, in contrast, were stark and undeniable. Although I no longer possess those papers, I know I'll never be able to forget the van's surprised, punctured headlamp eyes or how, with the impact, its back doors had sprung wide-open, spilling apples on to the road.

Apples on the road – really, it was ludicrous. Among the chaos, they were surprisingly distinct.

Pathetic, how I can see it all, still. How, as we weave through the sluggish traffic, I find myself recreating that ancient scene through my smeared window, imposing a fallen bumper on to the grille of a parked Transit – even uncovering childish apple-shapes in the leaf shadows dappling the curb.

But perhaps I go on clinging to those newspaper pictures because they were the only evidence I had? Because I was so far away, so uninvolved. After our Drama Club play was over, I didn't leave for my sleepover right away; when the accident itself was happening (*'At approximately 9.30'*), I was backstage, drawing extra greasepaint hearts and stars across Jemma's cheeks. In the post-show clamour of a poky, airless dressing room, the pair of us had giggled, louder than anyone else. We'd wilted together. Despite the unique privileges of my upbringing, all my supposed 'sophistication', I was practically ordinary then. Innocent.

My cab jolts, and the flat blare of an impatient horn shoves me back into the present. With a start, I'm fully returned, though still in my familiar London Square, stuck in traffic. Outside, sunshine leaps from windscreen to hot windscreen; we're hemmed in by gleaming chrome and wound-down windows. From somewhere unseen, but nearby, I hear the frustrated sputter of an aging motorbike.

I tell myself that I'm ok, still. That I'm almost as adept at suppressing the crash as I am at invoking it. Yet when I come back to myself, so the old loneliness returns. It creeps through me, an almost tangible wave, like steam. For a moment, my face feels wet with it. Heavy.

I try to rise above it, above everything, but I don't like the rubbery seat covers; they stick to me self-consciously, holding me in place. And I don't like the fact that I'm sitting, alone, in the back seat either, my young driver having pointedly held the rear door open as he waited, his black hair oddly faded in the August glare. Having been manoeuvred here, I feel more like a little girl than ever, though there's no luggage wedged beside me now. No Girl's World head or shiny pens. Even so, I feel about as invisible as a child, as small and insubstantial. Partly, I realise, it's the driver's silence.

After all my worrying about explanations as I packed, I know that I ought to feel grateful for his reticence, but I don't. There's no relief. Instead I'm finding myself longing for this man to speak, or to look at me, at least. I want some attention (maybe I *am* a little girl still), or perhaps I'm simply seeking a distraction.

"Busy morning?" I try, feeble even to myself.

He *mmm*s, inclines his head, perhaps. I plough on, regardless:

"I don't remember the traffic being this bad, not for a while… The time of day, I suppose?"

He doesn't even bother murmuring. In the rear-view mirror, there's not the briefest glance. I hardly blame him. I raise my fingers to my lips to prevent the next inanity and as I shift, the plastic squeaks. The cab's air feels as clouded as that misted rubber, clogged with the saccharine, floral scent of my own perfume. Even my perspiration, seeping out from underneath it all, smells artificial. *Unbearable –*

But then the driver reaches for his radio. He twists on the bright, bland chirp and jangle of a local music station and I feel instantly released. I don't need to talk anymore, and I don't need his eyes. I welcome the disposable melodies, the lyrics that mean nothing. I sit back, reclaiming my emptiness, that blankness, which is perhaps my oldest friend. My recoveries are always like this, swift and all encompassing. I am resilient, after all, I remember. I do not break.

I gaze beyond the faded marks on the window, a spattering like ghostly freckles speckling my reflection, to the yellow world outside. We still haven't made it out of the Square. If I were to turn around and crane my neck, I'd be able to glimpse the long, blank windows of my bedroom. I picture black gaps here and there where I drew the curtains too hastily, and the empty window boxes. I don't look back. Instead I watch the people beyond the railings, wafting across the grass. A woman on a bench air-kisses the man sitting beside her, before gradually rising, then sinking away.

31

It's only once we've turned the corner that we begin to pick up speed. The tall Edwardian townhouses give way to smaller, gaudy shops, doors propped open to the sunshine. I see a rack of London postcards and a rack of cheap sunglasses, row upon row of dull, plastic eyes. There are buckets of roses and carnations on the pavement, brown bananas in a crate. Pedestrians float by: more drifts, more waves.

We slip through a set of traffic lights, winking amber, and then another. We pass a pub with old, gold lettering scrawled across smoked glass. *Lounge Bar*, I read. *Ladies Welcome.* I stare at the people outside, busy clusters obscuring the wooden tables, others milling around the gabled entrance. Not one of them feels me looking.

But as I stare, all the people at their separate tables seem to throw back their heads and laugh at once, as one. Men with pink clown cheeks and women with long, bare arms and toffee coloured legs, with wide, red mouths and blazing hair. All of them, making life look easy. I can't hear them from inside the car, but briefly, sharply, I wish I could be with them.

I think how it would be to sit outside, laughing and drinking, telling stories and flirting, losing track of time as the late afternoon gradually transforms into a warm summer evening. A precious evening, this August, which has been mostly wet or clouded, it will pour like a ripple of silk into a soft and proper summer night.

And my thoughts return, irrepressibly, to Richard. To Richard in Venice, where it's bound to be even hotter. I imagine a greenish humidity rising from the canals, rubbish outside restaurants. I think of rats and flies and the clamour of children's voices sticking with the sweat to his sun-ruddy face. A ring of tourist grime around his neck.

And as if it were simple, I tell myself that I don't understand why he's refusing me, why he is refusing to return. After the years now, that we've spent together, all the grief that we have shared, surely his place ought to be right here, travelling beside me? Unless he should have prevented me from leaving in the first place – *how can he allow me to go back?*

My mobile's lying on the seat beside me, black and sleeping, but I know I shouldn't call. I mustn't. *Not yet.* I promised that I wouldn't, except in an emergency. And even then, not until nine, at least. Ten o'clock, Italian time, when his kids should be in bed.

I try to refocus on the car to stop myself from considering what counts, exactly, as an emergency? I concentrate on the smooth, brown skin on the back of my young driver's neck, but my gaze slides

32

inevitably from his carefully clipped hair down to my hands, rocking together in my lap. They remain cool despite the stuffiness, chilled even as we leave the pub behind and the car's air presses closer. Tighter. I feel it in bands across my face and throat. There's a headache growing behind my eyes.

Across the white lines, traffic blurs, running backwards. Although we're reeling along now, juddering queasily over speed bumps without pause, the cars on the other side move faster and there is the illusion of suspension, as if we're neither pushing forward, nor moving back. And then before I can stop myself, I'm wondering if perhaps there will be only this, this journey? Perhaps I'll never actually reach the loch house; *something* will happen on the way.

It's all too easy to imagine the accident again. A screech of tyres, a flat, metal bang. Glass spraying and flying, like rain, like music. A flash of red, and then black. Because wouldn't it be so apt for my cab to crash right now, this instant? *And perhaps not such a bad thing, after all?*

But leaning forward, my waistband digs into me, sharp and uncomfortable, and I'm reminded that I'm no longer allowed such thoughts. And when the car skims the curb as it swerves clumsily around another corner, causing a woman on the golden pavement to hop back and drop her phone, I don't feel fated, but instead a moment of pure panic. Of course it's nothing, nowhere near a collision, but I'm freshly aware of the heat – and of a strange, frail darkness, hovering overhead, just out of reach. As if it's always there.

Cowering against the sallow plastic, I try to pull my thoughts together once more, but my mouth is filled with that rubber taste and there's something else, another ugliness, rising from within.

"Stop the car," I say, but the driver goes on ignoring me. I'm not surprised. I can barely hear myself, though I'm clutching my waist blatantly now, rubbing and kneading and hardly caring how it must look. As if from a great distance, I hear myself moan. My fingers are abruptly, surprisingly clammy. My blouse creases beneath them like an extra layer of peeling skin. Except there's not enough of me. Not enough flesh, pushing back against my hands. I feel that darkness, as fine as cobwebs, brush my neck.

"I said *stop the car.*"

I'm growling. It's absurd. My voice is thick, sickeningly so. "Stop now. Please. I'm going to throw up."

At last the driver's eyes find mine in the rear-view mirror. They're big, wet boy's eyes; it's his turn to look afraid.

He yanks the wheel down hard. I'm flung forward as he pulls over, my moist forehead bumping the front seat. Heat and rubber merge. There's a rushing in my throat and I fumble for the door, scarcely managing to open it before the heaving begins. Vomit spills out of me in a thin, pale gush, spattering the gutter and the secret dazzling twinkles in the concrete curb. My eyes burn, but gradually the heat subsides. The spasms slow.

There's nothing touching the back of my neck now but the hard, gritty sun and the quick disgust of passers-by. There's no reason to be frightened. I've thrown up, that's all. Nothing else is happening. And this kind of nausea isn't even anything new; there have been several such incidences lately, if not quite as violent. It's a common thing, isn't it, in the early weeks?

My blouse hangs before me, un-tucked and twisted and baring a clear new stain from the press of my hand. I feel the driver standing close by and I struggle against a new cloying wave of shame. I force myself to look up and his gaze skirts over me, his eyes thinned. I spread my fingers slowly and deliberately across my stomach, smoothing taut my puckered blouse. *But of course he can't understand.* My belly's flat, there's nothing of me…

Yet I want him to grasp the possibility, to suspect regardless – except that then it occurs to me that perhaps he smelt the wine on me, and my shame doubles. I sag beneath its oily weight. A small pulse seethes between my eyes. *Only I don't deserve this; I know I don't –*

I clear my sour throat. Swipe my hair clear of my face.

"It's not my fault," I say, and my appeal is calm. My words don't crack.

But with a gesture of someone much older, someone deeply professional, a maitre d' maybe, or an old-fashioned butler, my driver turns smartly away. He blinks up at the buildings. Adjusts his cuffs.

For the rest of that first week at the loch house, I didn't remember my dreams. Yet each morning, I awoke damp and dirty, my mattress stained. My face remained dry though; my night tears had crept back down inside. There was, admittedly, the odd, flushed moment when I'd wobble and seem to feel them waiting – but mostly it was as if those secret sobs had never happened, as if my tearless state was something natural. Perhaps it was, for me.

At the time, I didn't stop to wonder. I had my stinking covers to deal with. Practical things. Grim-jawed, I'd wrestle my wet sheets into baggy packages and drag them from the bed, bundling them into the wardrobe to wash them later, surreptitiously, when I could.

But although I was determined to clean up as efficiently as possible, my self-disgust often slowed me down. It was a heavy, solid thing and I was too bumbling before it, too flimsy. My hands shook as I tugged and folded and I found myself berating my untrustworthy body with the same vehemence with which I cursed Marie.

Throughout the whole humiliating process, I listened in dread for her footsteps, convinced that she was about to burst into my room at any second. I pictured her eyes widening as she grasped my grubby secret, before her dumb shock gave way to something more sinister. Satisfaction flickering across her plain, plate face.

While I scrubbed at the mattress with her unforgiving soap and a thinning flannel, words flew, as if unbidden, from my mouth. I didn't even know what half of them meant. They were phrases I'd picked up from my parents' friends, and from their parties, from my other, better life, and their power lay simply in the fact that they were forbidden. Words like rocket fuel; my hatred for Marie flared with them, as it did with the cloth's crude swipes. And although my stepmother never actually came anywhere close during my frenzied clean-ups (there was no ponderous shuffling on the landing, no hesitant tap at my firmly shut door), that anger helped. It cleared my head and drove me on, except –

Except, sometimes.

Sometimes, afterwards, even as I hung, panting, over my stripped bed, my mouth gaping, my curses finally crumbled, it wasn't enough. Having ripped off my covers, I wanted to keep on tearing. There was such a surging inside me that I'd pull clumps of fair, fleecy hair from my scalp, or rake my fingernails along my arms. But even when I left livid marks, another scrawling set of unfathomable words, there were mornings when I wanted, needed, more.

At yet it was often at such times that the walls brightened and as the light shifted, I'd manage to release my grip on my hair or skin. My breath catching when the shadows lifted altogether, when with a magician's flourish, the windowpanes blazed gold.

That first week at the loch house, the way in which the sun returned was like a gift, a dazzling surprise after that dark first day of rain. Outside, the fading summer landscape assumed a renewed lushness. Colours had deepened. Ignoring the proximity of autumn, the trees' leaves appeared thicker and somehow greener. There was only the finest auburn within the coiling bracken, while the furthest hills had softened to a spectral blond. Down at the water's edge, the smaller waves stretched silver and jumped like stars between the rocks. When evening set in, the rock pools rusted as they faded. An amber twilight oozed across the grass.

And gazing from my bedroom window, it was as if the water shimmered within me too; I'd feel a corresponding prickling, a sweet stinging, in my chest.

That first week at the loch house, Marie tried to talk. And not about the television, or the weather, or what we might have left for lunch. Or at least not just about those things.

She'd come looming up behind me as I stood transfixed before a smeary window, or else she'd catch me on my way out, slipping with the shadows through the cool patch in the hall.

"Libby, how are you doing today?"

"Libby, I don't want you to feel that you're alone."

"Libby, you know that if you ever want to talk . . ."

Talk, talk, talk.

Of course, it was a ridiculous notion, as Marie herself was ridiculous with her feeble voice and her blinking eyes – but she didn't give up. Even when I pretended to doze or read, or when I sat down to eat, she'd be there, although I turned from her as often as I pushed away her food.

"Libby, I think I can imagine how things are for you."

"We can get through this together Libby, if you'll only let me in."

36

And still, it was always "Libby" this and "Libby" that, and never Liberty; I felt reinvented in her mouth. Her frail, appeasing tone seemed more suited to calling a pet than a child – some wilful, uncooperative cat, prone to hunting and scratching and staying out all night. And I thought how much easier it would have been for her if I had have been an animal; she could have caged me up with Mr Whiskers then. Left me weepily, gleefully, behind.

Her feigned kindness didn't fool me. Aside from the obvious emptiness to her words, I suspected that most of the time she was simply talking for the sake of it. Skimming over our vacuum.

Unlike me, Marie didn't like the quiet; she couldn't live inside it. And there was no telephone line connected to the loch house, a fact that she'd remembered with what had seemed like genuine relief on the day we'd arrived. She'd tried the stormy television repeatedly, but had eventually given up, snapping it off and replacing her thwarted attempts with reproachful glances at the dull, dead screen. Sometimes, to fill the void, I heard her singing flatly to herself. Scraps of romantic nonsense, clichéd tunes that quickly fell apart, scattering dryly from her cracked and bitten lips.

On the afternoon when Marie found the radio, she rushed to the living room, where I lay sprawled on the worn red rug, drawing.

"Look, Libby!" she cried. "It was at the back of one of the kitchen drawers. In with the light bulbs and wires and a load of old cake candles."

Standing in the doorway, she waved it like some victory flag. A dented, tinny-looking thing, not much bigger than her hand, its aerial crooked – but her face was flushed, her eyes actually shining, and I found myself thinking about my old friend Alice. How once, when we were digging through her rockery for broken china, we unearthed a coin that we initially believed to be Roman – how we'd convinced ourselves that our discovery would be life-changing. We'd be rich, surely. Famous. Marie was that excited. That stupid. I went back to my drawing.

"The lead's a lost cause," she said. "It looked chewed right through. But I did find some batteries, though God knows how long they'll last. And the signal's terrible, I can only get some local station and that cuts out all the time. I haven't a clue what it is – Radio Fort?

Radio North? Their jingle's hilarious... For a minute, I did actually get it to speak."

But now as she bowed over it, the radio released nothing but static. Hot, thin, spitting sounds like something frying on a griddle.

"I don't know, perhaps it's worse in here. The reception..."

"Probably," I said.

Only she didn't leave. Instead she shuffled deeper into the room, still crackling, and her shadow fell over me, blocking the light. I concentrated harder on the black felt-tip in my hand, on the way that its small, fluffy nib had splayed and greyed. The squeak that it made as I pushed down against the paper.

"But Libby, hey," she said. "What are you up to?"

Of course I didn't bother to reply. She didn't care, didn't stop fussing with her new toy even as she slumped on to her knees on the rug beside me. And anyway, aside from the fact that it was blindingly obvious, drawing had been my sole indoor occupation since we'd arrived.

I hadn't the attention for books and after that first day, Marie's ancient box had hastily disappeared – not that I needed it, it had served its purpose, but I'd found that I couldn't face my own things either. Despite insisting on bringing so much (stuffing that tired, scruffy Girl's World head into the car at the last minute), my beads and games and comics lay untouched in a corner of my room. They demanded too much effort somehow; even the idea of them made me tired.

But with drawing, it was different. I'd already filled two A4 pads with dense, rambling doodles and unfinished fragments. Stylised female faces, or patterns, odd animals and plants. I was hardly aware of what I created; I drew because occasionally it allowed me to drift off towards a kind of nothing-place. A place beyond thoughts, beyond daydreams, where it seemed I might escape –

Except that on that particular afternoon Marie was there, as she was so often there, yanking me back. Her radio sizzling.

"Colouring again?" she said. "You're not too bored here, are you? How are you feeling today, Libby? Are you ok?"

I kept drawing. The outline of a branch, or an arm. A small, crosshatched palm. I'd recently learnt about crosshatching, about making the shadows darker by degrees. It was my latest obsession. Marie leant closer. Her hair dripped over my paper. Her static blazed. She smelt of her plain, hard soap – of my scrubbed mattress; I thought of it waiting upstairs. The stain on the cotton, hidden beneath fresh sheets. That morning I'd used too much soap; the patch was blotched with frosty streaks, ridged as if with snow.

"Wow," Marie said. "That's good, Libby. You're a proper little artist, aren't you? Just like your Dad..."

I gazed down at my picture, seeing it clearly for the first time. It wasn't good. It was hardly anything. Perhaps swollen trees, a forest, or else a group of long, vague-faced figures clustered together in a boneless row. I put down my pen and ripped it from my sketchbook, intending to crumple it.

"Don't," Marie said. "Can't I keep it – would you mind?"

I shrugged and let the picture fall, creased, between us. "It's nothing," I said. "Rubbish."

Slowly, carefully, she set down her radio to pick up my paper. She stroked it smooth across her thighs. But abandoned, the radio emitted a fine dog-whistle-whine and she snatched it back – while I turned to a clean page in my thick, white pad. And with a new awareness, I began.

Just three figures this time. A man, a woman and a child.

The lines emerged with confidence. There was nothing else in the picture, no background. Nobody else. I linked them together by joining their hands.

Marie held the radio up to her ear, to her looping hair, as if that might help.

"I don't honestly know why I keep trying," she said. "Even when it worked, it died as soon as there was music –"

But then, between its sputtering, a hollow voice interrupted her, barely audible: "This is Micky McBride, riding through till two..."

"Here we go!" Marie said. "Here we go!"

And for a few seconds, Micky McBride became suddenly clear, his tone filling out, revealing a practised warmth. Spilling words like tea, just the right side of lukewarm.

"If you're free tomorrow, and up near Sterling, don't forget about those windsurfing heats," he said, before the crackle once more began to mount. "Beginning at noon," he called through it, "or thereabouts. And all in the name of charity, folks..."

I went on filling my page. I took my drawing to its edges. Mother and Dad in broad strokes, with their daughter between them. A simple family scene of the kind that children often draw – except that when I added flesh, shape, to their rough stick bodies, goose bumps ruffled my own skinny arms. I saw suddenly that Marie might have been right after all; maybe I was *a proper little artist*. Although crude, the resemblance was there already. Undeniably so. It was uncanny.

"Windsurfing!" Marie said. "Imagine that, around here. Mind you, I don't think it is. Around here, I mean. Actually, I'm not entirely sure where Sterling is... There's the map though, in the car. We could – we could. If you wanted..."

Her chatter fell out of her, her words growing faster, stumbling together as she watched my picture unfold. Because naturally, she watched, despite what she feigned. A ceiling beam creaked overhead, as if the house was watching too, mildly amused.

And as I drew on, the radio's hiss rose, swamping Micky McBride altogether. And the static wasn't simmering anymore, but snapping and rushing. It made me think of cold, of rain. Of the rain that had puckered the skin of the loch. That merciless battering.

"Oh, well," Marie said. "We don't need his windsurfing."

But she didn't turn the radio off, or even down. Instead she talked alongside its popping, its fizzing, as if she was some kind of presenter herself. Although a presenter of what, exactly? The thought made me smile. She didn't even possess the charisma to advertise her porridge.

"It's another beautiful day," she went on. "I can't believe how fortunate we've been with this weather, how it's changed. It's becoming a right old-fashioned 'Indian Summer'. Perhaps I'll do some more in the garden. There's loads more weeding to be done...I don't know where they all come from!"

She paused to laugh lightly, falsely, though she was racing the rainstorm now and couldn't stop chattering for long. "I don't really know what I'm doing out there, but the roses are looking a bit sorry for themselves. They probably need trimming. Deadheading. Or something. You could help if you wanted, Libby? Or perhaps we could do something in the kitchen? Cook something up together…"

Glancing up briefly, I saw that her hairline was strung with beads of sweat. She clasped the radio to her knees, her thumb still pressed intently on the dial, disregarding its senseless clamour. But I knew where her hands truly wanted to be – back on her belly, stroking there, comforting there. Holding on.

I welcomed her panic. I thought it would urge me to keep going, to keep drawing – except this was different from when I'd driven her toy cars. I could no longer altogether grasp that strange eager fluttering, that sense of triumph. The truth was that my picture was disturbing me too.

However simplified, it was unsettling to see my parents there, like that. They were undoubtedly recognisable; there were my mother's high cheekbones and the sweep of hair that fell across her eyes – there were the distinct lines of Dad's strong brow and his almost-boxer's nose.

I had never drawn so well before. I should have been proud, except that since the crash, hadn't I been avoiding looking at any pictures of my parents? Although my mother's image was everywhere back in our London house, I'd done my best to avoid her. I had kept my eyes averted, my head lowered, as I walked between Dad's editorial shots, down the stairs. Except for in my dreams, where I couldn't help it, I'd been trying not to visualise my parents at all; it was too painful. But this wasn't about me now. It was about Marie, *about getting Marie*. And besides, I couldn't seem to stop now that I'd started.

As Marie could not stop talking.

"A cake!" she sang. "We could bake a cake. Something big and chocolaty. There were those candles after all! And we've got plenty of butter and eggs left. There's hundreds-and-thousands too, and some silver balls. I don't know how long they've been there, mind – it's like the batteries. But there's jam, we could use that for the filling…"

On the paper, our mouths were still missing. I drew in our mouths. I gave us smiles. I made the smiles wider, blacker. But the pen was running out, the ink fading. I pressed down so hard that the page wrinkled. I dropped the pen and snatched up another.

Briefly, Micky McBride returned from his wind-tunnel, his voice fading in and out of the static, easily overridden by its gusts.

"Those brothers Kemp..." he said.

"...Harvest –" he said.

"...a missing white border collie. Called Blackie."

I took no notice. I corrected the angle of Dad's shoulders and remembering the fine gold chain he always wore, I drew a line across his throat –

And then my fingers froze, remembering.

Remembering –

Dad's chain. How cold it had always been.

How it had felt when he held me.

When I nestled against his chest, burrowing, with my face turned into the curve of his jaw. The iciness of that metal always a shock, such a direct contrast to his solid, smoky warmth.

And as if he was just there, a breath away, I pictured the fascinating bob of his Adam's apple. The small, smudged mole tucked beneath his chin –

He was everywhere.

I drew on, although I could hardly see the paper anymore. As I couldn't hear Marie anymore, or her radio, either its faltering messages or its over-riding white noise. I was too caught up with Dad. With Dad's flesh, his scent. Vividly, I remembered the line-dried sunshine in the cotton of his shirt. The steady, reassuring heat of his body underneath. I smelt the tobacco on his skin and a sweeter, browner odour, as if the leather of his armchair had rubbed off somehow. Or perhaps it was his whisky and coke –

Marie lifted the radio. She shook it and I realised its whine had grown more definite, high-pitched and skin-crawling.

"I think we've lost it altogether," she cried. "It's gone, it's gone."

Her words caught, and twisted. They became a gasp, a short half-sob. They stopped.

She was staring openly at my picture now, at my mother and me. And at my Dad. *Her husband.* It was all so wrong. She shut her mouth with a snap, and when she attempted to speak once more, her voice was different, small and gruff, clogged with its own interference.

"I loved your father very much."

My fingers jerked from the paper. From the corner of my eye, I saw the pen fly, and then heard the flat clatter as it hit the floor beyond the rug. Marie sat before me, her shoulders bowed, her stringy hair mere inches from my face. I wanted to strike her so badly that for a moment I actually persuaded myself that I was doing it. I even saw my hands rise. I felt my hard, determined palms meet her chest and the resistance of her woolly breasts as I pushed her. I saw the radio tumble from her lap. Felt her heartbeat rock between us –

But of course I never touched her. Instead my chilled little hands found the paper once more. I twisted the picture round to face her. I pushed it towards her. I wanted her to look at it, to truly *see* it. To feel it. *Mother – daughter – Dad.* I refused to let her turn away.

Look at what I've lost.

Look at what you stole from me.

Marie shook her head. "Libby…" she began.

But I wasn't even going to pretend to listen, not to anything, not anymore. I rose. Although I didn't bolt from the room this time. Instead I walked quietly to the door on purposeful feet. Quite deliberately leaving her with nothing. Nothing but dead air, as she started to weep.

43

The train to Edinburgh has been delayed. I gaze up at the digital board with all the other gazing people. We're packed closely together, a tight, craning knot, only divided by our cases. Kings Cross is noisy, the air busy with shouts and mutters, with heavy footsteps and slamming doors and the sudden whirr of pigeons' wings. Every now and then, there's a screech from beyond the barriers, a rattle from the tracks. Passengers for other trains whistle past as if released and although the sun remains bright outside, the concourse still smells of London rain, as if the dirt has been embedded.

Briefly, up on the screen, the Edinburgh train's 'Expected Arrival' slot flashes with a time over an hour from now. A groan blooms, mushrooms, from the people around me and then I feel myself sagging involuntarily alongside them. My journey has stalled already, but I try not to read anything into this – or into the words I overhear next, from the passengers mingling by Information.

"A body on the line apparently."

The girl talking has a blond ponytail plucked through a baseball cap and a toddler curled against her shoulder. She's leaning towards an older woman, another blonde, but brassier, perhaps her mother. The girl jiggles the toddler absent-mindedly as she speaks. His big blue eyes flicker open like a doll's.

"Some bloke jumped outside the station, the man said. It would have to be *our* train he was waiting for."

I yank the handle from my suitcase and turn away. My heels clip-clop across the forecourt, while the wheels on my case purr expensively behind. A group of older men in suits nod and smile and step aside. I smile back as I move on, imagining that I look as if I know exactly where I'm going. As if everything's ok – *I'm holding this together.* I look nothing like a woman who's just thrown up on the street.

But regardless of my resolve, and my determinedly dismissing the fact of a body on the tracks, the station remains full of associations. And it isn't fair; there shouldn't be such reminders here. There shouldn't be *anything* personal or private in such a public, transitory place. Yet there's another strong retro feeling to the fashions this season and many of the girls stuffed into magazine racks and hung in

44

advertisements across the station walls, seem to bare at least a passing resemblance to my mother. Those beads and tunics and dramatic turquoise eyes could have come straight out of any number of her old modelling shoots. Even the poses seem familiar, the haughty tilt of a chin, the suggestive slide of a shoulder. An impossibly long leg rising delicately, precariously, from a hulking, stack-heeled shoe.

And there's something almost mocking in the models' billboard glamour, in the direct and brutal contrast between their poise and beauty and looming stature, and all of us little travellers, shuffling in droves, below. It's as if even without their theatrical make-up and fancy-dress clothes, those women belong to some different, better species. My mother had that too.

But I should probably be used to such reminders by now. Certain pictures of my mother remain iconic, in their own small way. My father, behind the camera, happened to capture a particular soft-focused moment of an era that could be seen to be definitive – as for a little while, they themselves were perhaps definitive. A 'Golden Couple' in a less cluttered and supposedly more innocent media age. Before their deaths, their time in the spotlight hadn't lasted long though – but I can't blame Marie for that. After all, she came much later. Although my Dad's reputation as a photographer continued to grow, my mother's promising career actually ended with her pregnancy. With me.

The carefully cultivated disdain of one particular model's gaze goes on needling the nape of my neck long after I've drifted past her. The discomfort crawls down my spine until I feel it in my belly. A thin, shivering thread –

But I keep moving. I heft my case downstairs and then upstairs. I negotiate escalators and commuters, until I find myself in the adjoining St Pancras where I pause, finally, to blink. I haven't been to the station for several years and the glass and gloss is startling. I catch French voices amidst the general calls and chatter and I remember that there's the Eurostar now – and I think of Richard. Of *Richard in Venice* – and it occurs to me that I don't have to go to Scotland after all.

I could buy a new ticket. I could board a train to Brussels or Paris. My case is packed with all the wrong clothes, but I could do it anyway. I could run away. Or run back to him. I could catch a plane from Charles de Gaulle to Marco Polo – or perhaps take more trains; I could cross Europe by rail. I picture a wood-panelled sleeping compartment, a long, white linened dining car – wouldn't that be the most romantic way to hunt him down?

It probably wouldn't be a good idea to call first. If I told Richard I was coming, he might argue; he might impose his real life on me. It would be much better to simply turn up at his hotel. In the hotel restaurant at breakfast maybe, as if I'd followed him straight from his dreams.

I can imagine it so easily; it's as clear and polished as one of his movie scenes. I'd wear a new designer suit of crisp Italian cotton, but allow my hair to spill loose over my shoulders. Tumbling and tangled, the way he prefers it. *My bed-hair*, he says...

I picture towering windows, or perhaps a balustrade to lean against. A backdrop of low, gold light and lapping water. A gondola probably, weaving past.

And when Richard walks into the room, his eyes will obviously find mine, and perhaps it will be like the very first time we met? When I was only twenty and just an extra, another pretty piece of background on his set, while he ducked and dived between different cameras so that I'd assumed at first that he was some minor crewmember, someone's assistant. He'd looked so ordinary, with his shirt hanging from his broad shoulders, his glasses winking as he pressed them to the bridge of his nose. I had no idea how important he was, not right away. Nor how truly handsome.

Although of course I'd know it now. I imagine the look that we would share if I found him at his hotel. The concentration of that look. And how his mouth would fall open with the surprise of me, and with the force of all that has passed between us. While a cool, disdainful model's smile, my mother's smile, might flit across my lips.

"Richard," I'd say. "I have something to tell you."

"It will be different this time, Richard. You'll see."

Except that then I'm struggling to imagine what he might do next. What he could possibly reply.

Because I am not stupid, or truly childlike, never mind this daydreaming. I understand that it could never actually happen that way. Because his wife would be there too.

Perhaps she'd come gliding into the dining room before him and then I'd have to hide? Or worse still, they might enter together, emerging slowly with their arms linked or maybe just their fingertips brushing; they'd hardly need to speak... I scrunch my eyes closed as if both husband and wife really are about to appear before me. Spectres drifting between the bags and marching bodies of all these other travellers, these strangers.

46

And clearly, I don't want to think about Richard's wife. The last thing I want to do is conjure her into my fantasy, and yet somehow, over the years, her neatly streaked hair and rounded, vapid prettiness have become imprinted across my imagination. She's like a stain, a shadow. She refuses to be forgotten, or discounted. And it isn't only his wife with him in Venice, but his children as well. His children who are more of a barrier than even she, *Amanda*, could ever be. Because Richard is a good father, a *devoted* father. Of course, right now, this should make me happy. Of course, it does not.

But perhaps I should be grateful that the children are on holiday too, that the whole family is together? After all, they're in the world's most romantic city; I should probably thank god for his kids right now. With the children there, hot and demanding and trailing doggedly alongside them, Richard's wife won't be able to take his hand as they wander through a maze of alleyways. They won't be able to pause, side-by-side, on little bridges, leaning into one another and sighing as they gaze out. Instead they'll be poring over maps so that they won't get lost, checking their guidebooks for accessible pizza places and child-friendly bars. Perhaps snapping at one another as the day grows hotter and the children more fractious – their small, sun-creamed legs beginning to ache.

Be selfish, I will Richard's kids now. *Be selfish as only children can be.*

Be indifferent to the buildings' beauty and to the green of the canals, to the way that the old, corroded steps disappear into the water, as if consumed by smoke. Stamp on those ancient cobbles and throw your cross, little heads back. Make the gulls and pigeons flap. Open your red mouths wide and *scream*.

"Excuse me, are you all right?"

With a jolt, I come back to myself, to a foggy voice in the background announcing more delays, to all the bustling station brightness – and to a girl peering up at me, holding a baby. She has cropped blond hair and can't be much older than twenty.

"I'm fine," I begin. "Completely fine..."

But I feel myself blush and hastily attempt to relax the muscles in my face. I'm sure that I've been scowling and grimacing. My mouth twisting and my brow furrowing as if I, myself, am a furious child.

"You were swaying on your feet," the girl explains. "I thought you were going to keel right over."

She goes on talking, but I find it hard to focus. It occurs to me that she might be about to explain about that body on the line, about more bodies, maybe. And I don't know how to tell her that I don't want to know. But instead, as if it's a perfectly ordinary thing to do, she takes my elbow. She leads me out of the general throng towards the bars and boutiques that line the walls. As she guides me, I realise that she's not the same person as the young mother in Kings Cross. She isn't wearing a baseball cap and her baby is much younger. Strapped across her breasts, the infant strains around to look at me while his mother chatters, his movement lizard-like.

"You want to get yourself a nice cup of tea," the girl says. "Something to eat."

"I'm fine," I reply. "Really."

But even as I'm protesting, a queasy dizziness overtakes me. I grip my suitcase handle in a sweaty fist, fighting to suppress a queasy wave. *Not again. Please.* The station wobbles as if through a heat-haze, but the baby's gaze remains steady and the intensity of those eyes is somehow familiar. I think of the toddler in the capped girl's arms. It's as if these children are interchangeable, as I thought their mothers were. Such frank blue stares.

I clench the handle tighter.

"Yes," I hear myself murmur. "I should probably eat something."

It has, in fact, been hours since I forced down a slice of toast at breakfast. It isn't good enough. The baby's scrutiny is cold and assessing – but his mother smiles.

"You could get something here, maybe?" she says and I realise I'm standing beside a café bar.

"Yes," I say. "Thank you."

I scrabble to push the door open, my palms slipping on the glass. "Thank you. You're very kind. Thanks…"

I go on muttering as I stumble into a tight, laminated space, twinkling with halogen bulbs and reeking of coffee. A waitress materialises and wafts her hand at the nearest cramped table. I sit and then glance back to the door. The baby and young mother are already gone, but as I ask for bottled water and scan the menu, I continue to struggle against an absurd urge to keep looking. To double-check those windows to make sure the pair of them aren't lurking about there still, spying, possibly. Judging. I try to focus on the food.

I'd like the chef's salad, but then recall some vague worries about restaurant salad. No soft cheese either, I remember. No seafood, nuts, or liver. I settle on a plain chicken sandwich in the end – *just in case* –

48

although when it arrives, it looks cheaper than it should, and synthetic, and as I chew, I'm too aware of the white paste of it circling my mouth. Yet somehow I manage to eat half, and I steadfastly refuse to allow myself to read the wine list. *Although the way that baby stared ...*

Don't, I warn myself. Just stop this.

Stop.

My unease is exasperating and especially laughable considering my usual attitude towards babies. Up until a few weeks ago, until I started to wonder about myself, my broodiness had grown to such an extent that whenever I found myself in close proximity to some other woman's baby, even a stranger's baby, I'd stare compulsively, greedily, as if I hardly had a say in the matter. And each time my gaze raked over some tiny, nestled body, scratching at the details – a nuzzling head spun with wispy hair, the instinctive clutch of a soft-curled hand – the pang would catch me first in the oesophagus. A sob almost, hastily swallowed. And although I frequently attempted to mock my desperation – I felt such a sad, ticking cliché – it made no difference. The sheer power of that need easily overwhelmed my humour and my reasoning. All my small defences.

But now, in my current state, it seems I can't even stand to glance at a baby without panicking. I hardly dare. It's a whole other kind of foolishness. And yet didn't I experience something similar the last time? Maybe it's natural?

Perhaps after all the fantasising, after secretly imagining the warmth of my own child, how my very own baby might fit into my arms, *how it might fill me*, the actual possibility makes it too much to bear? There's too much to lose.

Or maybe it's simply one of the odder, un-discussed pregnancy symptoms? I hope it's that. And of course I hope it isn't truly like the last time. I pray it's not just me –

But: *Stop.*

I need a distraction. *Anything.*

Wine, I think –

No, I think.

I take out my phone to check the time.

But I don't ring Richard. I won't even consider ringing Richard. I fumble through my tickets instead. I run my finger across the black printed numbers and words, *that* destination. I go over the journey details once more, though I scarcely believe them.

I think about the smaller connecting train I'll take tomorrow after tonight's stay in Edinburgh. And I think about how lucky I'd been to book a hotel room at such short notice, what with the festival. How a stranger's last minute cancellation had almost felt like fate.

Tomorrow, I think. *Tomorrow.*

I'll reach the loch house.

But there's no way I can genuinely convince myself. And perhaps it won't be until I'm back in Kings Cross, finally confronted with the flickering information that the Edinburgh train, *my* train, has arrived (at last!) that the truth will strike me. *That I'm really going back.*

After shoving my drawing at Marie, I went straight down to the loch. To the beach, where I might escape.

The beauty down there often turned everything inside out, as if anything else was insubstantial, a distraction. No more than a string of dreams. With the sunlight, even the truth of my loss could sometimes flutter in the distance, shifting with the blinking waves, swirling with the shadows underneath.

It was little wonder I spent so much time there. I could have explored the woods that began further along the shore, or the overgrown fields, but always, I found myself turning towards the water, my feet slipping eagerly across the stones. It went beyond beauty. In the loch's shine, like spilt mercury, I frequently experienced a sense of dropping away. As if it was me somehow, and not the light, that was fragmenting.

And there were practical purposes to my visits too. Some days, I washed my lathered sheets there. I told Marie that I was making dens before carrying my incriminating bedding away in wadded bundles. I rinsed my linen in the cold shallows and afterwards, stretched it out across the larger, flatter rocks to dry. It didn't take long when the sun was out. And although it was unnecessary (Marie never seemed to come that far, not all the way to the water's edge), while the sheets paled, I had twice found myself turning them into dens anyway. Pretending they were tents as if I was still some little wondering kid.

It seemed harmless enough. Although I was far too old for such games, there was nobody to see me, to judge me, and there was an undeniable satisfaction in those crawlspaces between the rocks and cotton. Taut, white pockets, which smelt of waterweeds and soap. Once inside, I could imagine I was anywhere. Or nowhere. I clung to the idea of their protection from the swelling midge clouds, and from Marie and all her talking. From her stupid, searching gaze.

But I didn't have my sheets that afternoon. And of course I didn't have my drawing things either. Nonetheless, I kicked off my shoes, as I often did, in order to clamber more freely across the rocks. I found a dryish, crooked space between them and settled down inside.

51

For a while, I fidgeted with the stones there and with the water that squeezed up from underneath. I redirected glimmering channels, building dams and tiny, sparkling canals before smashing their banks and burying them, and then creating more. As the sunlight softened, settling gradually across the rocks' worn surfaces, I sorted the stones by colour into small, clicking piles. I set up miniature cairns of brown and orange, of grey and startling blue, although the biggest mound was of that lunar, bone-like white. I loved those pebbles most of all. Their clean smoothness, *mint imperials.*

Now and then, unable to resist, I paused to press one to my lips. And they tasted better than sweets; they tasted of winter. I touched one with my tongue and shivered, and thought of Alice.

Before Jemma, Alice had been my best friend. My very best friend in the entire world – until two terms ago when she'd had to move away, after her mother had remarried. If I'd have been younger, with Alice beside me, those stones might have been diamonds or emeralds, treasure cat-burgled from a museum. Mermaid-pearls, perhaps.

A long, long time ago, at least four years back, we used to pretend we were mermaids; we used to pretend a lot of things, although mostly we rode imaginary horses. We were cowgirls or highway women, some kind of outlaws – even at the time, I wasn't quite sure. But it didn't matter. As soon as we started to play, the school's pockmarked tarmac and wet railings melted away. Together, we galloped and reared through lightning-ripped nightscapes. We fled fires and floods and baying mobs. We fell magnificently and died until the bell went, surrounded by lavish skirts and pools of blood.

"Alice, don't leave me! You can't leave me. You're so beautiful. So talented. You've so much to give!"

"But you must be brave, Liberty... You must go on without me. The pain's too much!"

We took it in turns to break. It was the best part of the game. The funniest...

Perhaps only beaten in terms of giggling by the grisly adventures we sent our Barbie dolls on. Days when Alice's Ken became our serial killer, pushing an endless stream of overdressed or naked girlfriends from chair-mountains, or strangling them, or poisoning them with plastic grapes. Sometimes he removed loose arms or legs, a crudely hair-cut head, and we would bind such treasures in toilet roll and Sellotape; we held funerals for hours. And when one silvery February afternoon, a supply teacher read Bluebeard to our class, Alice and I became obsessed. Ken was never ever just Ken again, and we

52

unearthed a tiny diary key. Felt-tipped many of our Barbies' fingers an incriminating scarlet –

Except, I realised, I couldn't even think about those games anymore. About playing. *I couldn't even keep Alice.*

Nothing was the same.

I stood abruptly.

Stones hailed from my chalky hands, my dusty lap. The sun had grown heavy on the back of my neck. My head was swimming and my eyes burnt. I stared at the water for a long time, until the jagged fragments of pebbles and sky and eddying light merged into one again. It took a little while to put everything back together, but I finally managed it. I wiped my nose on my sleeve and then climbed determinedly out of my crevice and onto one of the largest rocks.

It was even hotter against the stone, surprisingly hot, but I no longer cared. I spread myself out as if I was one of my sheets. While I lay there, I could hear the smaller, looser pebbles tapping and clinking together without me, turning with the bubbles in the shallows. I closed my eyes and waited. The inside of my head seeped and flowered, black and red. Black, and red.

I dozed, as I often did on that small, white beach beside the loch, but when I woke, I felt flushed and sticky, although the sun was already beginning to set. And there were midges everywhere, flecks and dashes muddled with my own sketchy, waking floaters. The insects fell and crawled across my vision. They seemed intent on eating me alive. Scratching and slapping at my bare arms and then waving my hands, I walked back and forth between the rocks, watching as the midge clouds followed and then dispersed, as they regrouped and then followed me once more. Beyond my irritation and the scribble of their tiny bodies, the huge, spreading loch drank in the lowering sun. Its orange looked otherworldly. Too thick and still.

But as I stared and the insects parted, that great expanse shimmered and in the distance, where the far shore cut into the water, a small, dark shape emerged, only to glide, just out of sight. Briefly, rubbing my eyes, I thought of monsters, of those grainy images of snakelike necks and blurry humps. I thought of ominous shadows rolling just beneath the water's skin – but I told myself that I believed in monsters even less than I believed in ghosts and besides, everyone knew that the monster myths belonged to a different loch. And yet I went on staring, but the shape (if it had truly existed in the first place) was gone. It must have been a boat, I decided. A little boat, with a fisherman, that was all.

I imagined him sailing by while I slept, and I wondered if he'd noticed me, my small body, lying curled among the rocks? He might have glanced past me to the loch house, remembering the rumours, the spooky stories… Ignoring the midges, I turned to look myself. And I gasped at what I saw there. Gasped – and then began to laugh.

It wasn't unusual for me to track Marie while I wandered the shoreline. Between rearranging my sheet-tents and pebbles, I'd keep half an eye out, and I was usually aware of her when she came edging slowly around the house. The garden was her territory in the way that the beach had already become mine and I'd pause occasionally to watch her potter, crouching with a trowel among the straggling geraniums, plucking at the heather. Sometimes, she'd stand and gaze out, as if looking beyond me, one hand lifted to evade the water's glare, scanning the vast sky or distant hills – *expecting what, exactly?* Other times, she'd drag a chair from the kitchen and simply slump inside it, knees spread wide and arms lolling, her large hands hanging, empty.

But that afternoon, she was doing none of her usual things. She wasn't her usual self at all – but then the loch house wasn't quite, either.

The sunset had turned the building into something from a fairytale. The whitewashed walls appeared gilded, while the windows flared as if there were actual flames crackling within, and yet the house had also been bisected by a very prosaic looking ladder. All the same, it had taken several seconds for me to spot Marie, or perhaps to absorb what I was seeing.

She was standing, flapping, right at the very top of the ladder, like the awkward pigeon that she was. With her big feet clamped to the highest rungs, she clung to the roof with one hand, while the other flailed. She was trying to grab the television aerial, bent coyly against the chimney, just out of reach.

This is how desperate she is for TV, I thought. For something that, unlike her radio, actually worked. *For noise and other people,* I thought. *For anyone, but me.*

And in her condition too…

My mother would have called it pathetic. We'd hardly watched television at home. At least, not until the start of that long, impossible summer, when Dad had removed the last of his things from the house. When he'd finally married Marie in that hasty town hall ceremony (laughing, as if he hadn't minded, describing the purple plastic roses on

54

the registrar's neat desk). It was only in those weeks of realising that he'd truly left us, when our spacious North London house grew yet larger, *cavernous*, that my mother had started switching on the television.

I'd rush home from school each afternoon to find her spread across the sofa cushions in a hazy half-light, watching the tennis. Or at least appearing to watch it. My mother kept the room so dimmed it was sometimes difficult to tell. While the French windows often stood wide open, the curtains were always drawn. The garden's heat and buzzing drifted in, in small, squeezed pieces, though now and then, the lined hems quivered with a more persistent, fruit-tinged breeze.

And from the television, that very English murmur:

"*Fifteen – Love.*"

Before the furred, steady thud of the ball resumed, on and on, like a heartbeat. Back and forth, like breath.

My mother had watched the screen and I'd watched her. I don't think I'd ever before seen her looking so blank, or pale, or still. Not in the flesh, anyway. She looked like an old photograph of herself, perhaps one of the perfume campaign shots, when they'd swathed her in silk, behind a misted lens. She was just as dreamy and beautiful, and as unnervingly unreal... Even when the telephone rang she hardly stirred. She'd glance up, but that was all, maybe rearrange the cushions at her neck, but she wouldn't rise. She never answered.

While it trilled though, she sometimes smiled in my general direction and once or twice, she raised her glass to me. She winked. Or seemed to wink, through those blowsy shadows, that uncertain light. And in return, I'd cross the room, not to answer the call either, but to sit on the rug beside her, beside her glass, filled with gin and tonic and shifting ice. When she lifted her drink over my head, I'd hear its hiss and icy tinkle, while the ball-girls ran in circles, and then ducked hastily back in place.

For those brief, long Wimbledon weeks, before school broke up and she enrolled me in Drama, there had been just the two of us. Although I went on loving Dad, perhaps more fiercely than ever, for a little while my mother and I had seemed utterly united. It was us against the world, almost. I knew it wasn't her fault that he had gone.

Now, standing on that bright, cracked beach, listening to the swill and slide of the loch water and staring at Marie up on the roof, at stupid, clumsy, crawling Marie, I felt those moments again acutely. It was painful, but I wanted them back anyway, precisely as they were. I wanted everything, the heavy curtains and the scent of flowers, the slam of rackets and the polite applause. I even wanted my mother's sighs and her sadness – the cool, quiet fear that I'd carried about back then, like an overfilled vase, ready to spill.

I saw how small and precious that fear was now. How lucky I had been.

And I had no idea what I was doing standing there. Standing alone, before the loch house.

How could the world have changed so much?

And while Marie continued shuffling away from the ladder, out across the tiles, I heard the short, high cry of some water bird and felt a sudden darkness flutter over me, like a hood tugged briefly across my face. The sensation lasted seconds, but even after it had cleared, a shadow went on flitting along the loch house's gold-lit wall, quick and loose and mischievous. I turned away, to face the loch again and the setting sun. To the tremors of a rising breeze, and to the light caught in flames across the water.

I didn't hear the ladder fall. Instead I seemed to feel it within, as gentle as the arc and bounce of a distant ball. But a minute or so later, I definitely heard Marie calling out, from behind me, above me – how could I not?

"Libby! Libby, *help*."

I half-turned to glance over my shoulder. Sure enough, the wall of the loch house was blank and clear again, the ladder lying on its side among the heather, while Marie remained hunched against the roof. There was no way that she could climb down and if she jumped, she'd surely break a leg, at the very least. She moved as if to lift an arm to me, to wave her distress, but only her hand managed to flutter. Like the guttering, she seemed haphazardly nailed in place.

"The ladder!" she shouted.

I gazed back out, towards the water. I imagined a little black boat floating in the distance. I imagined it bobbing closer. Closer. I thought about sailing away.

"Libby, look at me! I need you – *look at me…*"

I realised that the midges had gone. I didn't know where they had gone, but I noticed how dim the trees were already growing on the far side of the loch, and yet the fading light only seemed to make the white stones around me glow even colder. Brighter.

"Libby, *please*. Libby –"

The loch smell rolled over me, green and close.

"My name is Liberty," I whispered.

56

Eventually, I would go to her. But not just yet.

When I think about those weeks with Marie, about the loch house, with its shadows, and about the loch's green fingers slipping across its lunar stones, I know that my loss was so large that sometimes I too simply vanished underneath it. There were hours when I hardly knew who I was, or what I did, when I didn't even try to quiver free. And yet it's all flooding back so easily. Especially that cold intent.

"You have to find yourself to free yourself," Dr Gilchrist once told me.

And I had wanted to slap her, even then.

Because what happened at the loch house wasn't my fault. It remains my mantra –

Or not all my fault, at least.

It turned out later that no one had quite understood what Marie was thinking, packing us off like that so soon after the accident. Stealing us so quietly away.

"I can't handle any more goodbyes," she'd told me, when in truth she was avoiding confrontations with several of my relatives, including my Grandfather, who never would have condoned her plans – and yet what exactly had she been planning?

She claimed our escape was what my father would have wanted. "For us to be together, to help each other," she confided, her gaze softening with a secretive light.

But looking back, Marie seems so full of strange ideas and secrets; it makes me wonder if her sadness and madness weren't one thing, the same thing, from the very start? I think how young she was, how isolated... And how nobody would have dreamt of arguing for her sanity in the end.

Nonetheless, there is another version of events in which she hauled me off not because she was already becoming 'unbalanced', but as an act of protection. She was attempting to escape a hungry media, way too interested in the crash. She was saving us from journalists and photographers of the type who lurked around the crematorium gardens on the morning my parents' bodies were burnt.

I didn't see such vultures for myself of course, since I wasn't allowed to attend the service, and yet I find myself visualising them with the same knife-sharp focus that I'm able to look back on so much. As if my longing somehow transports me.

I picture turned-up collars and cigarettes, the burst of a flashbulb through the trees. Such a stylish send-off would have made good copy – and maybe I really did glimpse some of their photographs? I seem to remember clusters of ridiculously tall, thin women draped in black. Endless dark-sheathed legs and giant sunglasses. Patent stilettos gleaming wetly in the sun.

I do genuinely remember the sun. I remember it vividly, although I was kept inside the house on the morning of the funeral, with only the consolation of some muffling medication and a pair of strange, vague relatives downstairs.

After the accident, my house had drifted with people I hardly knew. Faces I couldn't quite place, or didn't really care to. I had met my American Grandfather, my mother's father, for the first time the night before the cremation. His flight had arrived late and he was as pale as parchment with fatigue and grief. He wasn't at all what I'd been expecting (some brash, Stetson-ed businessman, I suppose, like a character from 'Dallas'), but frail and slump-shouldered. Kind. "She was my Princess," he told me, his papery fingers on my hair.

But of course my Grandfather had gone off with the rest of them that morning, and the people who were supposed to be looking after me (perhaps, after all, nobody I even half-knew, but paid child-carers from some agency, maybe one of them a nurse) didn't bother to check up on me. I had swallowed their tablets and so they'd probably assumed I was sleeping, but I clearly recall kneeling up on my duvet to gaze from my window. I remember how, between my rainbow-shaped stickers, the sky was blue and cloudless. A perfect swimming-pool sky. My head had lolled towards it, resting on the glass, and it seemed like days passed before the cars reappeared. While my breath filled the panes with slow white plumes.

There were no separate services; Mother and Dad were cremated together. It made a kind of sense, I suppose; after all, they had died together, and they'd lived together, previously. Apparently, the new wife, the second wife, made no objections. Marie had agreed to everything before she fled.

And perhaps that was all there was to our leaving – maybe Marie had simply panicked? She'd run, as I am running now, as if compelled, and then become caught inside the loch house –

Maybe I'll never be able to unravel her motivations. There is so much about our leaving, about everything, that doesn't make sense. I can't possibly begin to untangle it all right now. Not while I'm so exhausted, not while I'm still moving. And certainly not here, in this ridiculous cubicle, where in a much more prosaic way, the walls are closing in.

I'm locked in the toilet on board the train to Edinburgh. It's an ugly, panelled box. The cold metallic walls are probably meant to offer an impression of scrubbed cleanliness, but the stainless steel effect is, quite frankly, stained. The entire cubicle is smeared and dented, scored with small, deep gashes. Splintered words. A wad of damp tissues and paper towels erupts from an inadequate bin beneath the sink. The air is dizzying with the stink of urine.

No bigger than a coffin. The thought arrives seemingly unbidden and yet exasperatingly predictable. I push it away, and yet I can't even bring myself to throw up in here. It seems almost miraculous the way that my latest bout of nausea has passed. *I must use train toilets more often...*

I try to smile at myself in the smeared mirror, but my reflection waits a moment before responding. And my skin remains pallid, green about the gills. The paler streaks in my hair have taken on that greenish tinge too, and I can't see anything of my mother in my features this evening. There's no quick wit, no easy beauty. In the past, people have claimed I have her eyes – although not the glint in them, I know.

I touch my collarbone lightly where my shirt is open. My breasts are tender. And I think how this might well be a part of it, as the sickness is a part of it. I consider Marie's apparently symptom-less pregnancy and I wonder if the lack of evidence frightened her? Perhaps she knew no better.

It will be very different with me; this is what I tell myself. *If this time...*

But I shouldn't dwell. It's too early, maybe. And it might only lead on to other more dangerous thoughts – thoughts about babies who were not babies. About blood and bloodlessness and a blank space, a terrible emptiness, amidst swirling pixels on a screen –

My breasts hurt.

This is what I focus on as I turn from the mirror, as I duck my eyes that have never truly been my mother's eyes. I fumble for the lock, impatient now to escape, but when I finally manage to flick the latch, something else returns to me. For a jolting instant, I'm opening another door into another bathroom. It is the loch house bathroom. I recognise it straightaway from the cobwebs flapping like bunting across the ceiling and the way that even the light feels cold. There are blue tiles over the sink. Stains like handprints across the walls.

And in the midst of it, there is Marie.

She's cowering before me, a pink shape through the steam.

There is steam...

My hands are wet with it, but despite the fug, Marie's face is irrepressible. It's far whiter than the rest of her, and shining, and so suddenly startlingly like my own that it's like looking into a whole other mirror. I understand that we share the same expression – a look of horror and vulnerability. A terrible guilt –

Nevertheless: *I hate you*, I remember, and then a strange, dark, gusting triumph.

The metal door bangs open and as abruptly as it came at me, the memory is gone.

I'm back on the train, clinging to the doorframe, swaying with the clatter. I close my eyes briefly, wondering, but Marie has vanished, and I'm more than aware that such images, such flashes, frequently mean nothing. The loch house bathroom, Marie's face, they're probably no more than dream remnants. My tired brain overflowing.

I am, I realise, exhausted – *and my breasts hurt*. I need to collapse now, not to think.

The train rocks and jostles as I hurry back along the aisle to reclaim my first class seat. It's quiet in my carriage, the clack and rattle feels cushioned and the passengers are few and far between. There's an older, suited man sleeping at a table near the door. With his chin nestled onto his ruddy neck and a middle shirt button popped open, he looks oddly defenceless and I'm careful not to disturb him as I slip past. A little further on, a younger, crisp-shirted man is tip-tap-tapping on a laptop. Every now and then, impatience flits across his face as he types or retypes. An earpiece hangs from his ear, like a part of him, come loose.

There's a woman too, buried behind an enormous paperback. I can see the top of her bowed head, her badly dyed red hair. Utterly absorbed, she doesn't glance up as I swing by, but the laptop man does. I catch his gaze briefly and he loses his frown. I feel the tug of his eyes all the way to my end of the carriage.

Perhaps I'm not completely lacking my mother's sparkle after all, but I'm too tired, too distracted, to talk to anyone right now. And a complimentary half-bottle of wine, along with a packet of cashew nuts, sit waiting on my table. I carefully set the packet to one side as I slide into my seat.

At the window, the swimming twilight has solidified into a flat, black emptiness. It's peculiar, this effect of travelling through open country by train at night – it's as if the only light in the world is the light from our carriage, unless it's coming from another train. Some ghost train, racing alongside us.

More mirrors...

But instead of picturing Marie's face, I think about my mother, about how relentlessly I've searched for her in my reflection, over the years. Although for a while, during my teens, after Grandpa had sent me to boarding school, I developed an absurd little fear of mirrors. I was particularly afraid of confronting them after dark. Obviously, it began at the loch house – where everything started, or else ended – but fleetingly I remember the other girls at school, with their sharp elbows and sharper voices, battling one another for space before the glass, while I stepped back.

I was always so different, so separate – though unlike the more regular misfits (the poorer girls and the fat girls, the girls who were too stupid or ugly, or too intelligent), I was never bullied, but instead treated with a kind of extreme politeness, a deference bordering on wary indifference. I've never known how much they were told about me, but there was always that undercurrent, that un-whispered knowledge that I had come from tragedy. That I was 'Something Else'.

Although now as I lift the wine bottle, I deliberately face the shadowed glass. I study my slim arm as it rises to pour and the way that the satiny folds of my blouse curve around my tender breasts. My reflection is doubled and rippled, gently distorted. The tumbler meets my hazy lips. With a familiar sense of defiance, I watch myself drink –

Then realise that someone else is watching me too.

It takes a moment though, to identify the hiss and quiet click of the internal automatic door seizing open. I lean around the arm of my seat to get a better look, but it's another second or so before I'm able to focus on the child there, and to understand that he is real – that an actual child is sitting, legs splayed, on the grey, quivering floor of the intersection between the carriages.

A round, blond toddler. A boy I think, though I don't know why I should think that, with softly lapping, milk-steeped flesh. He's only wearing a nappy. His chin glistens with drool. I have no clear idea how old he might be, eighteen months, perhaps – two years? He's really just a baby, and yet there's a startling solidity in his settled posture and putty-like limbs; in an odd way, he appears over-grown. His mouth hangs slackly as he stares at me. Tiny glimmers to its darkness. Emerging teeth.

But where's his mother?

Perhaps she'd been using that narrow passage to change him and has vanished momentarily to fetch clean clothes or cream? I look past the toddler to the space around him, and to the closed carriage door beyond our open one. The panelled ceiling lights bob with the train's onward rush, but there's no sign of anyone else, not a shadow. However, even my own carriage looks deserted from this angle. Each of my fellow passengers is hidden, burrowed between the empty tables and spare seats. I crane back towards the open door. I wet my lips.

"Hello," I say. "Where's your mummy then, eh? Where's Mummy?"

I try to keep my voice steady. I tell myself I need to remain calm for this child, that I mustn't alarm him – although he doesn't actually appear anywhere near as disarmed as I'm feeling. He simply *looks*, while inside, ridiculously, my own heart has started to race as it does when I'm preparing for an audition or a doctor's appointment, or if I'm about to meet a new crew on Richard's set. It's the familiar beginning of one of my panics, my absurd panics – and of course the child does not reply. His big blue eyes encase me.

For a few seconds, I think I know who he might be. I recall the young woman at the station, the first woman with the cap and the ponytail, talking to someone else (her own mother?) about a body on the line...

But how stupid all this wondering is – there is a baby out there. And he's alone.

My hesitation is madness. Especially after all the time I've spent gawking at strangers' babies. Those days when I'm hardly able to pass a new mother and her infant on the street without feeling that ache, my palms sweating, literally itching, to take hold. Only a matter of weeks ago, I'd have scooped that child up without thinking, purely grateful for the excuse to hold a small, warm body close. I've done it often enough, insinuating myself with women I hardly know, the wives and girlfriends of Richard's friends, offering to take their tiny children, especially their newborns, as if I'm the one doing them a favour. Painting on a reassuring smile as I do so. Pushing through the hurt.

My fingers curl, hovering above my stomach, but I don't permit them to land. Instead, drawing breath, I force myself to rise and step determinedly, if a little shakily, around the seat towards the passage. I'm about to sink to my knees, to reach out to the toddler when the door at his back gasps open. And a second child appears.

This one's a girl. She's older, perhaps as much as nine years old. She possesses a similar messy halo of shining hair – his sister, I suppose. She looks at me before bowing over the little boy. She's wearing a tight navy skirt and a T-shirt decorated with a peeling pattern of red balloons. A pastel-coloured necklace (a candy necklace?) pinches a loop around her thin, grubby neck. Freckles burst across her nose. Behind the freckles, her skin is very pale. Even her eyebrows are pale, and her fleshy mouth; she looks dusted with powder. But her eyes are surprisingly deep for someone so fair. As night-filled as the windows.

And I feel surrounded. Beside her, the blue of her brother's gaze is all the more startling.

The girl stoops to lift him, without taking her eyes from me. The boy seems more than half her size and I expect her to stagger with his weight, but she doesn't. Still, I think I ought to speak, that I should offer to help. *She's looking at me.*

I ignore my banging heart, my clammy palms, and: "Are you ok there?" I ask, "Would you like me to take him? Or fetch your mother? *Where's your mother?*"

That's the pertinent question, I think, and almost laugh. I can actually feel the laughter gathering inside me, brittle, little, shell-like shards – except that then the girl's gaze drops away and instead of any sense of release, I feel suddenly worthless. *Hopeless.*

It's as if this girl on the train has seen directly into me, straight through to my jangling nerves and my panic – and she isn't impressed, or even convinced. She heaves the baby, that giant baby, higher, so that his chin (practically the same size as hers!) rests on her shoulder. His waxy feet dangle around her scuffed, scabbed knees. There's a brown stain bleeding through his nappy. I try not to recoil, but my stomach flutters. A tiny flutter that I'm sure means nothing.

For God's sake, I should know better.

With an awkward shrugging gesture, the girl clasps her brother tighter and spins around, away from me. But before they disappear once more into the next carriage, she glances back. The dark glass of her eyes twinkles as her gaze catches mine, and then her whole face brightens as she breaks into a smile.

And it is such a true smile. A beautiful smile –

I cling on to it long after the children slip away.

"We need to start facing facts," Marie said. "If we can't talk about what happened, about the accident, about how we're coping, or not coping – we at least need to talk about this baby."

But she was struggling to even look at me and I could see from the smudges around her eyes that she'd only recently stopped crying. And her hands went on shaking too, just as they had been when she'd finally let go of the ladder, stepping awkwardly from the last rung. I'd watched her fingers tremble when she'd lifted them to cover her face before she had walked unsteadily back into the house. I'd left her huddled on the roof for five minutes, maybe ten. That was all.

"You did already know about my pregnancy, didn't you, Libby?"

I stared at the kitchen table, at the expanse of scored, greyish wood stretched between us. Although it remained dry outside, the wind had risen with the night. It bustled back and forth in Marie's narrow garden, rifling through the bushes, whining into the walls. The kitchen felt muggy in comparison. Above the table, the air had thickened. I imagined it settling like sediment. Grainy layers.

"I asked you a question, Libby. Please. I'm trying."

I shrugged.

Then flicked my gaze back up, to Marie's face. Her nose was blotched too, and when she drew in a breath, she half-gasped, half-shuddered. She wasn't quite back in control. Her hair had spilt loose from its elastic and there were several strands sticking to her jaw in a series of small s's. When she sighed, they writhed and I thought of mouse-tails again, and then, deliberately, of worms and snakes.

"If you knew I was pregnant, I don't understand how you could have…"

She stopped again and glanced at the window, although there was nothing to see there. Just black, with only the shine of the sink taps mirrored in the glass. From where we sat, we couldn't see the rest of the room, or our reflections. We'd vanished. But I suspected that if I went outside, the darkness would be different, less dense. It would open up before me, especially with that wind hurrying the clouds along. Especially if there were stars.

I'd never seen such stars as there were above the loch. Most evenings, they filled the sky with shattered glass. Before climbing into bed, I'd open my window wide and lean out as far as I could, simply to gaze. I found comfort in the loch's nocturnal rippling too. Even when clouds faded the sky's twinkling, the water's glinting, those smooth liquid sounds were soothing, and somehow silvery in themselves. Hanging over my sill, I'd inhale deeply, as if I could suck down some of the bigness of the night, some of that endless black. I imagined it cleaning me out inside, as the pounding rain had done. And I had never worried about heights.

But there, in the kitchen, the air went on condensing. The things around us, the cupboards and the humming fridge and the old scorched oven, seemed to have taken sneaking steps closer. And there were too many pans stacked precariously on the draining board, too many of Marie's coffee cups queuing in a brown-rimmed row.

"Aren't you interested in this baby, Libby?" Marie said quietly. "I'm surprised. I thought you would be. After all, this baby is a part of your father. And a part of you too."

I closed my eyes, holding on to the sky still, to my stars and the loch below. It was what I needed then, that swilling void. That emptiness, which filled me.

"*Your* brother or sister, Libby," Marie said.

In my head, I rose; I strode away from her again, away from the table and this 'conversation', and out of the kitchen altogether. I went outside.

In reality, I stayed exactly where I was. My legs, tucked awkwardly beneath me, felt claylike. Her words weighed me down. They were what had thickened the air, I realised – and I pictured those layers more intently. Suffocating layers, like her coarse, grey wool.

"Well, I'm going to tell you about this baby, Libby. Whether you want to know or not."

I found myself staring at the bin. I could smell the rubbish where the bag was overstuffed and the swing-lid couldn't shut. I realised that I'd been aware of the odour for a while, another thing, pressing us too close. Sickly-sweet and meaty, it reminded me of cat-food and with a jolt, I thought of Mr Whiskers. So far away from here. I imagined the yowling cattery at night – *all those bewildered animals* – and a warm wet wave of sadness swelled inside my chest.

"You probably *need* to know," Marie continued. "It might help explain a few things. It might help you to understand if I'm overtired, or anything. And it might actually help us too. It might bring us together. Help us get through this."

She'd focused now, but I refused to look back at her. I was concentrating; I couldn't let myself spill over.

"Also," she said. "If something *were* to happen . . ."

There was a stain on the wedged-open bin lid; it was moon-shaped, milky-looking. The air quivered with another of Marie's lengthy, hitching sighs.

"I'm beginning to show more," she said, and there was something new beneath her beleaguered tone now, something unexpected. A quiet pride.

"The baby's due in January. I thought I'd be bigger by now. Other women, other pregnant women, always seemed bigger, earlier. But I suppose everyone's different, and what with everything... For a little while, I almost seemed to forget I was pregnant. And I haven't had any sickness, any of those 'normal' things. I suppose I've been lucky, except that it hasn't helped the baby feel very real. But then, not much has felt real lately – but I'm sure you understand that, Libby. Don't you?"

I wouldn't nod; of course I understood, but why should I help her? I reminded myself: *no eye contact*. Besides, what I was actually thinking was that January wasn't far away. *Just after Christmas* (although Christmas itself was unthinkable). I tried to work it out, counting backwards. They had only married in July.

Marie carried on, as if she'd guessed what I was wondering.

"I'm nearly five months gone," she confirmed, and again I heard the lilt in her voice. A secretive *happiness*.

"Yesterday, when I was working in the garden, I thought I felt something. A kind of flickering. Like a bubble growing, and then popping. You know, I think it might have been the baby. The baby moving. Kicking. I think I've started believing in it now. At least, more than I did."

I thought of her clambering across the roof and I hardly believed *her*. Her stupidity was overwhelming – and yet I didn't know that I was about to speak until I did.

"And exactly how long were you with Dad for, then? How long before he left us, when he was supposed to be with my mother, still? With me?"

For a few seconds there was nothing, only the slinking wind outside and the fridge's drone, but then Marie swallowed. I felt her shuffle in her seat, perhaps considering reaching out to me. I slid my

67

hands from the table, and they fell like separate things. Two beanbags, heavy in my lap.

"Oh, Libby," Marie said.

I held myself carefully, although that white stain seemed to peel and lift away from the bin lid, smearing before my eyes. I drew in a shivering breath of my own, and a new scent came at me, startlingly different from the cat-meat stink. I smelt earth and sap and musky flowers. A familiar, heady perfume –

The rhododendrons in our London garden.

It was the scent of lost things, the scent of home.

An age ago, at least three summers back, when Alice had been away, staying with her father, I'd spent much of my lonely school holidays inside our ancient rhododendron bush. For a while, it had been my favourite place to play. There was a perfect space near the centre (*my first den*, I thought now), which you could only reach if you knew the right way to crawl between the sprawling branches, if you were small enough to duck beneath the swathes of green.

At first, it had been a brilliant hiding place, the air inside was rich and flecked with pollen; half-glimpsed fragments that tumbled like algae through the emerald light. Sometimes I went there to escape the ringing phone, or my parents' shouting, their noisy friends. Other times, I'd read or draw in there. I'd arrange collages on the powdery earth, transforming silken petals and waxy leaves into seascapes and faces and intricate feasts. I once constructed an entire elaborately tiered wedding cake from fallen flowers. I could be as silly or as earnest as I pleased; nobody could reach me inside those rhododendrons. They held me safe.

Until one afternoon when I heard Dad outside. From my hidden pocket in the garden, I heard the French windows clatter and then his distinct footsteps swinging out across the lawn. It had taken me a minute to realise that he wasn't alone; his companion's tread was quieter; she shuffled where he strode. She was perhaps barefoot, and I knew immediately that she wasn't my mother. Her voice did not ring out, but only murmured, and while this woman's laughter was frequent, it was also nervous. A separate self-conscious breeze.

Dad's voice had been familiar enough though. Deep and resonant and velvety. It bowled over me with that dusty light, although he had no idea that I was tucked away, close by. That I was listening. And:

"I want you," I heard him tell that woman, that stranger.

"I want you now. Come here."

Sitting, huddled, in the loch house kitchen, I forced my hands from my eyes. Marie gazed at me, her head cocked bird-like to one side.

"It wasn't just you," I told her. "He had other women. You weren't the first."

I was careful not to shout. I wanted to keep my words cool and clipped, as if I were the grown-up. I didn't want Marie to guess how small I truly felt. Dad's voice had returned too vividly. His thick tone felt wedged inside me –

"Come here".

It was like fur, sticking in my throat.

"My mother knew all about them," I went on hastily. "She told me about them, or she might as well have. I'd hear her talking, on the phone. And I heard him too – they'd shout. But that didn't matter. None of you mattered, not really."

Except even as I said these things, I wondered. What if it had been Marie who Dad was with that summer's day so long ago? I tried to remember when exactly it was that she began working for him, when she was no more than another eager photography student, one of his 'dogsbody volunteers'? Maybe it had been Marie, *only Marie*, for all this time? The possibility twisted my stomach, and then it hit me, as it hadn't before:

She has Dad's baby in her.

She's like my mother, with that baby in her –

The idea flared through me. I didn't know where it had come from or what it meant exactly, but my whole body felt livid with it. I was burning up, although when my voice emerged, it remained short and cool.

"I wish," I said, "that you had fallen from the roof."

And then I was standing. Glaring.

For a few seconds, Marie stared right back, her beady eyes shining. Her chewed mouth twitched and then her pink nostrils flared and she rose too, slowly and shakily, until she was towering, quaking, over me.

"I know you do," she said. "And I know what you did, too."

Despite everything, I felt a small, bright flicker of curiosity. I wondered what would happen when she blew.

"I know you pushed the ladder," she hissed. "I knew you were there, Libby. I could feel you there, and I heard your footsteps too. *Pitter-patter, pitter-patter,* as off you went again, running away. And when I climbed down, I saw the footprints in the flowerbeds – for

69

God's sake, Libby, what did you think you were doing? This isn't a joke. I'm carrying a *baby*. Doesn't that mean anything to you? *Your Dad's baby*."

"What?" I said. "What are you talking about?"

Confused, I pictured Marie back up there, on the roof. I saw her arms flapping towards the aerial. I saw her begin to crawl across the tiles. I thought about the clouds of midges and how they'd parted, and the stealthy way that the sun had crept. Orange sliding down the whitewashed walls.

"I didn't push your ladder," I told her. "I was on the beach. You know I was. I came and put the ladder back up for you. It was heavy. I could hardly lift it. I helped you to climb down."

I watched doubt inch over her. It fogged her eyes and creased her forehead.

"You're crazy," I went on, although I remained careful not to shout. "Footsteps. *Footprints* – Marie, you saw me down there, by the loch. You were shouting for me. How could you have heard someone running? There isn't anyone else out here. There's us, that's all. Just us."

"B-but," she said, "but, then – even if you didn't push it, let's say that you didn't, and it was some freakish accident, a gust of wind or something, and I heard – well, I don't know what, I know that *you heard me*, Libby. You must have heard me calling. And you didn't come. Not for ages. You didn't come."

As if she'd been toppled, Marie sank abruptly into her chair. Her bewildered gaze snapped away and she put her head on the table and began to cry. Huge, heaving, little-girl sobs. I stared, trying to resurrect the disgust I'd felt when she began this talk. I remembered the scruffier kids at school, the ones who nobody would partner. The ones who avoided eye contact, even with each other, who were always at the back of the queue at lunchtime, or standing alone by the playground wall.

But, although I resisted it, I felt lost too. And I was exhausted, almost as helpless as Marie.

Ignoring the clenching inside me, I turned away, but I was no longer thinking of her calling, and the way that I'd ignored her. I wasn't thinking of Dad anymore either, or the rhododendrons, any of that. Instead I recalled how just before the ladder fell, I thought I'd seen a shadow flutter across the loch house wall. And then it came back to me distinctly – that brief sense, which quickly dissipated, of darkness, closing in.

70

I open my sticky eyes to the amber glow of the slumbering carriage. I've been dozing and muddle-headed, I sit up, taking in the empty aisle and sealed doors. There are no signs of any children. But then, there's barely a clue that anyone else exists at all.

I check my phone. There's well over an hour until Edinburgh and the train's judder sinks right through me; the loneliness seems to tap against my bones. It's late enough to call Richard, but I won't, not yet. He wouldn't like it; *she* might answer. And besides, I half-promised myself that I wouldn't. *Not till I'm certain.* However shaky I might feel.

So instead, I strain against the clatter, listening out for a snore or a sigh. Any suggestion of life, of other people, will do. I don't hear any such sounds, but after a moment, a gentler clicking separates itself from the general rattle, and I recall the laptop man.

With a flicker of relief, I remember the bold slide of his gaze as he stared after me and before I can think it through, I down the last of my wine – acrid now against my sleep-soft mouth – and rise. I pad quietly, but purposefully, between the seats. And it's a simple thing, I tell myself. Quite harmless. It's just that I can't sit there on my own for another minute, let alone an hour, waiting for children to reappear, or not appear. Waiting for my past to crowd back in.

And even before I've reached his table, the man is looking out from his keyboard. Blinking up at me. And there's a bottle beside him too, and it's not some pithy, mini complimentary wine, but a gleaming, full-sized single malt –

And: "Hello," he says, his voice low and conspiratorial, so that I feel almost expected, justified, as I slip into the opposite seat.

"Do you mind?"

I echo his hushed tone. I'm polite, deferential, although it's not even a real question since I'm already seated and staring pointedly from his hands, paused beside his laptop, to his whisky.

He keeps his smile small, but I can see how clumsily it's restrained, and his gaze dips to my throat and then lower, before darting back up to my mouth. He's very young, a few years off thirty. I take

71

in his fair, cropped hair and good cheekbones, the traces of bronze stubble patching his jaw. That careful suit.

"Not at all," he says. He touches his keyboard lightly. "You'd be doing me a favour. Can I offer you a drink?"

I nod. Obviously, I nod.

"There's only the one glass, I'm afraid. But if you're not worried about sharing? I'm not contagious, I promise." He flashes a brief tight line of teeth.

It's not even a proper glass, but a plastic tumbler swiped from the buffet car, already clouded with his fingerprints, his lip-prints. I return his smile, however. And he pours.

Nearly half his bottle, I notice, has already been drained. But even without the bottle, it's clear that he's been drinking from the smudginess to his muddy eyes and his ready hospitality – the way he has to concentrate to keep his grin from slopping wider. I go on studying him openly as I knock back my measure, hardly feeling the scorch. *Half-cut*, I decide.

I've always liked the phrase, the way it implies damage, but not necessarily irretrievable damage. He offers me his hand.

"I'm Tim," he says.

He folds his fingers over mine. His grasp is warm and surprisingly steady, but for a moment, I hesitate. Then: "Lizzy," I say.

I don't know why I say it. And then I wonder if he's actually a Tom or a Tony, and how little difference any of it makes. It's all a game, I think, and all too easy; the way he's looking at me, his blurry gaze shambling between my hair and face and breasts. Picking at my buttons. I think of Richard.

I think of Richard explaining how when he first saw me, all those years ago, flitting through the crowd on set, he felt knocked sideways. He couldn't stop looking, he said. I moved like water; *I shone like water –*

But what if Richard were to lay his brown eyes on me tonight? (His paler brown eyes, his lit-clever eyes.) Even if he saw me sitting here, exactly like this, determinedly drinking with an attractive younger man, I wonder if he'd feel anything at all.

With the next sip, the whisky blazes, heating a path from my tongue, through my chest, to my tingling centre, and my hand jerks involuntarily, protectively, towards my waist. I snatch it back. I grip the table instead and keep drinking. Once more, leaning across for his bottle.

"Thirsty girl, eh?" Tim says.

I nod, although my smile has begun to ache. I want this to stay simple, to be normal. Whatever 'this' is. Whatever *normal* –

I try harder.

"I'm sorry," I say. "Barging over here. Drinking all your whisky. I don't know what you must think."

"No problem," he replies slowly. "I understand. Long journeys. You get restless. Lonely. Trains at night."

I murmur agreement, feeling a rush of gratitude that he's playing his part. For the sheer cliché of him. His laptop clicks quietly as he presses it closed.

"I've interrupted your work too," I say.

"Fucking reports," he says. "It's a blessing. Honestly."

And it's going to be ok, I think. I can manage this.

"What do you do?" I ask.

He begins explaining about the nightmare he's had since being promoted, how he has to travel all the time and how he's no longer one of the boys. He's meant to catch out his co-workers, he explains. Report back... And I nod or shrug whenever he pauses, although I can't quite grasp what his job actually is. Not that it matters. He's happy to keep talking, maybe because of the whisky, and I hardly need to listen. It's such a relief.

Generally, I'm more used to staving off advances than making them. Aside from Richard, I've only attempted to approach men twice before, in my whole life. The first occasion was an age ago, perhaps during my second year with Richard, when I still believed I might make him jealous. I made a pass at one of his friends at a party. That man was older than him, far older than me, with a rather too burnished chestnut tan, but in good shape. He was one of the producers, I think. I didn't know him well. We were standing just outside the kitchen, sipping margaritas. I can't remember what we talked about, but I can still recall how his leg felt, the surprisingly firm curve of it when I reached out and touched his thigh. And the strange, strained moment when he stopped talking. And how I'd almost laughed...

But he wasn't Richard.

I tried, but his kisses felt wrong in my mouth. In contrast to his eager fingers, knotting in my hair and squeezing down, inside my dress, his tongue was oddly tentative. Unsettling. And once I realised that Richard wasn't coming to find me, that he wouldn't discover us, I backed off, pleading dizziness, too much tequila. With a single regretful sigh, the producer released me. Probably half-afraid anyway that I'd throw up on his hand-made shoes ...

73

But with this Tim, I don't want to go anywhere. There's something soothing about his tipsy openness, his ordinariness. His forgettable day-to-day problems.

The tumbler passes back and forth between sips now, instead of shots, and I realise that his complaints about middle management are coming to an end. And I think I made the appropriate sympathetic faces throughout and only grinned in the right places, though often real lives, other people's lives, seem so odd and funny to me. And if not exactly drunk, I am a little woozy. Tim's outline has grown sketchier, almost as feathery as his reflection in the dark window and when he leans towards me, resting on his elbows, wrinkling his sleeves, the whisky on his breath smells duskier, more enticing, than the raw swallow in my throat. I draw in his warmth.

"How about you?" he asks, but he's no longer discussing work, and the question throws me –

"Where are you going?"

Fleetingly, I consider the lines I rehearsed back in my flat, that ridiculous explanation. *An old friend...We used to holiday together when we were children...* Of course, still the words won't come.

"Edinburgh," is all I say, and he nods.

Then begins to tell me about his own journey, which turns out to be nothing to do with his job, but a short break for his step-brother's stag celebrations. He chuckles, flushing as he goes on, his cheeks as rosy as a little boy's. Although it's such an old-fashioned comedy standard, he says, they might actually try pulling the naked lamppost trick – for that very reason, in fact. He has a rope, he tells me, in his bag.

"A rope?" I say.

And while he continues, sniggering over the plans he's been concocting with a third naughtier brother, I think about the last time I made a move on a man I barely knew. About how messily it might have ended.

It was after Richard's daughter was born. His second child. We hadn't seen each other for several weeks and I was on the tube when I read about the birth in the paper. It wasn't much, a few pathetic lines in the Metro, tagged on to the end of a brief piece about Richard's first short film award. Naturally, I'd known about Amanda's pregnancy, and yet, to see it there. Like that.

I didn't get off at my stop, but stayed on to Leicester Square and walked to Soho. To the first dodgy bar I could find. It didn't take long; there are still such places, not too sleek, not too busy. Almost quaint. In order to enter, I had to negotiate a black-painted stairwell and a cluster of plump businessmen, smoking in the doorway. I let the first man who asked buy me a drink.

Two double gins and when I crossed my legs, he cupped my knee. I uncrossed them and his hand travelled slowly, like a spider, beneath my skirt. Shortly afterwards, we went outside to hail a taxi together. And as we waited, I did feel something.

His kisses certainly weren't cautious, and to my surprise, I found myself stirring, softening, against him. Despite his thinning, silvering hair and the probability that he had his own wife and kids folded into a pocket in his wallet, I almost wanted him. Until we were in the cab and he began nuzzling into me. Then I burst into tears.

"Never you mind, Love," he said, sitting back magnanimously, playing the gentleman.

But when he dropped me off in the square neighbouring my own (naturally, I didn't give him my exact address, he was a stranger after all), for a few intense seconds, he held on to me too hard.

"Look after yourself," he murmured, and his fist tightened on my arm.

I found his fingerprints later, pressed small and mauve above my elbow. They were still there the next time I met up with Richard. But he didn't ask. He rarely asks. That used to be part of the attraction.

"You're beautiful," Tim says.

And I laugh, wondering how obviously I've been drifting. As my thoughts spin back to this boy, this train, I realise how airy-headed I've become. There are haloes blossoming around the carriage lights, golden, minutely-pulsing haloes – while a pair of ghosts huddle in the black glass beside us, laughing and drinking too.

Double spirits, I think; it's a terrible gag. It makes me giggle harder.

"No, I mean it," Tim says, only slurring slightly. "Truly beautiful."

And then in the middle of my laughter, he kisses me, as I knew that he would, and it's clumsy at first, but as warm as his handshake, and I like that warmth. His heat's in my mouth and then spreading against my palms where they're pressed against him, flattening his shirt to his chest. Pushing closer. His fingers find the back of my neck. They squeeze. His wristwatch catches in my hair. Finally, he sits back,

75

almost panting, his eyes shining. They're mahogany coloured now. Concentrated.

"Not here," he says.

"Will you come with me?" he says.

As we stand, a little unsteadily, I glance at the laptop he's abandoning, along with a coat and a rucksack bundled haphazardly beneath the seat. I think of my own case stranded further down the aisle. My mobile left open on the table. I imagine Richard calling in my absence. I think of his wondering, his voice, and those words play through me once more.

"You moved like water..."

And I think how ignorant, how innocent, he was back then, to have said such a thing. How little he understands of me, even now.

Because it's not just about the loch house, or the other men I might have had. There are so many secrets. There's Dr Gilchrist, my teenage years. Richard knows barely anything about my time at boarding school – nothing whatsoever about the disgrace in which I left. Or how though my Grandfather went on paying for everything, he wouldn't see me anymore. His bewilderment and shame...

But there's too much of it. Too much to explain –

"Come on," Tim says, and he links my hand into his, as if we're children.

And I like that too, although the heat from his fingers is sticky now – until we reach the end of the carriage and the automatic door whooshes open and I realise where he's leading me. With a sinking sensation, I confront the toilet cubicle I visited before. I don't want to go back in again. Except I do.

But it is ok, or as ok as it can be, because Tim hardly allows me a second to re-assess that dull, cramped space. He pushes me backwards, ahead of him, smearing kisses across my jaw and throat, while scrabbling to close and lock the narrow door behind him. The sink edge digs a bar into my back, but though the battered cubicle's stink is the same, at least there are no more visions of Marie. And still not a hint of my mother in the glass.

"You're gorgeous, Lizzy," Tim says. "I can't believe you..."

He leans back, as much as he's able in that tight, ridiculous space, and tilts his head, studying my face. But I don't want him looking anymore. I pull him to me. I taste his tongue. I breathe him in, sucking down his whisky kisses.

He wastes no time, but fumbles with my blouse, my buttons, and I shift awkwardly, trying to help. I realise my breasts are no longer

76

tender as his fingertips trace the fine, silken line of a bra strap. As they slip beneath the border of lace.

And this was meant to be a simple thing, I remember. *Harmless.*

Nonetheless, I loosen, giving in to his stroking hands. A shiver rolls right through me. A thin, delicious wave that spreads out to touch my edges. That ripples deeper too –

But then Tim dips his head. He opens his mouth to my skin, and at last it hits me.

I can't have this.

I can't have his lips, his tongue, his breath, anywhere near my breasts. As I can't have his fingers anymore, the damp hand that's slipping over my hip now, over my stomach, reaching closer. Panic flares through me, a dazzling knife-line of sobriety.

I can't have him inside me.

What am I doing?

I can't risk him inside.

I'm wedged between the wall and basin, and so I can't step back. There's nowhere to go.

What was I thinking?

I watch my hands lift, my old, cold hands, and before I quite understand what I am about to do, I'm shoving this boy aside; I'm banging at the lock. I'm barging out –

"Lizzy," he says, raising his own arm, perhaps trying to catch me. But there is no way I'll let him catch me. Not now.

Not.

Now –.

I don't even attempt to explain. I'm too angry at myself, too frightened by myself. I charge out through the dreaming carriages, feeling stupid, disgusted. Knowing I've been dreaming too.

In the night, in the loch house, someone came into my room.

During the smallest hours, the blackest hours, as I drifted awake, or almost awake, when I shifted in some frail, unknowing space between.

The darkness was so deep that I felt gagged and blindfolded, sealed closed. I tried blinking and then rubbed my fists into my sockets, but the room remained dank. Elusive. There was nothing to hold on to. When the shadows finally began to separate, they turned in drifts, in heavy waves, and although it had been so warm lately, there was a biting iciness to the dingy air. A November frost, already, in my room, and –

And –

There was someone in there with me.

The window was the only solid patch within those wintry tides. An ashen square where I'd left the curtains open (but had I left the curtains open?), with another shape, a distinct person-shape, imprinted against it. A figure who appeared to be staring out as if they belonged.

"Marie?"

My voice slithered away from me. It was more of a gasp than a word, but still I regretted it. Those thick shadows ruffled as if I'd sent a pebble skimming across the empty loch; the ripples spread out and out – and yet the figure didn't turn, or reply, or even stir.

Whoever this was, it wasn't Marie.

I sat up slowly, my heels and knees locked together, the quilt drawn close. My nails dug into the bunched, cool cotton, already moist against my palms.

And once more, I was keenly aware of the loch house all around me. Around *us*.

I could feel its thick walls and whistling spaces, and how we were contained. I heard the gentle rattle of a window from another room, a door bumping against its frame. I smelt the familiar, sweet-sour odours of old stone and beams and boards and I thought of softening wood, its stale bread odour. Of the creeping, cobweb-spread of mould.

I strained against those shadows. I scrunched my eyes shut, imagining that when I opened them, that figure would be gone –

But it was there, still. Standing right there, staring, beside the glass.

Too tall to be a child.

Nevertheless, I recalled that flitting shadow again, and the amusement that I sensed sometimes coming from the house. I thought of the way the air had tensed when I'd smashed Marie's old toy cars together, that taut quivering as of suppressed laughter, giggles. A kind of glee... And how when we spoke, the house often seemed to listen, eavesdropping with a bad-mannered delight.

Except wasn't this figure an altogether different thing? A solemn thing?

Around its glimmering edges, the darkness was setting, congealing, and: *A man*, I thought, remembering Marie's stories.

A drowned fisherman?

A man, I realised, who wasn't studying the window after all – but gazing directly, possessively across the room. Staring right back at me.

"Dad?" I breathed.

And then shouted: "*Dad.*"

Shoving aside my covers, I jumped up and leapt two steps across the room –

Suddenly finding myself rawly awake, finding myself curled and shivering –

And still lying in my bed.

Awake, I realised.

Only just awake this second.

And alone, of course. Alone.

Another dream, that was all. Another nightmare. Yet I couldn't stop trembling. My small frame vibrated against the mattress, against its stains and stiff patches, its freshly wrinkled sheet.

While my heart went on skittering, I sat up once more, like an echo of my dream self – except that now the darkness felt thin to me. I rubbed my face, as if for the first time. I blinked. But there was nothing unusual in my room. No one stood before the glass.

There was no man, or child. *Nothing.*

I climbed from the bed. I reached out through the chilly air and the softer fug of my own catching breath. My bare feet stumbled. Although the night appeared flimsier than it had in my dream, I hurried across the boards to flick on the light. For an instant, the room flared like a photograph of itself, the yellow rug blazing, while the walls seethed and glared, bone-white. At first, the ceiling seemed higher than it ought to have been, but rapidly, it dropped.

It took a moment for everything to settle back into its proper place, as if the house had been playing another game with me. Hide-and-Seek, or 'What's the time, Mr Wolf?' And I had almost caught it.

Swiping once more at my tired eyes, I made myself walk back across the room towards the window, to where in my dream that man had stood. Although the shadows had been swept into the corners, with each step I took towards those dim panes and that floating sill, I kept expecting something to melt past, to touch me –
but there went on being nothing.

Nothing except sallow walls and shadows, that bare and waiting glass. My own reflection no more than a gauzy stain, bisected by the frame.

But where I should have felt relieved, there was only sadness.

Because he's gone, I realised. *Dad's left me.*

He'll never stop leaving –

And it would only keep on growing blacker. That hole where he had been.

My fingers squeaked against the icy pane as I gazed out. The night wasn't endless after all, but beginning to pale. A smoky blue band rimmed the matt hills beyond the loch and there was already a scattering of pearls across the water. Higher up, where the sky remained inky, there weren't many stars left and I caught the scent of the breaking day even through the rot in the window's wood. A tang of forest foliage, of browning ferns and new, cold dew. It was similar to the smell of Mr Whiskers' fur when he returned, sly and hungry, after being out all night, back in London. The gift of a headless mouse left on our doorstep, arranged like something precious.

I glanced down to Marie's garden. The light moved in hazily, in fleecy strings and I wondered if I might be able to make out the loch path, or the chalky rocks down at my beach –

Instead, I saw a child there.

I almost laughed.

A child, standing just outside the house.

Not a girl like me, but a boy I thought, as I took in the shape of his head and shoulders and his open, solid posture, his legs spread wide. He stood amidst a tangled mass that during the day would be nothing more than rocks and heather. His head tilted and I glared right

80

back, no longer afraid – *because what was this, anyway?* Yet another dream?

Through the silt of the fading night, I couldn't see the boy's clothes, or his expression. He had no detail, but merged like feathers into the grass and shrubs at his feet; he dissolved with the loch beyond. And in the next blinked moments, he began to vanish more completely, in broader and broader patches, as he backed away between the stones and bracken. Until finally he too was gone.

But there have, I remind myself, been ghost-less times. Good times. *Whole happy years.*

And I make myself think of them, the old days, when I still imagined I might have a career, a proper life. Before I began to give up on everything, except waiting for Richard. And alcohol. And hoping for a child...

I remember the fine, floating feeling that the whole crew used to share at the end of a performance or after a particularly long day on set. The after-show parties with their drinking games and laughter, ripples of laughter that grew quickly into waves and torrents. I remember how that sound used to hold us together, lifting us and driving us on into the small hours, when some girl would usually end up dancing around the empties on a table, singing some twisted show-tune. Although inevitably there'd be some other girl weeping her heart out in the bathroom, but no one minded that.

They were perhaps the very happiest times, when I was in my early twenties, when I appeared to have friends, whole crowds of them, or at the very least drinking buddies. They were the nights when Richard first sought me out, bundling me through the coats in a stranger's hallway, pressing me into a spare bedroom, his eyes both greedier and more nervous than his considerate, expert hands.

After our first time together, he held me all night; he stayed all night. He clutched me so tenderly against those sheets speckled red, where perhaps we'd been a little too rough, too eager, despite his clever fingers. But we only noticed the bleeding afterwards, and it was nothing beside how deliciously my body had slipped beneath his, rising so easily with his touch that it felt like the flesh of a stranger, as amazingly beautiful as Richard had claimed. And I can still remember the hope of that, the wonder.

That I could be remade.

But now.

Who am I now?

An unbalanced woman. A frightened woman. A woman so lonely she's reduced to propositioning strange men on trains.

82

Undressing in my hotel room, my fingers fumble with my blouse and when I finally tear the fabric loose, a button snaps free of its thread. I watch it spin for a fraction of a second before it vanishes forever, lost to the plush silence of the carpet's pile.

Even this elegant room, with its heavy drapes and pictures and antiques, its gentle lamplight, doesn't offer any comfort, but simply stands in pointed contrast to that stained cubicle. There's a kind of mockery to the fine furnishings that somehow brings to mind my cab driver. How he turned away, as I hung, pathetic, apologetic, from his car door.

I struggle out of my underwear and then send more clothes scattering as I untangle my nightdress from my case. My hands aren't just bumbling, I realise, but freezing still, almost as chilled as they were when I began this journey, although it's just as ridiculous. The hotel's tastefully hidden heating system is chugging out waves of near-tropical humidity and the rest of my body is flushed, my skin assimilating the room's rosy glow. I find myself staring at my pink-blotched belly –

Happy times, I remind myself, hastily. *Ghost-less times.*

But I've absently knotted the dense, brushed cotton of my nightdress around my hands, binding them together, probably in some feeble, semi-conscious search for warmth – and I recall the rope that Tim told me about. A rope kept coiled and waiting in his bag... My stupidity astounds me almost as much as my desperation. *Anything* could have happened.

"Prone to self-destruction," Dr Gilchrist once pronounced. And I hadn't bothered arguing, not even back then. But it's not good enough anymore. Not now that the way I live may no longer just affect myself.

I yank my nightdress on, quickly covering my shallow belly, the fabric trembling in my icy fists, and then I creep across the giant bed, towards the pillows. I'm too tired to deal with any of this, and too sober now. The irresponsibility of my actions only truly hit me when I arrived.

When I'd left the train, after snatching up my things and hurriedly changing carriages so as to avoid Tim for the last ticking minutes of our journey, I'd made my way from the station to the hotel in a kind of trance. It wasn't far, a couple of streets, but somehow (yet another example of my distraction) I'd forgotten about the festival, so that Edinburgh itself rolled over me like yet another dream.

The castle's firework display had taken place a few hours earlier, and although most of the crowds had long dispersed, the air hung in misted veils. The sweet, burnt aroma of gunpowder had clung to my clammy face as I wandered the cobbles. Such an evocative scent, a smell straight out of anybody's childhood – I'd let it tug me along – and through the haze, the beautiful old buildings had towered, more fairytale and higgledy-piggledy than I remembered. Their windows twinkling in tinsel pieces.

And even when I encountered other people, stumbling groups of more determined festival-goers, I'd continued to float. Drifting through their laughter, I had actually found myself smiling back. None of it felt real. The way their eyes shimmered, as if they'd held on to those fireworks. As if they were still burning, somewhere within.

I draw back the slippery counterpane and wriggle down between taut, creamy sheets. And as I click off the bedside lamp and the shadows and bedding merge, I think about how Richard looks when he reaches for me, his expression so much more layered than Tim's easy leer. Because despite everything that we've been through, and even on that final night when he tried to say goodbye, Richard's gaze went on glittering. Embers flickering inside him too.

He still loves me. I know it.

I cup my hands between my thighs.

I'm sorry, I think. *I'm so sorry.*

But one hand slides up, as if of its own accord, to touch my stomach, and I understand that Richard isn't the largest reason for this sweeping guilt. My shame goes deeper, to the thrumming flesh beneath my fingers. To that idea of a new life. That shining secret of my own.

The first time I believed I would have Richard's baby was also the occasion of our only real holiday together. A holiday, which wasn't a snatched extra night or two when he was working on location somewhere, but a proper break in a beautiful white house in a remote Greek village by the sea. It was to be just the two of us for a whole week. I never knew what he told Amanda, or his children. I didn't ask. I was too grateful – and too pre-occupied, wavering between fear and a feverish kind of excitement because of the pregnancy. I had no idea how Richard would react when I confessed.

I had bought an over-the-counter pharmacy test on the morning of our flight, although I hadn't really needed the confirmation. When it came to taking my pills, Richard had no idea how reliable (or not) I might have been, and my periods had vanished and I was sleeping more, sleeping better, in fact, than I had in my whole life.

84

But on the night we arrived, late, in Greece, Richard was distracted, busy with his phone, while denied my recent early bedtimes, I was overtired, on the verge of weeping. After we'd dragged ourselves from the airport cab, he remained outside on the step to take one final call.

"Sorry," he mouthed, "two minutes."

So I had no choice but to leave him there, with the moths and the mosquitoes. Their tiny, flapping bodies snapping and then fizzing as they hit the blue porch light. I locked myself in the tiled bathroom. Tried to pull myself together.

"Hey, Angel," Richard called through the door. "Come to bed."

Angel, I had thought.

Blinking back at my red, used-up reflection, I felt far from angelic. Yet I'd imagined that Richard would go on waiting. He'd throw back the covers, open his arms, but by the time I emerged from the bathroom, he was already asleep. Age and exhaustion rubbed plain across his face. It wasn't until the following morning that everything felt different, *miraculous*, once more.

I was the first to wake and I watched Richard for several minutes as he slept on. The day was warm already, but I tugged our lone sheet over the curve of his brown back, across the rising muscle in his shoulders. Before I rose, I tucked him in as if he were my child, and then padded barefoot through the darkened rooms. The air was soft, the tiles smooth beneath my feet. I opened the wooden doors, which led to the garden. I stepped out into the light and the true, waiting heat.

The bright new day, the buzzing foliage – it was overwhelming. The beauty there struck me physically; I reeled backwards on my bare heels. Because we'd arrived at night, tired and irritable, I had hardly glanced at our surroundings. But that morning, I discovered a garden full of flowers, full to bursting-point with life. A vine heavy with dusty grapes wound across a trellis overhead, but looking closer, I saw how most of the crowded plants were no different to those found in any common British garden. There were marguerites and geraniums, fuchsias and roses, except there, they'd been transformed. They were so much blowsier, their faces big and bawdy, their colours deeper, their layered scents intoxicating. Woozily, I turned. I caught the waxy sweetness of a great, glowing camellia. I could taste it even, a rare honey on my tongue.

And there were insects everywhere. Black murmuring bees wheeled clumsily by, dodging jewel-like beetles. Ants striped the terracotta. Beyond the insects' murmur, I could hear birds, singing and chattering – and beyond the birds, kept safely distant, the lap of waves.

My body led me deeper into that garden. My thoughts seemed to follow behind it, questioning and twittering and irrelevant. Between the splayed green vine leaves, the sky was a washed ceramic blue. Later it would deepen. I blinked up at it and felt the sun slide across my skin. My heart lifted. My head was dazed, but my body had never felt so awake before, never so completely alive.

In the centre of that garden, I paused and spun in a slow, wondering circle.

I thought about Richard, tucked away sleeping in that quaint, solidly built house. *Our own little house*, I thought. A magical place of chocolate-coloured beams and snowy stone. And as I walked on, breathing in the lush sap and the pollen, and only the slightest tang of sea salt, I thought how protected I felt, and how happy. I had thought that everything would be all right.

I didn't tell Richard my news until night began to fall, when we were sitting outside a beachside taverna, sipping sticky red wine. Watching the sun set over the water, the pebbles' deepening blush.

"I'm pregnant," I said. As if it was simple.

Because that's what I'd believed the garden had revealed to me – that my secret was a simple thing. Something pure and good and nothing more. Throughout the day, waiting for the right moment, I had cupped that knowledge inside me like a pearl. And surely, I'd finally found the right moment, with the evening unspooling so delicately, the afternoon giving way in threads of pink and blue.

I had wanted my announcement to be as gentle as that unfolding, as warm, but as soon as the words left my mouth, my fear returned. I drained my glass and then stared down at it, at the crimson caught within its curves. I couldn't look out to the soft-slapping waves. I couldn't look at Richard. I didn't want to witness the shock and anxiety that was bound to be fluttering his features. The twitching panic as his thoughts skipped from Amanda to his children, and then on to his job, his reputation. Back to his wife.

"And you want," he said. "You want to keep –"

I cut him off with a nod. Suspecting now that the hope I'd been carrying since morning wasn't solid after all, but no more than light. Changing, quavering, melting light.

"A baby," Richard said.

And I could almost look at him then. Because he hadn't said *another* baby. *Another kid.* And because I could feel him leaning closer too, and there was a surprising tentativeness to his packed body. Something like shyness as he touched my chin, as his hand lifted to push the fallen hair back from my face.

"My Liberty," he said, and when almost accidentally, I braved his gaze, I found myself inside him, silhouetted in his eyes.

And I don't think he glanced away, or even blinked, until the dog appeared. A stray who entered our silence, by way of that narrowing strip of sea-licked stones.

As she trotted closer, I took in her hunched shoulders and her prominent ribs, and how she lifted her snout to the twilight and then to the ground, turning over pebbles, as if searching, with her nose. Everything about her seemed hungry. It was only natural that she came over to our table, to the scraps left on our plates.

And her eyes were heartbreaking, as dogs' eyes so often are. I reached out to pet her without thinking, as Richard also leant in close.

Except it was then that I noticed the true, strange, swollen shape of her, the uneven bagginess of her flanks. The row of huge, un-suckled nipples, so distended they almost dragged along the ground. I saw how Richard stared as she snuffled closer, and then how abruptly his gaze tipped away from her, and then away from me too –

And suddenly it was unbearable, the feel of her wet face against my hand.

I sit up with the shadows.

The hotel room wades towards me in blurred pieces. I tug at the sheet and wipe my cheeks with it, and then my mouth and eyes. My throat feels clogged. My head aches. Everything aches. There is too much sadness, always. It keeps the happy times at bay. Nonetheless, I can't believe that after everything, it is the thought of a stray dog that has undone me. A pregnant or not-pregnant *dog*. A memory of a thumping tail and dumb nuzzling – it's laughable. I ought to laugh.

Instead I curl into a ball. I wrap my arms more tightly around my stomach, holding myself, as no one else will. I make myself very still in an attempt to pinpoint that new warmth. That possibility. A sense of hope within the hopelessness.

"Are you there, baby?" I murmur.
Please be there.

87

It's a kind of prayer, but I try to remain practical. I consider the evidence. My tender breasts and sickness. The lack of blood, not even spotting, for well over two months. And all those weeks previously of course, of casually unprotected sex, so meticulously, secretly timed...

Firmly, I tell myself that I'm only just beginning, that there's no reason to believe that anything is wrong. Things will work out this time, regardless of what I might deserve. And after all, I didn't really let that boy, Tim, touch me. I didn't let him in. And I won't drink anymore either. From now on, not another single drop –

"I'll give you a proper chance," I promise. "*I will love you.*"

Another wish, another prayer, quickly swallowed by the dark.

She has brought me here as a punishment.

Hard and crystal-bright, the thought came at me on one of the last dazzling mornings, as I stepped out of the loch house. I paused between Marie's dying flowerbeds, my gaze trailing over the fallen, shrivelled heads of her failing roses. Even the heather was parched-looking and spotted yellow, as if instead of using plant-food, Marie had sprayed her shrubs with bleach.

She knew about the ghosts, I thought. *And that's why she brought me here. She wants to frighten me, to punish me. She wants revenge.*

Marie and I had hardly spoken for three days, not since the night of her little pregnancy 'chat', the night when the ghost-boy came. She'd continued to feed me and to look after me in her way. She went on picking up my wet towels and clipping the lids back on to my felt-tip pens, and if she made herself a sandwich or a bowl of fluorescent cup-a-soup, she'd leave one out for me too. But apart from the basics ("there's hot water if you want a bath", "could you stop scratching at that please?", "Bedtime"), she'd been keeping herself to herself.

I knew that she was watching me though. I felt her watching and now and then, I caught her. If she passed the doorway of a room that I was in, she'd stop sometimes to stare, her slack, plain face contorted, momentarily concentrated. A prickling wonder to her eyes.

She wants to make me as crazy as she is, I thought. *As crazy and as frightened because already she doesn't want me – and because Dad loved my mother so much more than her. That's why she's trapped me here. Perhaps she'll keep me trapped in this house forever, until I'm one of them.*

Earlier that morning (before breakfast, but after I'd hidden the previous night's reeking sheets), I had unearthed my old 'Misty' annuals from the bottom of the boxes where they'd lain, waiting so patiently to be unpacked. I pored the thumbed-soft pages, looking, I think, for clues. I reread the story of the girls who went caving and found an alternate world but could never go back home, and the tale of an evil governess whose angry spirit lived on inside the cupboard where she'd been locked up to die. But although I still loved my comic books, especially for the lurid, stylised glamour of their artwork, I also couldn't help seeing how ridiculous they were. Even then, *how childish* – especially set beside the cold fact of a boy beneath my window.

I thought about how real he'd seemed, and yet how he'd appeared to be such a part of the landscape too. He'd melded with the slinking shadows even while emerging alongside those smoky chinks of early light. And I wondered if, before he'd faded, I'd truly sensed his anticipation (sweet as the chill of that breaking day), as if he had been waiting outside the loch house, waiting for *me*, for a long, long time...

Briefly, I pictured myself as one of those wide-eyed, scared-brave, young 'Misty' heroines. I imagined myself reproduced with heavy crosshatching and splashed with gaudy colour, one finger resting in the corner of my boldly shaded mouth as I stared out across the empty loch.

Except that those pictures weren't right, as nothing was right. If there had been a thought bubble drifting above my head right then, it would surely have read *'But being haunted isn't like any of those stories. It's not like them at all!'*

But before I could consider my ghosts any further, Marie materialised behind me. She filled the doorway and my thoughts scattered.

Her nothing-coloured hair was freshly washed and flyaway, its wispiness jarring with her loping bulk, her sagging shoulders. I smelt her brash, blue-flecked soap as she bundled past, and then the underlying odour of Marie herself, a somewhat softer, but seedier, earthy scent. I pressed myself flat against the wall, but she ignored me anyway. She kept going, past her struggling garden and down the drive, without glancing at me once.

I gazed beyond her to my little beach, and then further out, to the other side of the water. The clustered trees and bushes there were stealthily changing. They'd grown mottled and a little sparser. One or two were even woven through with red, although the distant hills remained summery-pale, a pencil sketch. The loch light danced, drawing me back. I saw that Marie was standing now, beside her car.

I returned to studying the garden, its drooping shrubs and all those crumpling, browning leaves like torn-out pages. I found myself searching the stiff, powdery dirt between the plants for signs of footprints, child-sized footprints, but after the dry weather we'd had recently, the ground was so cracked and hacked and broken looking that I could no longer even distinguish the groove-marks from the ladder. No wonder nothing wanted to grow. The soil was brittle and jagged, littered with tiny stones. Like shattered bird bones, I thought. *Thousands of teeth...*

I turned, once more, towards Marie.

"Your flowers are dying!" I called.

She didn't reply. She was bent over her car bonnet with her nose in her bag and her hair in her face. Finally she straightened. Her keys flashed between her fingers and then she was opening the driver's door, ducking out of sight as she clambered awkwardly inside.

She's leaving me, I thought.

And I wouldn't go after her.

I was determined I wouldn't, although I felt a renewed awareness of the house, its bulk gathering around me, too close. And while I stood there, frozen, a breeze whisked into the dim hallway. It swirled between my knees and tugged at my shoulders; it lifted the fair, frizzed ends of my un-brushed hair. The hall shadows twitched and I pictured thin, grey hands. Long fingers.

Caught on a wave of giddiness, I swayed and reached out clumsily. The wood of the doorframe held me; it kept me there. As if helpless, I stared out.

Beyond Marie's poised car and the pebbled drive, and those great, pale slabs of rock, the loch blazed suddenly, brilliantly, brighter than I had seen it all morning and then as rapidly, it faded. *Like a giant's winking, silver eye*, I thought, except that it seemed too vast and ancient for a mere fairytale giant. It was more like the eye of some timeless god, or of the land itself...

Marie leant out of her car window. Her elbow made a perfect triangle on the sill.

"I'm driving into the village," she shouted. "Are you coming?"

And almost before I realised what I was doing, I was running towards her. I hauled open the car's rear door and practically threw myself inside.

"Oh," Marie said. "But it feels good to get out. Doesn't it feel good, Libby?"

We were back on the twisting high road, only we weren't driving the way we'd arrived, but in the opposite direction. Yet the same landscape smeared my window; there were fields and fields, and rocks. A gold-laced copse. Birds. I was back on the back seat. And once the loch house had dropped away below the ridge, something had happened to Marie. Her face had rediscovered its colour, and then, in a rush, her relentless empty chatter had returned. That grasping optimism.

"I hope I've got enough cash. But then, there's sure to be a bank there, don't you think?" she said. "Won't it be great, Libby, to get the things we need?"

She began to make a list. "There's bread, of course. And milk. Stuff for the freezer... Chips."

It was hardly the most exciting of prospects – and yet as the fields gave way to a tawny forest, I caught a little of Marie's flutter. It had been a long time, I realised, since I'd been shopping. Or walked on pavements. Or seen any other people.

"What's it like then?" I asked. "This village?"

"Oh. It's small. I can't really remember... We didn't go often when I was a kid. There wasn't much there. But it's bound to have changed a bit. There are more tourists now, I think. Better access –"

Her head jerked suddenly, her frizzed hair swinging.

"Batteries!" she cried. "I could get batteries for the radio – maybe that would help? Or a new aerial? Or just a whole new radio. Or a cassette player! Imagine that... I could play my tapes then. I could buy more tapes..."

I leant forward, tuning out her babble. I'd caught a chalky smear at the next turning, a glimpse of cottages through the trees. There was the village, *right there*, before us – it struck me that I was actually grinning a little. It was ridiculous –

And then: *Dead*, I realised, before we'd even climbed out of the car.

Although the village was pretty enough, consisting mostly of pale, stumpy houses with squinting windows and slate roofs, it had a shuttered look, and it was just as tiny as Marie had remembered. Hardly more than a single street. Driving to the end of that street, we'd found a squat church and a single, smaller pub, but then the buildings had petered out again, the landscape quickly reverting to further forest and rusting scrub, and Marie had had to hastily reverse. We'd left the place without fully understanding that we had entered it, and perhaps it was genuinely deserted these days? A proper ghost town? *A ghost village*, I amended, of the kind you might find in 'Misty's' pages...

Except as I unclipped my seatbelt and stepped out into the light, the day felt too fresh to be haunted. The air was lush and organic, rich with grass trimmings and pinesap, and there was the sky too, weighing down on us, pure and enormous. A floating block of dizzying blue. A crow called out, rude and rasping, ignoring the trees' gathered shushing and I turned from one poky, net-curtained window to another. But even the pub and the church shared the houses' closed and sleepy look.

The pub's windows were dark behind veils of dust. Its sign, 'The Plough', was stained and faded, while the church's graveyard was overgrown. The lopsided headstones were streaked with green, as The Plough's benches were greenish too, and weather-beaten and warped.

"What now, Marie?" I asked.

Of course she was busy dropping things as she clambered from the car; there was the familiar jangle of her purse, and then her keys. Scooping them up, she shrugged.

"Shop?" she said.

As we walked, I was very conscious of the slap and shuffle of our shoes. The quiet blanched between every sound – and along with our footsteps and that crow, there was the inevitable creak of the pub sign, whinging on its hinges, and I found myself recalling the boat that we'd been told about at school, the one remembered in a Conan Doyle story. A boat that had been discovered drifting in the middle of the ocean with nobody on board.

With each daydreaming step, my sense of dislocation grew until I honestly started to wonder if I'd actually woken yet that morning. The slanting heat didn't help. A circle of blown leaves skittered alongside us, and it occurred to me how the little things might be merging. Connecting. Yellow leaves and yellow light –'The Marie Celeste', I remembered. *Another Marie...*

I slid her a glance, and was almost grateful that there wasn't anybody around to see us together. Although she'd washed her hair, she hadn't properly dried or combed it. Mine, I supposed, was equally matted – more so probably, since it was thicker and hadn't been shampooed for days. In fact, I could feel the snarls at the nape of my neck, stiff balls like tangled straw. But Marie was meant to be a grown-up, a grown woman; it made all the difference. Her slovenliness was inexcusable, and naturally, she was wearing her same old terrible cardigan. Her porridge cardigan. Her pigeon cardigan. *This season's must-have colour*, I thought, *must be vermin grey*.

I smiled; "Dressed up for the occasion then?" I could ask. Instead I picked at some of the loose skin on my smirking bottom lip and kept walking. It was Marie who faltered, and then stopped so abruptly that I almost bundled into her. She'd found the shop, I realised. We were in the right place, a real place, after all.

'Post Office and General Store'. The notice was handwritten and smudged, pinned up behind the bifocal glass of one of those narrow windows. Apart from the sign, the shop looked no different from any of the other houses, pretty and deserted. *A shop in disguise,* I thought.

A bell ding-a-linged when we pushed the door open. It sounded like the bell on a bicycle from some distant era, a bike with great, wobbling wheels and a wicker basket. The smells that hit us were old-fashioned too, a mixture of sawdust and tobacco and wood smoke, and something like biscuits from the very bottom of the tin. From its scent, I expected the shop's walls to be lined with homemade preserves and brown-baked loaves. I imagined a rainbow array of penny-sweets in proper jars and huge help-yourself canisters marked 'SUGAR' and 'FLOUR'.

But in its own way, the shop was disappointing. After that strange combination of eerie quiet and postcard-charm on the road outside, this place was shockingly ordinary. It wasn't trapped in some time warp, and nor did it look like some haphazardly converted living room. There were just shelves and racks displaying the usual corner-shop fare of sliced white bread and cans of things – beans and sardines, pies and peaches. There were cartons of UHT milk and matchboxes and giant bottles of cheap cider, and in one corner, propped up against the humming chest of the 'Birdseye Freezer Selection', a cardboard cut-out advertisement woman brandishing an enormous packet of washing powder and an aggressively dazzling smile.

There was a real woman too, but she sat half in shadow, behind a cramped counter at the far end of the room. She was thin and pasty, with rather froglike eyes and a tie-dyed scarf wrapped tightly around her head. She blinked wetly at us and then bobbed back behind her magazine while Marie hesitated between the aisles. I paused inside the doorway for a moment, listening to the slow, thick flick of the woman's pages. After the emptiness outside, it was unnerving to see an actual villager. She somehow seemed less substantial than that cardboard woman, who dominated the strip-lit space with her orange face and her rubber gloves. With that ultra-violet, beaming mouth.

"Good morning," Marie said at last. "H-hello."

In turn, the counter woman took her time looking up. Finally, she nodded.

"I wonder if you might have a basket, or a trolley, or something? I'm afraid we've got rather a lot to buy."

"Set it here," the woman said. She swept her magazine before her in a gesture like a sigh, clearing a space between a stack of stamp books and a pile of rubber bands. After a moment, she tossed the magazine to one side too.

94

"I'll bag as you go," she said and yawned.

Catching a glimpse of her small, greyish teeth, I wandered closer, pretending to look at the jams and the Marmite and the shortbread slices. I stopped at a picture of a monkey dressed in chef's whites on the dented side of a packet of tea.

"We've been here a couple of weeks now," said Marie, "and things are growing desperate. I feel like we've been eating crackers instead of bread forever – and now we're using my old puzzle books for loo roll! I'd absolutely kill for some proper coffee too. People said I'd probably go off it. But I haven't."

"Is that so?" said the woman.

From the corner of my eye, I watched as she opened her till and drew a packet of cigarettes and a neat black ashtray from its heavy, sectioned drawer. I couldn't see whether or not the till also contained any money.

"I'm pregnant," Marie explained. She tugged at the wool around her stomach – and there it was, her clear, round bump. Not huge yet, not by any means, but distinct, nonetheless.

"The baby's due in January. I felt it kicking the other day... and perhaps this morning too. At least, I think that's what it was." She paused to laugh a little. She sounded breathless. Over-excited or nervous, even weirder than her usual self. "I'm afraid I don't really know what I'm doing. This will be my first."

There was the scratch of a match as the counter woman lit her cigarette. I had already turned my back on the pair of them, and now I started walking away. I ran my eyes and then one hand along the shelves, hoping that something, anything, might claim my attention, but I'd somehow ended up beside the cocktail sticks and paper napkins, a thin section of accessories hemmed in between rows of alcohol. *Grown-up, boring things.* Cold bottle after cold bottle slipped by beneath my fingers and Marie just went on talking as if she couldn't stop.

"We're staying at the old loch house – I don't know if you know it? We're a little bit cut off out there. It's pretty remote."

"There's a few of them," the woman said.

Her words followed me. They drifted alongside the fluorescent bulbs striping the ceiling in a slow tumble of exhaled smoke. I watched the smoke roll and fragment against those stark, cobwebbed lights, and then I wandered over to the cardboard-cut-out woman, both drawn and repelled by her relentless grin.

"I beg your pardon?" said Marie.

" 'Loch houses'. Tourist places. Fishing places, some of them…
But I don't suppose you've come here for the fish?"

"No."

Marie was moving heavily about now, rustling packets and
banging boxes together, piling things obediently up on to the counter
before foraging for more.

The washing powder woman stood more-or-less the same height
as me. Reduced for display purposes, so that we stood eyeball to
shining eyeball, face to bright, flushed face. With her perfect hair
caught mid-swing and her marigold gloves and that apron, she looked
ferociously domestic, desperately so. I told myself that if my mother
had continued modelling, she'd never have allowed herself to be shot
that way, and I considered rapping the cardboard woman (just once, but
sharply) right in the centre of her unlined forehead. Would it really be
as satisfying as I imagined watching her fall?

"So, who's she then?" the shopkeeper asked. "Are you two
sisters?"

I froze with my right hand trapped in a half-made fist inside my
pocket. It was a pathetic fist – really, I could do no harm at all. I felt
them both looking, but I couldn't turn around. My scalp starting to
crawl in the slow seconds before Marie answered.

"No, no," she said. "I'm her stepmother."

And then she let out a shorter, gasping laugh, which must have
sounded slightly crazy even to her.

"Is that so?" the counter woman repeated.

In that confined space, her cigarette was beginning to turn my
stomach. I wanted to leave, but at the same time, I didn't want to draw
any more attention to myself. I didn't know what I'd do if she
addressed me directly. Something about the way her indifference
combined with Marie's contrasting, needy chatter had been gradually
unfolding the loneliness inside me, and now that loneliness seemed
everywhere. The whole shop felt infused; even the grubby strip-lights
appeared to fizz and flicker with a sadness of their own and each shelf
seemed lined with loss as well as dust. I felt the heat of unspent tears
behind my face. A weight against my chest too, a heavy door shutting.
It pushed against me, pressing me small.

"We've been here over a fortnight," Marie murmured, as if she
was practising her script once more, taking us all the way back to the
start.

Except I realised that I was terrified now of what she might
babble next. Yet I couldn't say anything. I couldn't move. I simply

96

stood there, staring like an idiot into some cut-out woman's face. Those cardboard eyes held me, although they were bland and way too white, and hardly beautiful at all. Really, this model couldn't have looked more different to my refined and stylish mother; there was no resemblance whatsoever – and yet, as if they were somehow genuinely linked, I couldn't dampen my thoughts of her. And when Marie began clinking jars or bottles, I found myself giving in completely, as if to spite myself.

And what came to me, in devastating detail, were my mother's hands.

Her slim hands, her tapered fingers. Her perfectly filed and polished, pearly nails. I saw the ridges of every knuckle, and the long, defined lines of the fragile bones caught beneath her clean, creamed skin. I remembered the fascination of her wedding ring, its buttercup glow, and the vanilla scent of the lotion that she used. I remembered how she touched me.

Her touch, which was always so smooth and cool and certain.

After administering one of her rigorous brushings, her hands would slip like cotton over my head, her fingers softening as they lifted and turned my freshly tamed hair. I remembered how she'd stroke my forehead as she murmured... And then there was the way she'd drum her nails too; it was perhaps her only habit. She'd tap unconsciously, distractedly, creating a rain-like scatter on armrests and tabletops. A fairylike tinkle on a frosted glass... And how elegantly she always held her glasses, lifting a fine-stemmed flute or crystal tumbler to the light, turning it and swilling it between each careful sip –

"Something happened," Marie said.

Her voice sounded muffled as if she was standing much further away than she actually was, but it brought me back nonetheless, back to her and this stuffy shop, and to my own un-bathed, untouched skin.

For a moment, the musty air buckled. The washing powder model blurred and I felt flimsier than her cardboard, damp and breakable. Far too easily torn.

"There was an accident," Marie said.

And without thinking, I swung around, my body suddenly all too present once more. I stumbled past the washing powder woman, who rocked on her heels, but didn't fall, and then on, past the tins and bottles, the packets of cakes and bread and OXO cubes. Without looking back, I burst out into the sunshine and the murmur of trees. I was more than happy for the door to slam behind me, to slam so hard it might come crashing from its hinges. Except there was no crash, just a bump and a click, and then the thin, nervy ting of that outdated bell.

But Marie's words remained with me.

"There was an accident."

They were unforgettable. Unforgivable. Her disclosure echoed on through my head so that even outside, I couldn't escape her breathlessness and her stupidity. Her husky, wretched voice.

I stormed back up the yellow road with my head bowed. I couldn't have cared less about the village anymore. There was nothing there, nothing to distract me. There was no escaping anything, not ever, although it wasn't sadness that surged through me anymore, but hatred. It rose out of my stomach and up through my small, squeezed throat. It blazed in my nose and mouth, hotter than the threat of tears – and it wasn't only for Marie. My hate was also for that shop woman with her easy distance and her wall of smoke, and it was for the sun that wouldn't stop shining, and for the fallen leaves that went on tumbling around my impatient feet. And it was for my mother too. And Dad –

It was for the way that they had left me; *how could they have left me?* It was for time that could never be turned back.

I'd already reached the church. I paused beneath the overhanging trees there, but for several seconds, the world seemed to keep moving, rushing on. Overhead, the sunlight was liquid; it expanded and contracted in white-gold droplets through the branches. I leant against the church's low stone wall and gulped at the mulchy air, *breathless and bumbling, just like Marie.* With my hands still curled into fists, I stared into the graveyard. I stared at all those dumb, lopsided headstones, and at the bracken, coiled like wire between.

Then, mindless of the thorns (or perhaps welcoming them) and of my dizziness too, I scrambled up on to the wall. Beneath my palms, the stone was cool and damp. Gritted. I dropped awkwardly to the other side, landing with a gasp on a mound of drifted leaves. There were more dead leaves than I'd seen anywhere yet, as if just here, autumn was properly arriving, despite the heat. I crunched and kicked my way around the graves.

Let Marie come looking for me, I thought. *Let her have to find me here with all the stupid dead people.*

I pictured her straddling the wall, with her hand hovering limply over her slack belly, calling out to me with her crumbling voice, using the wrong name – "Libby, *L-Lib-by*", because even now, she knew no better. I imagined the light dipping from her eyes as it had when she'd climbed down from the loch house roof. I imagined her face paling too, greying like the rest of her, and I was pleased.

I stopped before one of the more recent looking headstones. This one wasn't like the others, but black and shiny, made from some kind of granite or marble. There were twinkles amidst its darkness, but it appeared far less dignified than the older stones. It reminded me of a kitchen work surface, a modern chopping block. I leant closer to read the inscription.

ELOISE CROWN

BELOVED DAUGHTER

THOUGH SNATCHED TOO SOON,

YOUR LOVE REMAINS

Without understanding why I wanted to, I slid my finger along the cold, cut curves of the final S.

I knew that because my mother and Dad had been burnt instead of buried, they didn't have a grave, but I'd no idea, I realised, whether there might have been a different kind of memorial, a tree or a rose bush perhaps – maybe a plaque on the crematorium wall? I realised too that if they did have a plaque, I hadn't a clue what I would have wanted written there. 'LOVING PARENTS'? *'SNATCHED TOO SOON'*?

I felt how inadequate words were, and how inadequate I was too, grasping about in a kind of fog, not even certain whether there was anything to cling on to.

I looked around then, scanning the trees and leaves, the huddled church and grave mounds, viewing the scenery as if it was no more than a painting, another stage village-backdrop, paper-thin. And beyond it, *beyond all this*, what was there?

I tried to think past the surfaces, but all I could imagine was something cave-like, bottomless, a deep, black well, without even the distant flickering of outer space.

At any moment, I thought, *we could go falling –*

"You!"

The shout came from behind me. It was a harsh, half-strangled sound. Unmistakeably angry.

It wasn't Marie's voice. I didn't recognise it at all. My feet caught in the knotted ground as I wheeled around, and I grabbed at the headstone to regain my balance.

A blurry figure bounded towards me.

A man, I thought at first, from the way in which he ran, from the sway of his torso as he ducked and dived between the graves. The gate lay on the other side of the church and so, like me, he must have clambered the wall. There were leaves leaping and whirling around his feet like waves, a blustery tide of tan and red. He came crashing through the brambles without slowing. But it wasn't until he drew much closer, when he was almost on top of me, that I saw that he wasn't a man at all, but a boy. A skinny boy. Only a year or two older than me, but much taller, and his face was practically luminous, it looked so thoroughly drained. A glaring, livid white.

That blazing, bleached outrage seized me even before he did – I was already trembling hard and close to sobbing when his grimy hand closed like a clamp around my wrist.

What had I done? Perhaps I was forbidden there – or maybe that black block was his sister's grave? Or a friend's? What rules had I broken?

The boy's eyes were huge, the pupils massively dilated. His short hair stuck in wet feathers to his gleaming forehead. He was breathing as heavily as I was, and trembling too. Our hands shuddered together, though mine was like a rag, not even squirming, caught in his.

Still, he shook me harder, deliberately. I rocked against him. I couldn't speak.

The smell of overturned leaves rose thickly around us, carrying the sweet muskiness of bonfire night, but with that edge of dirt and mould too, which came from the slimy, blackened layer that lay buried underneath.

He shook me again and I felt the wrenching all the way to my shoulder, but I didn't cry out. I couldn't cry out. Then as suddenly, he released me.

"Shit," he said.

"You're real," he said.

He didn't step away from me. But he started to laugh. And as soon as he did so, he was just a boy again. *A skinny boy*, skinnier than me in fact – and I was the one left fuming.

"What d'you think you're doing?" I shouted. "What -"

"It was you!" he said, when he was able. He held that filthy hand mid-air, it hovered before his mouth. His voice squeezed out of him in pieces between the laughter. "I saw you!" he said. "I saw you at the window. The other morning. At the window in that house down by the loch. It was dark."

I stared into his face. Purplish shadows ran along his cheekbones, but his eyes shone. They glistened, no longer flooded black, but brown. I watched his pupils shrink. I didn't think I'd ever paused to see a person's eyes do that before.

"I thought I'd seen a ghost!" he told me. "So, just now – seeing you again, here – *I thought you were a ghost.*"

And then, without for a second realising it was about to happen, I found myself doing something I hadn't in a very long time. I started laughing too.

But this is hard, possibly the hardest part of my return.

I still struggle whenever I think about Kyle – even about Kyle when he was happy and laughing (perhaps especially about Kyle, happy and laughing). He didn't deserve what happened at the loch house. Some of us might have, but not him.

And on top of that essential, unspeakable injustice, it's become a strain simply remembering what he looked like. It's yet another layer of betrayal. Although I can conjure up the basics, Kyle's angular cheekbones and his general scrawniness, these memories in particular remain hazy. I want to trust them, but loss has filled my head with clouds, and there have been times when I've worked with certain young actors or passed a particular type of boy in the street (an awkward, rangy boy, on the brink of puberty, staring out from beneath a hood perhaps, his expression hooded too), and I have wondered: *Are you like Kyle? Or you? Or you?*

There seem to be so many of those lost, defensive boys out there. Boys with startlingly frail wrists and brooding faces, boys who slouch beneath the weight of their frustration. They merge together until I become afraid I'm constructing Kyle from scraps of other people, from strangers and stereotypes. Sometimes, it's as if he has never been anything more than an imaginary friend, a rough doodle in my sketchbook.

But I don't mean to do that to you Kyle.

Please understand; I have tried to hold on to you. *I did try.* I'm certain.

I flick on the bedside lamp. This fretful, sketchy wondering isn't getting me anywhere, but with the light, my hotel room tumbles in oppressively. The walls heavy with their rose-wood panelling; the wallpaper above, burgundy silk, twined with creamy vines. *Way too many tangles.*

In the fug of my arrival, I'd ignored such details, but now, because I can't think about Kyle – not right now – I'm floundering for distractions. Yet I'm not entirely sure the decor helps.

There are several oil paintings, all appropriately old-looking, finely lumped and cracked and dominated by their curved, carved frames. But they're not quite the Victorian rural idylls I'd expected. I had imagined harvests, cattle, hearty peasant girls. Instead, I realise, they form a singular celebration of hunting.

My tired gaze itches over them, across glossy horses and scarlet jackets, the black mirror-shine of spotless boots. Matte eyes meet mine, contemplative against leathery faces, posted between helmets and silvery moustaches. There is fist after gloved fist, each bound casually by reins.

One painting, which I'd taken at first to be no more than a brown smear, reveals itself to be a crowding flock of hounds. *Not a flock*, I correct. A pack. Although there is something undeniably bird-like about that animal mass, the way that some nose the ground, how others cock their heads. A lifted, scratching paw.

Dogs, I think. Seeing all over again that pathetic creature, wandering our Greek beach –

No more bloody dogs.

I glance away, comprehend the flat-screen that takes centre-stage on the opposite wall, equally as important, as imposing, as those prints. I hardly ever watch television. And yet how fast I grab for the remote.

Although the first programme that I'm offered is News. More loss, as a voiceover describes another suicide bomb, "further carnage" in the Middle East, while a truck rumbles by, close to the camera, a truck loaded with men holding guns. The men are swathed in black, but above their scarves, their eyes appear strangely thoughtful, considering, *more hunters...* But then the desert puffs up around their tyres and in a magical swirl of sand-smoke, they accelerate. They're gone –

Giving way to a weather forecast, the UK map as neatly dissected as a cow in a butcher's manual. Yet there's a kind of restfulness to its rain-lines and wind arrows, to the odd, coy, cloud-peeping suns. I pull the cloaked duvet tighter around my shoulders. A little girl, again.

For once though, I think, I'm not that twelve-year-old Liberty; this isn't about the loch house, or Marie, or even about Kyle. *Thank god it's not about Kyle.* These feelings, I realise, rare and precious, are from before all that, from before the accident. When I might still have been a proper child.

Days when my mother kept me off school, when she'd let me sleep, or pretend to sleep, padded in blankets, in her place, on the sofa.

Quiet mornings when we both pretended I was sick, that there was a valid reason for me to stay at home.

Although: "Lazy-itis," I heard her tell my father once, laughing. As if she hadn't wanted me as much as I had wanted her. As if, that.

I'm sure her need was, sometimes at least, just as powerful as mine. And mine for her could be ferocious. Such an intense tugging, I'd feel it beneath my skin, in all my ragged nerve-endings, threatening to burn.

Mother –

When she was alive, when she was with me, there were those flashes. Flashes of fear and dread, as if even back then, before everything, I was aware of her slipping away from me. Piece by perfumed piece.

Mother.

The longing so much bigger than the word.

I make myself lean forwards, towards the screen, trying to concentrate, to keep here-and-now, although I'm far too conscious of the way that the duvet's pooled, hot and heavy, on my lap.

And the weather has melted back into News. I'm shown aerial footage of huge, walled buildings – state buildings, I think. When the camera closes in, I see, as I am meant to, that certain blocks are roofless, scorched black. I can't quite grasp the story, the reporter's words, but the inflection of tragedy is clear in his voice. And I should probably switch off, I know I should, but I can't yet face the swooping silence. Because it will be full of Kyle. Because Kyle's waiting. I can feel him waiting, a quivering pressure in the over-heated air. Right now, even more present maybe than my poor mother.

With what seems like a rush of inspiration, I consider the possibility of a mini-bar. But obviously, I mustn't think about drinking either –

"The charred remains of two bodies have been recovered," the newscaster announces.

And I realise that these buildings aren't some governmental structure, but a private home. A farm, the television informs me, although it's actually more some grand estate. It was only the yard beside the stables that offered the impression of a compound, a prison. I glimpse the age and elegance of a mansion in the walls and windows left standing, un-eaten by fire. Remains that appear alien in their grandeur, bewildered.

"With the forensic investigation underway, police refuse to speculate," I'm told. "But all three members of this close-knit family are missing."

A fresh wave of stuffy heat engulfs me. This room –

I pluck at the duvet with my thin hands, ignoring the contradiction of their chill. Carefully, I loosen it around my stomach, around my baby. *If my baby...*

But: Stop. *Just stop.* Reminding myself all over again: I must not do this. I will not do this.

And while I resist the urge to slide my cool fingers across my skin, a reporter stands at a roadside, suited and sombre. Still talking about arson, and of how the mansion's gates were locked from the inside, the ground floor boarded. He licks his lips.

And it's enough. More than enough.

I don't need this, this further ugliness. Even the emptiness would be better, even Kyle, maybe. Maybe?

But as I grapple for the remote, shaking it free from where I tossed it, half-hidden in the cotton, the bedstead creaks and I think of boats and oars. *Kyle's way too close –*

And I am not strong enough.

Or fast enough, it seems. Because before the screen shrinks into black, the reporter's nodding. "And alongside the shot horses," he tells me. "Police have recovered three dead dogs."

Kyle and I were walking back towards the village shop when I spotted Marie, although judging from her expression, from the way in which she gawped, she'd seen us first. She appeared to have stopped in the middle of the pavement simply to stare.

"Who's that?" Kyle said. "Your sister?"

And before I realised what I was doing, I'd reached out and pinched his thin arm. I dug my nails in too.

"Don't say that," I hissed. "People keep saying that. That's nobody, that's who that is. She's just the woman I have to stay with. That's *Marie*."

"Oh," Kyle said.

He was making a big deal out of cradling his arm where I'd pinched it, tenderly stroking the milky skin protruding from the chewed-looking sleeve of his over-sized T-shirt, but he was smirking too. As I watched him, it occurred to me that I'd never really got to know a boy before, not properly, and I thought how although I liked this Kyle, he was also irritating – but already he'd somehow changed things, and that was good.

In the graveyard, he had talked to me with such indifference that I'd found myself replying as if it was an easy thing to do, as if I was some ordinary kid, without loss, or knowledge. Surrounded by the speckled headstones and all those burnt-brown leaves, beneath his burnt-brown eyes, I'd felt something loosen in my back. A tiny piece of tension peeling away like softened bark. Our conversation was probably easy mainly because he didn't know anything about me, and perhaps because I was secretly impressed.

Not many people, I'd thought, *would have the guts to grab a ghost.*

Not that I had told him that.

After we'd finished laughing, he'd commented decisively on the fact that I wasn't from around there, was I, what with that weird, posh voice? And I had guessed rightly too, that he wasn't either, although his accent remained mysterious to me, vaguely northern? It certainly wasn't in the least bit posh. I'd looked at him slyly.

"How old are you anyway?" I asked.

106

He gazed at me for a calculating moment before replying. I didn't glance away but went right on studying the patchwork of light and straggling tree shadows patterning his face. I noticed his narrow shoulders and the point of his chin, and a small purplish bruise flowering at the corner of his mouth. It wasn't a very prominent bruise; it wasn't angry looking. Except for the fact that his lips there were slightly swollen and a little too red, I might have thought that he'd been eating blackberries. Still, I wondered whether it hurt. I imagined reaching out and touching it. How might it feel?

"I'm thirteen," he said, at last. He looked down at the toe of his trainer, which was carving a circle through the confetti of leaves to reveal the darker mulch beneath. "Two months ago," he added, as if that made any difference.

He didn't bother to ask my age in return. Since he was bound to have assumed that I was younger, it probably didn't matter. *A younger girl* – even then, I think I understood that I was quite possibly irrelevant. It wouldn't take much for him to dismiss me outright, to forget me altogether. Briefly, I remembered the girl who had been at the loch house when we arrived. The girl with the turquoise beret and the cutting eyes. *He'd be different with her*, I thought. But then I blinked her away, aware of the panic that trailed after her. The cold ache of that first day.

"Thirteen!" I blurted. "Aren't you a bit old to be afraid of ghosts?"

With satisfaction, I watched him duck his head as he replied. He couldn't hide his blush.

"Well it was still dark, wasn't it? And it's weird out by the water, in the dark. And I was out there on my own. And I thought that house was empty. I didn't realise anybody actually *lived* in it. Who'd want to live *there?* And what were you doing anyway, standing at the window like that? Like some kind of loon in that long white nightie, with your hair all down around you and looking all stare-y. Staring out..."

Very quietly, I began to make soft clucking sounds beneath my breath.

"What?" he said.

I didn't reply, but clucked a little louder, and then after a moment, added some elbows too. A scratching foot.

"Are you saying I'm chicken-shit?"

"Chicken," I agreed lightly, although inwardly, I was impressed all over again by the natural way he'd added that "shit".

"Anyone would have been spooked," he said. "You woulda been."

I shrugged and then after a few seconds considering, I turned and walked away. As I walked, I concentrated on the brush and slide of the fallen leaves; I watched them part around my ankles. Aside from their colour, there was something about the slow way in which they spread and lifted that reminded me of the smaller eddies of water at the loch's edge. It was almost hypnotic. Their dusky scent rose around me, thickening the air.

"Let's prove it then," he shouted after me. "Let's find out who's chicken, and who's not."

I stopped, and looked back over my shoulder. I felt peculiar, there and not there all at the same time. It wasn't a bad feeling. It was a bit like being on stage again, playing a part.

"Alright then," I agreed.

He crunched his way towards me, through the tide. "It's fucking boring around here anyway," he said.

I nodded.

"My name's Kyle," he offered, when he was standing before me once more.

"Liberty."

And again, he peered at me as if he was trying to figure something out, but he didn't comment on my name the way another kid might have. He slid his bare, bony hands into the pockets of his jeans and together we wandered back to the wall and to the road beyond it, through the snap and crackle of dead leaves.

Passing once more through the shining village, I thought how different the place appeared with Kyle beside me. Although the houses weren't exactly bustling, I noticed signs of life that had completely evaded me before. I caught the twitch of washing on a line in someone's garden and a ginger cat weaving through a tattered hedge. A person-shape appeared behind a frosted door. It wasn't much, but still.

In contrast, Marie looked exactly as she always did. With her un-styled hair and clean-scrubbed face, she was more like some overgrown child than a proper woman. Except that the pink in her cheeks resembled fever spots rather than roses, and with her slumped shoulders and fraying edges, she didn't appear altogether 'right'. As we drew closer, her goldfish-gaping mouth gave a blubbery twist before resetting into a desperate tooth-filled smile.

"Hi Libby," she said. "I didn't think that you'd gone far."

She was mostly focused on me, but every now and then her gaze slipped across to Kyle as if she couldn't help it.

"I hope you've been having fun," she went on. "It's turning into such a gorgeous day."

I shrugged, wondering at her strained warmth, at the way she'd chosen to ignore my latest storming out. I thought about how she'd described herself as my stepmother too, back in the shop. Perhaps it was all a game to her? I recalled her mad, barked laugh and shuddered.

Maybe she was simply crazy, through-and-through. Or very stupid. Whatever her reasons, I wasn't about to join in her pretence. I stared down at her mannish shoes. She could play happy families alone.

"I'm going back to collect the groceries in a bit," she went on. "I need to drive the car right up to the door. Too much to carry!"

I caught her flashing her grin openly in Kyle's direction. Rolling her eyes at her own incompetence.

"I probably shouldn't be carrying too much," she went on, "what with this baby."

Her fingers scuttled across her woollen middle and I watched Kyle's eyes slide up from her hand to the slope of her breasts. I glanced away again, away from them both.

"Plus," Marie said. I felt her looking at my throat. "The lady back there, the one in the shop, she gave me the address of a local doctor. I thought I might pop over there. Register. Just in case of anything. Maybe I'll be able to get a quick check-up too. It shouldn't take long. It's only a few doors down. You'd be welcome to come with me if you like? The pair of you, if you want."

"We're going this way," I told her.

"Oh, ok," she nodded, her hair falling in its messy threads across her face. "I'll meet you in a bit then, I suppose. Around here?"

I shrugged.

"Well. In that case. Yes. I'll see you soon, Libby. Keep having, um, fun."

Kyle yawned then as if the tension between us meant nothing, or maybe because he was used to such things. Then, "Come *on*," he muttered, when Marie seemed reluctant to keep going.

She was just standing there, pulling at her grinning bottom lip with her teeth, and I felt a little thrill of pleasure at the boredom in Kyle's voice. Marie and I were nothing to him. Our worries were nothing. For him, the world stretched far beyond resentments between two strange girls on an empty street, and suddenly he seemed amazing.

109

Kyle was no more than an impatient thirteen-year-old boy with skinny wrists and a ragged T-shirt and a small, odd bruise – and yet he seethed with potential. He offered, I realised, the promise of Other Things, a kind of escape. And perhaps it was my imagination, but our movements seemed utterly synchronised as we skirted Marie, wandering away down that gilded street.

"Bye then, Libby," she called out behind me. "Bye for now."

Outside the shop, hovering beside its disguised-as-a-house front door, Kyle told me what we needed to do. The challenge was to steal two items. It didn't matter what they were, but they had to be larger than a fist (he showed me his knobbly fist), too large, basically, to slip inside a pocket. He explained that he might actually buy something small, so that it didn't seem too suspicious for us to be in there, and how we had to be quick – although not too quick.

"Want to enjoy it, don't we?" he said. "Have you ever nicked anything before?"

"Yes," I lied, and then pushed impatiently past him. Directly overhead, the little bell released its high-pitched jangle.

The shop had somehow grown starker and even pokier. Its old-fashioned layered scents struck me as dank now, more musty than sweet, and at the end of the narrow aisles, the woman at the counter seemed thinner and paler too. She leant forward as the bell's tinny echo fell away, craning to see past a shelf crammed with cereal boxes. She held us for a few seconds in her damp, blue gaze.

"Kids," she said.

It could have been either a greeting or a dismissal; it was hard to tell. She'd taken up her magazine again and she was still smoking. Her exhaled smoke created a fleecy halo about her scarf-wrapped head and when I squinted, deliberately blurring my vision, the misty tendrils weaved and wobbled the way the locks of a mermaid's hair might. For a moment, I imagined the whole shop rippling. We were underwater, sunk into a cave perhaps, far beneath the loch...

"You haven't come for the shopping then?" she asked me.

There were bags and bags of groceries, packed full to bursting and piled up on the lino beside the counter, at the end of the aisles. The bags were typical corner-shop bags, made of flimsy, crinkled red-striped plastic, with useless handles. One of them seemed to have split already and there were apples, rather greyish-looking apples, spilling out across the floor.

110

I shook my head, but the woman had already sunk back behind her magazine shield. My lack of response made no difference.

Kyle sidled up beside me. He nodded towards the shelves. He grinned. He was so obvious and so eager, but I felt tired all of a sudden. Laden down. Over his shoulder, between the racks and rows, the cut-out woman continued to beam from her place beside the freezer as if she'd known, all along, that I'd be back.

I turned hastily away from her, and from Kyle too. What *was* I doing back there? Wasn't I too mature for any of this? *Such a grown-up young lady* – except, in a funny way, I felt *too* old, and I was muddled. But I couldn't even consider leaving yet; it was a Challenge, after all.

My eyes skimmed over the produce, across the tea and the crackers and the household bleach and over the conspicuous gaps, the dust-furred shelf spaces, between them. I hadn't noticed those gaps before. Perhaps there was stock here that would never be replaced. Perhaps the shop was going out of business? The idea made sense; how much trade could there be in a place as dead as this? But maybe the spaces were simply down to Marie; she seemed to have bought up half the shop – the till woman probably loved her... Except then I recalled that woman's dull responses to Marie's gabbling and I doubted it.

I glanced back towards her, beside her till. She really was strange looking and as I meandered down the aisles, I found it hard to keep my eyes from her. That cardboard washing-powder figure had nothing on her now. As Kyle approached the counter, I saw again how tightly that tie-dyed scarf was wound about her forehead. I saw the stretch and strain within its running rainbow colours, and the fragility of her skin. There was a tracing paper quality to it; I imagined her easily smudged, easily ripped, and I remembered a teacher I'd had long ago at Infant school. Another thin woman who kept getting thinner, who had also worn a headscarf. I remembered how one morning she simply wasn't in our classroom anymore, and I felt a thickening in my chest as if I might be ill myself.

What if this shop woman was suffering as our teacher had been? I started to imagine what it might be like to be stuck there, surrounded by the clutter and harsh lighting of that suffocating shop. To be stuck in the middle of nowhere and to be sick, properly sick.

I didn't like this. I didn't like it at all. I'd fallen out of the habit of considering other people in any way, but now I'd started wondering, I seemed unable to stop. What *would* happen if she realised we were stealing? If she actually caught us? It might be her final straw. She might break down, start sobbing.

Kyle was talking to her, buying something small, as he'd told me that he might. I kept watching them, almost compulsively, out of the corner of my eye. When the woman lifted her frail hand to pass over his change, I found myself imagining the bones inside her fingers as if I could see straight through that translucent flesh. But when Kyle walked back towards me, he was beaming.

There was a little pink rectangle, a packet of 'Hubba Bubba' gum, clasped in his left hand along with a few pennies, but while I watched, he reached out with his right. He took something, something much larger, from one of the lower shelves.

I swung away. I heard his trainers squeak as he kept walking. I held my breath, waiting for the woman to say something. I wondered whether she was waiting too, maybe until Kyle walked directly out of her shop? For now, he just kept going, squeaking up and down the aisles. Maybe he was preparing to bolt – *and what would she do then?* Perhaps she might start screaming?

Because if she didn't weep, I thought, if she didn't burst into tears, then she might as easily become angry. Ill people, I thought, were surely angrier than other people, than *normal* people, especially if they were dying.

If she was dying…

All too clearly, I imagined how rage might transform that shop-woman, her mouth gashing, her spectral hands rising to claw at her cheeks, to rake the scarf from her head. I pictured a tufted, mostly hairless scalp, her face suddenly skull-like.

What would she do? How would she punish us?

I hadn't touched a single item, but my hands were sweating. My breath caught.

She'd definitely tell Marie. When Marie returned for her groceries, the shop-woman was bound to make her pay for whatever I stole. And Marie would cringe and cower, struggling with her purse, her big body hunched in awkward apology. If the shop-woman didn't cry, I guessed that Marie would – and what if the police became involved too? Marie would crumple. There'd be a scandal; they might take me away –

I began to study the shelves with a renewed interest.

Kyle drifted past and I followed him, skidding up and down those lino paths. In an instant, my flatness had completely lifted, my worries scattered. The pressure, which I'd felt since first stepping back inside

112

the shop, had snapped away. My heart was very much mine again, beating once more.

In fact, I could feel its beating as I hadn't for a while, a gleeful jumping behind my ribs. I pictured the hop and flutter of a bright-eyed bird. A sparrow or a finch. Maybe something larger – a magpie?

And then, right here, on a shelf before me, was the exact thing that I needed to take. I watched my fingers open. My arm reached out.

And as I unbuttoned my flimsy short-sleeved cardigan one-handed and shoved it clumsily inside, it hardly seemed like stealing. I felt utterly justified, if a little over-excited. I'd simply reclaimed what was rightfully mine.

I strode importantly from the shop with my head held high. The woman's gaze dropped away behind me. I pictured a pair of marbles skittering across the floor. I felt the grin growing on my face.

Kyle, I realised, was shuffling close behind me. His hand nudged between my shoulder blades, manoeuvring me along the road, away from the shop. He was talking in hisses, in biting whispers.

"*Keep going*. And try not to look so *guilty*. Stop giggling."

But I didn't pay much attention. I couldn't stop smiling. The trembling of his hand shivered across my back and the shop's little exit bell went on trilling in my ears. Everything was funny suddenly. Funny and sunny, dazzlingly bright. The vibrant sky draped nearer than ever. Blue mosaic pieces winked between the trees.

Just before we reached the church, Kyle stopped. At first, he made an effort at looking cool and unbothered when he showed me what he'd taken – one of those giant, sallow cider bottles and a whole six pack of Lion bars, but after a moment he started sniggering too. It was the Lion bars that set him off. It was the way that they danced and shuddered, dangling like a chocolate Jacob's ladder from his skinny, shaking hand.

When it was my turn, when I unbuttoned my cardigan to show him what I'd stolen, Kyle was incredulous.

"What d'you take that for? What use is *that?*" He shook his head, bewildered. "What else did you get?"

"Oh," I said. I'd forgotten that we were supposed to take two things. I shook my head back at him; I was still trying to suppress my laughter. That made him the winner, I supposed, but I didn't care.

He wound one pointed finger in a slow circle in the air beside his head. "You're nuts," he told me. "Crazy." But his voice was light, amused too.

113

"So?" I said, and then I started giggling all over again. I giggled unstoppably, triumphantly, my arms clutched possessively across my chest.

In the car, on the way back to the loch house, with the yellow fields unfolding on either side, Marie's eyes plucked at me in the rear-view mirror.

"What's the matter with you?" she said.

Her voice was clear and soft and she wasn't driving hunched over the wheel as she usually did. Instead she was sitting back in her seat and she looked languid almost, practically relaxed. She'd wound down her window and the bright, crackling breeze rolled the hair from her face and heightened the colour in her cheeks. Her eyes glittered in the glass.

I didn't offer a reply and I stopped smiling as soon as I realised that Marie was too, but for a couple of seconds, a fleeting moment, before I ducked swiftly away, our grins had met. Our glances touched.

Hastily, I transferred my attention to the nothingness of that enormous sky and the trees outside, to the synthetic taste of Hubba Bubba turning juicy circuits in my mouth. But as we dropped over the ridge, I caught sight of the loch house and I felt my heart lift again. Its windows were shining with the same deep blue light they'd held on the day we'd arrived. And I was glad that we were home.

At dawn the following morning, I waited for Kyle, as we'd arranged. I stood at my bedroom window exactly as before, but this time I saw him coming. It was a little later than that first glimpse, that ghost glimpse, and so the night had retreated further. The sky had already cracked open, revealing streaks of a pink so sharply beautiful that after a minute, I found myself blinking away.

Far below, in the water, the pink was looser, a gentler flowering, and when Kyle emerged against it, perched on the little oval of his rowing boat, he looked almost as tentative. Unreal once more.

Half asleep, I found myself swaying as I watched him pull closer. I rocked gently back and forth with the movement of his oars. Their rise and fall reminded me of the heavy flap of a moth's wings, a moth attempting to fly, having been knocked sideways by the light.

But when Kyle reached the shallows, he hopped out nimbly and then began to haul the boat across the monochrome beach. I was impressed then by how confidently he moved. *Like a real sailor*, I thought. *A proper fisherman* – but then I shivered. The shadows in my bedroom were also starting to part; the house uncurling and stretching, waking around me, and I pictured the man from my dream. His shape like mine, patched against the glass.

I trained my eyes back on Kyle. I became very still and very focused. But the glass between us remained icy-cold, and I could taste the dawn again, that secret tang, like winter frost.

I thought of what I'd stolen with Kyle's encouragement. The newspaper that I had tucked neatly away in the more stubborn dark beneath my stripped, stained mattress. If I were to go over there and take it out, it would remain unreadable in the half-light, but naturally, I'd already memorised the crude text, as the accompanying photograph was keenly imprinted in my mind.

'DEATHS OF LONDON FASHION COUPLE – INQUEST CONTINUES'

The paper had used an old professional photograph of my mother, taken during the unimaginable time before I was born. I assumed it was one of Dad's, since he was missing from the scene.

In the picture, my mother stood alone beside a stone column, framed by some Victorian-looking alcove. She was dressed in a strapless evening gown and her bare shoulders appeared illuminated by their own creamy light. Her hair had been gathered into a high, ringlet-dripping pile and the smooth curve of her neck was truly swan-like.

While I bent to tie one trainer, I remembered the portraits of my mother back in London, how they had threatened to undo me – and how differently I'd felt, discovering her today. She looked so beautiful in the newspaper, so self-contained and flawless.

I thought about her gleaming mouth, her liquid eyes.

It was like she'd wanted me to find her. Through the smudged print, she'd held my gaze directly – almost, I thought, as if she hadn't gone anywhere after all. As if, like me, and like the loch house, she was simply waiting.

And sleep goes on eluding me. Beneath my thick covers, my arms lie rigid at my sides. My hands are curled into little-girl fists, white-knuckle-tight, twisting the sheet from the mattress.

But I can't turn the light back on, and I certainly can't face the television again. Apart from the unease it brought me, it has struck me how pathetic, how *Marie-like*, that whole urge was – hardly different to my stepmother with her scratching radio. As if any diversion could have held back that tide of loss. Such a mass, pushing forward. So much that I've let slip away.

And my own last loss remains with me still. Yet another scar, a shadow inside me, a constant shadow, threatening to eclipse any dumb, new hope.

Except it can't happen again.

It just can't, I tell myself – although I go on lying here, as dazed and frozen as I lay before them, then.

"Hands by your sides, please," the midwife said. Carefully inching the waistband of my knickers lower with her latex fingers.

Too keenly, I remember the jelly she smoothed across my belly. The circling cool and warmth of it, and how Richard, standing at my side, had caught my eye and grinned like a naughty schoolboy. He couldn't seem to stop smiling, at first – of course I remember such details.

There's no possibility of forgetting the little hand-held machine that the nurse brought out in order to listen to the baby's heartbeat. Dark and rounded, it emanated static, crackling and hissing when she pressed it to my slick skin. Fleetingly, Marie's radio had returned to me then, too. Those thin snapping-popping sounds like oil, spitting and puttering in a pan.

Before we'd left my flat that morning, Richard had cooked me breakfast. A full English, which I'd done my best to eat. It was astounding to me how he'd started coming around to the idea of my pregnancy. Since returning from Greece, he had looked after me with a ridiculous conscientiousness. Obviously, he'd been through all this before; he was an expert. He thought I must have been at least twelve weeks gone, by then. That they would tell me we were safe.

But.

But the midwife kept moving that machine. Sliding it back and forth across my stomach, and those sounds remained. Fine clicks and whispers, but nothing more. After a couple of minutes, she had lifted the machine from me. She turned her back while she adjusted it and then she tried again. But it was the same. No heartbeat.

She dug her rubbery fingers into me then, squeezing and pushing and then she asked me to roll on to my side, but it made no difference. She took out a stethoscope. Wiped me off with a tissue and then pressed the metal end at intervals from one hip bone to the other. Trailing a line of icy discs below my belly button. She listened. Her expression, I remember, was very still.

And then she went outside and called the doctor. And then there was the scan.

Afterwards, after the devastation of that scan, the doctor had shuffled us into his tiny cluttered office in order to explain.

The table between us was piled with folders, overflowing with papers. A plastic scatter of chewed pens. There were strong hospital odours of disinfectant and vending machine coffee, and someone had stacked polystyrene cups into a careless tower in one corner. I remember a spider-plant on the windowsill, its tendrils sapped yellow, burnt-looking in the slatted light.

But more clearly than anything else, I remember Richard's face, how he'd paled as he listened to the doctor. It was almost cartoon-like; within seconds, his Mediterranean tan had vanished. And then his hand fell limp in mine.

Although he remained right there, sitting hunched and self-consciously too large in that spindly chair, it was as if Richard's whole body had melted away from me. But then, everything was fading. Inside myself somewhere, I could feel those lush Greek flowers hanging their heavy heads. The drone of fat, black bees disappearing, along with that tingle, that sunlit hope.

Beginning to panic, I turned to the doctor, who had finished his talking, his attempts at *explaining.*

"I don't understand," I said, but I was lying.

"This can't be happening."

117

But even my own voice emerged from somewhere far away. Like a soft scratching half-heard from beneath a rock fall, a sound perhaps imagined.

The ache was overwhelming.

I had to struggle to breathe around its edges. I battled in order to simply go on sitting upright, to keep my crumpling chin lifted, and to keep hold of the doctor's slippery gaze.

I had wanted you then, so much...

And for a moment, it was almost exactly like being back at boarding school. I was plunged back to my headmistress's study, to that final, terrible interview when she suggested that I should leave. Beneath the doctor's mess, lay the veneer of her vast desk, and I remembered how she'd crossed the room, as if casually, while she spoke. Evading my eyes, just like the doctor –

And a small, jagged part of me broke out from the grief and rose in anger.

I wanted to rally against all that grown-up reasoning. All those justifications, which meant *nothing*. And in the next few breathless seconds, I had to suppress the urge to rise and shake that doctor by his professional shoulders, to scream into his face.

It's my fault, nobody else's. Why are you pretending that you can't see that? Why don't you just say it? Why can't you see?

But perhaps the doctor understood perfectly well. After all, he had access to my medical records, a whole dog-eared, wadded folder of my secrets. Perhaps his quiet was an ethical matter? Maybe he'd guessed rightly that Richard knew next to nothing about my past, particularly the stark, incriminating fact that this wasn't the first time this had happened. That there had already been a pregnancy, which would turn out not to be a pregnancy.

That there had been a baby – at least one baby, lost before.

September rolled steadily towards October, but for a few more days (those days before autumn roared in, dragging along its rioting entourage of gales and storms), the sun went on shining as if it were still summer, and Kyle offered me a series of escapes.

They were brilliant, odd pockets out of time. Separate and surreal, like extensions of dreams – perhaps that's why, for three strange mornings, I was almost happy. Kyle somehow managed to give me that happiness, in amongst everything else.

He would pick me up at dawn and return me late morning so that if Marie noticed my absence, she'd merely think that I'd slipped out earlier to wander my beach, or perhaps a little further away, out of sight, in the woods – if she considered it at all. Not that I was concerned about Marie worrying, or even about her anger, but what I didn't want to have to do was to explain Kyle, to share him in any way. He was my latest secret and I guarded him jealously, protectively, as I did my memories of Dad, which I knew she'd love to paw over. I was determined that Marie wouldn't take anything else from me. Not a single thing.

I clearly remember climbing into Kyle's little bobbing rowing boat that first morning. I can remember how his hands looked as he tried to hold it steady for me, how bony-pale they were in the gritty light, and how we talked in whispers, although there was nobody about to hear. Our hissing giggles wound back and forth and tailed away like silk, like streamers, jostling with the other crisp, flitting breezes. Now and then, our voices disappeared altogether beneath the slosh and creak of the loch against the boat sides and the shuffle of our feet.

That early, it was cooler than I'd expected. I was only wearing my pyjamas beneath my coat, and the chill seemed to come as much from the water as from the wind. It seeped up in danker, invisible waves through the bottom of the boat, bringing with it the slimy odour of dead fish and waterweeds. But I shivered with anticipation as well as from the cold; even in the shallows, the water that closed in around us and sucked at our boards remained as black as ink. And when Kyle picked up the oars and guided us further out, I was acutely aware of that lapping blackness growing deeper, then deeper still.

My backside and thighs were damp, and there were things crammed around our feet in the bottom of the boat, objects that slid with us when we rocked more violently. As the night began to dissipate, falling away in sooty layers, I saw what they were. A metal box and an ancient fishing rod. A rolled tartan blanket and a Swiss penknife. A blank-eyed, rattling torch.

Every now and then, when the oars knocked clumsily, or when we wobbled and appeared about to keel, a fresh wave of giggles claimed me. Kyle's eyes glinted through the leftover shadows and when he laughed, his teeth shone too.

We were so small out there. The loch was vast, but although I was scared, I loved that feeling. Our insignificance. And I felt more awake when I was with Kyle, as if I was properly alive, actually *living*. Things were simpler and possibly worthwhile.

I turned back once that first morning. Like the water, the loch house held on to the night still. It was grey and rimless, dissolving into the rise of the hill. I struggled to picture Marie inside, sleeping – it was difficult to imagine anyone behind those walls at all. There was nothing about the building that was obviously broken or decayed, and yet it looked abandoned, derelict even. It was unsurprising that Kyle had fled when he caught me hovering at my window. I found myself thinking, ridiculously, how if I'd seen myself there, I'd also have assumed I was a ghost.

But what mad thoughts were those? *Leave it behind,* I cautioned myself and determined to ignore the house's pulling darkness, its solid, waiting presence, I turned my back once more and closed my eyes... And when I opened them again, the loch beyond the boat's small prow was flaming. The sky had torn completely open and the new day was waiting. A blaze of pink, of mauve, of gold.

Kyle took me to his secret island. It wasn't far. It wasn't much, a heap of rocks with a few straggling trees and shrubs and a well of claylike mud at its overgrown heart – but it was perfect.

There were a number of such uninhabited 'islands' out on the loch. Mostly, they were havens for water birds, for ducks and gulls and geese. When we arrived, there were several geese pecking about among the pebbles and scrubby, twinkling grass, but mostly they sat together in neat groups between the rocks, with their snakelike necks bowed and their wings tucked primly to their sides. As we dragged the boat up across their stony shore they didn't fly or even wander off, but went on regarding us sourly with their beady, button eyes.

The island wasn't really a secret either.

"Fishermen come here sometimes," Kyle said. He lifted the rod from among the puddles and muddy footprints in the bottom of his boat as if to demonstrate, but I could tell from the awkward way in which he wielded it that he had no more idea of what to do with it than I. It was his grandfather's, he explained, like the boat and the crudely sliced, baked-black Bannock bread wedged inside that metal box, along with a dazzling rainbow collection of fishing flies. Kyle waved the rod in the general direction of the mainland, where it curved far from the loch house and grew furry with forest.

"That's where I'm staying," he said. "That's where my Granddad lives... you can't really see it. It's just outside the village. It was probably alright once. One of them little cottage places."

He paused, jabbed the rod down into the stones. When they parted, clicking, he leant on the end and used both hands to grind it deeper.

"It's a shit-hole now," he went on. "Everything's falling apart. I come out here whenever I can. I'd live here if I could."

He took me on a circular tour of his island then. It was really such a measly patch of ground that it didn't take long, perhaps fifteen minutes, and that was mostly because there was the odd denser, creeping shrub to negotiate, and nettles, and that sticky mud. Following Kyle, slithering across clammy rocks and weaving between thorny, springing branches, I didn't ask him how he happened to be in Scotland, staying with his granddad, or where he came from, or why, like me, he wasn't back at school. I didn't ask why he hadn't once mentioned his mum or dad either, not even in passing.

Even then, I understood how explosive such a discussion might be. How words could open up so much, *too much* – and besides, Kyle became focussed as we wandered. Stopping several times to show me the odd treasures that he'd found.

"Here," he kept saying. "Look here."

And we crouched together, frowning.

We paused first beside the island's single silver birch, although it took me a moment to understand what I was meant to be seeing. That among the tree's pale, squirming roots lay a handful, perhaps two cupped handfuls, of bones. Fish bones and bird bones mostly; I made out several tiny duckling skulls, as fragile as folded paper.

"I collected them from all over," he explained. "Reckoned they should all be in one place."

I nodded, somehow seeing the sense in that, but Kyle was already off, leading me on. Taking me to the gouged out, rotted centre of another of the island's scant, battered-looking trees. A man's flannel shirt lay there, long abandoned in the undergrowth. The shirt had moss growing in its buttonholes, while a swirling pattern of tiny mushrooms speckled its faded plaid.

"Mushrooms everywhere," Kyle said.

He was right; along with those tiny brown-capped ones, great white monstrosities bloated their way out of the grass and heather. Black fungus ledges shelved the trees.

"Like hands, them ones," Kyle said. "Looking out."

And when I turned to him, confused, he lifted a squared palm to his brow and nodded, briefly becoming a proper sailor again. A Captain this time, scanning the unreachable horizon for the hope of land.

By the time we returned to that tiny beach, the warm musk of mushroom spores was clinging to my hair and fingers. I wiped my palms on my pyjama bottoms and took in a long, deep gulp of cool loch air. I stared back out, across the water.

I couldn't see the house at all anymore, just its shadowy hills in the distance, grey fist-prints pressed into the brightening sky. The wind murmured through the shrubs, while the water wrapped its gleam around us. Where it drew close, the loch sighed and gurgled, polishing pebbles, its surface patched with leaves. When I squinted, they transformed into a whole fleet of tiny boats. Kyle bent over his own vessel and began sorting through his things.

"I'm starved," he called. "Are you?"

He produced the tin containing the Bannock bread, and broke the loaf in two. The charred crust had turned leathery; "It's a couple of days old," Kyle warned.

The centre was chewy and riddled with raisins, and I wasn't keen on raisins, and yet I found myself hungrier than I could remember being for weeks. It might well have been the best breakfast I'd ever eaten, and Kyle too was wolfing down his share.

While we ate, the light changed, the blue deepened. The day's heat unfurled.

When every last crumb had been obliterated, including those crusts, I reached down into Kyle's metal box and ran my fingers over the bright, feathered fishing flies still in there. The flies' plumage was impossibly soft, and absurdly colourful – as if a parakeet and a peacock and a bird of paradise had been simultaneously plucked; there were feathers of turquoise and scarlet and brilliant yellow. Of emerald and violet and peach. Some feathers had stripes as bold as a zebra's, others were netted and speckled, like scraps of veil from a pillbox hat.

"So beautiful," I said.

Instinctively, I lifted one to my mouth. I stroked its down across my lips and everything felt reassuringly blank. Simplified. I was far from Marie and my stomach was full and the sun was shining. The loch lapped with a rhythm like sleeping breath against the stones. I held the fly up before my eyes and turned it slowly in order to study its glimmering hook. I tested the point with my thumb and pressed its cold flat side against my arm – and then I realised that Kyle was watching. Watching the hook against my skin. He looked utterly absorbed.

A duck released a series of short, blurting quacks from somewhere in the scraggy foliage. The sounds were strangely like the ha-ha-ha of a human laugh, but Kyle didn't look over at it, or even crack a smile. Beneath the concentration of his gaze, I pressed the hook down harder so that when I moved it, a small white curve like the letter 'c' remained imprinted on the tan of my flesh.

Kyle caught my eye. "Dare you," he whispered.

I shrugged. And then I nodded.

"Ok," I said. "But you go first."

He didn't take the hook from me, but bowed over the tin and selected his own. A fly as yellow and blue as the morning, misted with pink. Settling cross-legged on the stones, he lay it carefully on his knee and then began to fold back his cuff with a stiff precision. Like an old man about to dig, I thought. Like someone with decades of experience in rolling up their sleeves.

For a second, I wondered if I was glimpsing his grandfather, but then there was his arm, as long and pale as another twisting root, and there was nothing else in my head. Just that.

I found myself fighting the urge to giggle and then a deeper desire, to reach out. To touch him. To circle his knobbly hand with my fingers, to rub at the fine, sharp scar at the base of his thumb. But most of all, to cover the cool blue veins smudging his wrist.

His wrist –

But when he lifted the hook, he raised it higher, towards the bleached inside of his elbow. His tongue clicked against his teeth, and my own mouth was scorched, I realised. Warm and thick with thirst.

123

And then there was only the sound of our breath between us, flicking so fast I couldn't tell which gasp was his and which was mine. Then he pushed, and then the metal was inside him. The hook was inside him.

The skin strained and when it parted, the slide of it opening was so quick, so easy. I had never seen anything like it. Not in my whole life.

"How much does it hurt?" I said, hardly realising I'd spoken.

I don't think he replied, but I wasn't really paying attention, because now, the blood was coming. He must have cut deeply; it spilt so completely, so speedily. Like something from a nature documentary. Time-lapse footage of some glorious tropical flower, petals springing wide from where they'd waited, coiled in a nugget-like scarlet bud. It was as if his blood, too, had been waiting, exactly for this.

I felt that so intently as I stared. The air between us thrummed with the release.

"Now me," I said.

And perhaps Kyle shook his head. And then again, perhaps he didn't. I realised I had actually started to snigger, my torso trembling. It was all nuts, *everything*; I truly didn't care. When I put the metal to my own arm, I hardly felt it. I was too busy watching Kyle's blood as it went on flowing freely. Running in startlingly bright stripes, way more vital, more living, than his skin.

That night Marie asked what I had done, how I'd hurt myself. We were standing in the loch house hallway in a triangle of light from the kitchen. Beside us, the staircase twisted into gloom. I'd tugged on an old short-sleeved cotton nightdress, having practically ruined my pyjamas scrambling about in them that morning, and Marie had noticed the cuts when she'd handed me a mug of cocoa to take up. Now her hand rested in a ring around my wrist. I could feel the abrasions on her palm, small, swirling calluses where she'd been wielding a spade, with her endless digging. Her skin was both soft and stiff at the same time, like peeling cardboard. Corrugated.

"That looks nasty," she said, lifting my arm towards the kitchen glow. She grimaced. "I don't understand how you didn't notice doing it."

I shrugged again and pulled away. Her rough-rippled hand hovered mid-air, with nothing to hold on to.

"Libby." she said.

124

"I really do want you to be ok here, Libby. You know that, don't you? I want us both to be ok. I'm on your side. I truly am. More than anything, I'd like you to believe that."

I gazed down at the brown bubbles on the surface of my drink. And then past the cup, to my foot in its fuzzy sock, already poised on the first sunken step.

"Perhaps it was wrong of me to bring us here," Marie went on. "I only wanted…"

Her words trailed off as she bowed her head and released one of her grey Marie-sighs, but for a few seconds, the delicate way in which the shade and light shifted over her features almost made her pretty. Gold strings flitted through her mousy hair; a blush tinted her cheeks. Perhaps, I thought grudgingly, she was 'blooming' at last. She cocked her head and gazed back down at me.

"If you really want us to leave, Libby," she said. "If you honestly want to go back – then you know that you only need to say."

I stared at her, not altogether comprehending. Was she actually willing to give me up, to let me go? Or did she simply mean that we'd return to London together? My thoughts whirled; I didn't know what any of this meant, and right then, I could scarcely bring myself to imagine that other house, my London house. All those wide, white, airy spaces, and the quiet that would sift through them, now that my parents were not there.

I felt the emptiness rise in me. My mouth, I realised, had dropped open and I waited to see what words might fall out. The shadows on the staircase heaved. The thick walls curved a little closer, the loch house waiting too. But before I could begin, Marie was already blinking away from me, blinking up towards that darkness. Her big, dry hands plucked at the buttons on her cardigan and she wrapped it more firmly as she backed down.

"Although, not yet, I think," she said. Her voice had flattened, dipping into a murmuring monotone that I strained to hear. The colour faded from her cheeks. "I think we need to stay just a little bit longer. For a few weeks more, at least. There will still be so much publicity, you see. Television, the papers…"

I turned and climbed away from her. My feet silent as I crept up into the dark.

After that last loss, after the hospital, the doctor's office, the horror of that scan – Richard took me back to my flat and put me to bed. Although it wasn't even night, he tucked me in.

As if I was one of his children, I had thought. And the bitterness seethed inside me, in that aching space where the baby wasn't. Where nothing lived.

I had wrapped my arms around my waist, my too-narrow waist, and then dug with my fingernails as if I could somehow scrape and push that useless flesh into working. I drew in my knees too, coiling as tight as a spring, balling up, until I realised how dumbly foetal that position was. I made myself unfold, despite the throb. I stretched out against the mattress. Jammed my restless hands under the pillow beneath my head.

Richard lay on top of the covers, fully clothed. I don't think he had even removed his shoes. He stared up at the ceiling and didn't try to touch me. Nevertheless, he was so near I could smell the cigarette smoke on his jacket.

He rarely smokes, usually just at the very end of parties, but he had that afternoon, outside the hospital. Through the drizzle, in the shelter bordering the car park, alongside the other sad, grey people. People with closed faces, carrying plastic bags and sagging carnations, cowering into their own shoulders to shield their tiny flames.

As I'd watched Richard with his cigarette, feathers flitting from his small, tensed mouth, I had stood beside an old woman wearing a great tweed overcoat and slippers. She'd clutched a drip-stand in her spare, veined hand. But Richard had hardly glanced in our direction. I understood that it was difficult for him to look at me, right then.

My old bed-sheet beneath me smelt of Richard too. But of a different Richard. The one from the previous night. *Before everything.* The cotton was lightly imprinted with his sweat and his reassuring aftershave, with the scent of his skin under his shirt. A dusky odour. And despite all that had happened, it was still enticing. Only just beginning to stale.

His throat bobbed through his open collar and I thought about how easy everything had seemed the night before. I thought of how

126

he'd lifted me on top of him, the curve of his arms in the dim light. How he'd looked, below me, as he put his face to my breasts when I pressed closer, pulling him deeper. I'd felt so full then. And the shadows had echoed the fallen sheets, draping smooth lines across his shoulders –

"Liberty, hey," he breathed now, drawing me back. "Hey there, Angel."

And at last, he was looking at me.

Although his hands, like mine, were twisted somewhere in the pillows, he held himself steadily, carefully. He looked. His eyes wet and puzzled behind his glasses.

And I thought I'd wanted him to see me. To take me in. Yet there was something so teacher-like about his gaze that I found myself fighting to resist the plunge back again, to memories of boarding school, to my headmistress – all that professional concern. To Dr Gilchrist too. *Doctors...* It was suddenly so wearying, so exasperating, that hawkish inquisitiveness. The sheer effort of that *regard.*

"I want to help, Liberty. Please." Richard said. "I'm trying to take this in. I am trying."

It was the only time he'd ever come close to asking. But of course it was overwhelming. Impossible. I thought about the knowledge that I'd carried, even as a teenager, how it went beyond them all, beyond anything anyone could imagine. I thought about those places inside me that nobody could reach.

Empty spaces, I saw then – and for a moment, the whole universe had seemed populated with lucky, clueless, sturdy children. All of them too innocent. Not one of them able to understand. I couldn't bear it. And so I had leant up on one elbow, I licked my lips. I turned the questions back on him.

"Tell me what it's like," I said. "Becoming a father."

"What –"

"What was it like? For you and Amanda. When you had your first, especially. When you had Martha. You were there at the hospital when she was born, weren't you? What was it like?"

For a few seconds, Richard's eyes swam larger behind his lenses and then he tugged off his glasses. He rubbed one hand across his forehead, pinched the bridge of his nose.

"I don't see how," he had said. "This can possibly help."

"Please, Richard," I replied. "*Please.* I want to know what it's like to have that. This isn't about Amanda. It's not some stupid competition. I just want to know. What's it like? What did Martha

127

look like, as a newborn? Could you see then how pretty she was going to be? Or was she squashed-looking? Bloody? Floury?"

Richard groaned. "*Liberty.*"

But he wasn't going to stop me. He couldn't stop me. The questions seemed to rise by themselves now, twitching in my throat.

"Did she have hair then? What was it like to hold her? Was she solid? Or floppy? Did you feel safe holding her?"

I knew that there was no way he would answer me, not that day, perhaps never, but I went on regardless, pushing him and pushing him, until I saw his expression shift, tightening, lightening – and I knew that I'd taken him there. That he was remembering, visualising his tiny child, those first precious moments, despite himself. In spite of me.

"Were you frightened?" I asked. "How much were you afraid?"

And somehow, suddenly, I was right there with him, seeing that baby too. I pictured a small blurry face, a searching face. I felt the terror and the wonder. I took in those impossibly intricate fingernails on impossibly intricate hands. A doll-like body, which at the same time, was nothing like a doll at all. But messier. Softer. Skin so thin you could almost glimpse the blue of miraculous organs through a perfect, dappled chest –

I was right there, staring, alongside Richard. Because somehow, I did know. *I* understood. I could even feel the shape, the fragile weight, of a newborn in my arms –

But then.

Then darkness.

I felt its rise, old and familiar. A black hood dragged up, over my head. I couldn't see the baby anymore, and I had nothing. I held nothing. I thought of a flock of birds converging into a single mass. A descending shadow marring the sky. Muddying my vision. For a moment, everything connected. Nothing made sense.

And I did my best to fight it, to push it all away. I reached out through that blackness, from my very core. I reached for Richard.

No more questions, I'd thought. No more thinking, imagining.

And sure enough, the darkness thinned as I grabbed at him. Pulling his jacket from his shoulders, yanking at his shirt.

"Fill me up," I whispered, into his face, his skin. My lips at his jaw. "Please, Richard. *Fill me up.*"

I had wanted to be transported. Transformed. But afterwards –

Afterwards, lying scooped beside him, I felt grief settling around me. Coming in, in waves, with the ticking radiator and the reddening

128

light, with Richard's sleeping breath. And everything was just the same.

The second morning on Kyle's island, we attempted to fish. We didn't use the boat, but sat on one of the larger, sloping rocks, a giant's dusty boot plunged into the shallows. While Kyle untangled a snare in the rod's silvery line, I sorted through his grandfather's metal box, searching for the prettiest fly. Kyle cut his index finger and the pad of his thumb when he attempted to attach the hook, but there was no sense of ritual or excitement about the cutting this time, just a sudden queasy bubbling of sticky blood.

Kyle pulled a face and then wiped his hand impatiently across the rock and down the already-stained thighs of his mud-streaked jeans. There was something so reassuringly ordinary and easy about the way he moved, his distinct *boyishness* – I liked to watch him. When he was finally satisfied that the rod was ready, he jumped to his feet with an unnecessary energy in order to cast out and sitting beside him, swinging my legs, I had to dodge the line when it came whistling back, almost snagging my face as it arced past. There was a surprisingly loud, fish-frightening splash when it hit the water and huge, white ripples that went on and on.

"Bollocks," Kyle said as he hunkered down again beside me, and then we were both giggling.

"Come here little fishes," I sang. "Come on over and take a look."

Still grinning, he hushed me. Although we didn't know much, we both understood that you weren't supposed to make any noise if you wanted to catch anything. With an exaggerated gesture, I clamped a hand obediently over my lips and then settled back to study Kyle from the corner of my eye.

His eyes, I saw, were darting between the line in the twinkling water below us, and the furthest edges of the loch, where it melted from pale blue to a more fragile sheen, like smoke. The sunshine was hazier that morning. It was taking longer for the heat to break through and when Kyle had picked me up two hours earlier, the dawn had been so cold that we could see our breath. Kyle appeared warm enough now though, his face flushed, healthy-looking. I noticed that even the little

130

bruise at the corner of his mouth had almost vanished. It had turned a soft yellow, as if he'd been eating butter instead of berries.

Once more, I found that I was starving, but there was no Bannock bread today. The idea was that we'd build a fire and cook our own hooked fish for breakfast. I could see a matchbox wedged into the small, tight denim pocket on Kyle's hip. But already, I wasn't convinced. Neither one of us was very patient.

"Aw," Kyle groaned, after perhaps five minutes had passed. "We're *never* going to catch anything. How long's this supposed to take?"

"Give it here," I said. "I'll do it."

Kyle rolled his eyes. "Got a way with the fishes then, have you?"

But he passed the rod over anyway and as he did so, our fingers touched and I glimpsed the corresponding hook-marks on the inside of his arm, those few essential inches above his wrist. A series of fine, burnt-red lines – his cuts intrigued me in a way that my own did not. Mine had already scabbed over and looked hardly more serious than a playground scrape, but his appeared deeper; I wondered if they hurt. Although dried, they were still raw-looking, angry-looking. They were a bit like claw marks, as if he'd been taunting some vicious animal, a wildcat perhaps.

I wondered if anybody (his grandfather?) had noticed them at all, and if so, whether they cared or not, whether they had been as bewildered as Marie. But I said nothing; I asked Kyle nothing. I didn't need to remind myself that we hadn't come to this island to talk, least of all about our families. My fingers, so much smaller than his, closed around the rod.

Its weight surprised me. I felt it all the way to my shoulder. My arm seemed to bend with it and I struggled to keep it in the water, to hold it straight. A duck crunched across the stones nearby. It paused to take in my struggle with a long sideways, sceptical glance, before waddling on again, tail flicking. Somewhere beyond it, in the undergrowth, there were other birds stirring, rustling with the leaves, shaking out their wings. Intermittently, there were more of those short, loud quacking bursts too, that strange duck-person laughter. The wind picked up and the clouds started to thin and pull apart in their cotton-wool way, their edges stained with gold. And Kyle, I realised, was watching me again, and he was smirking.

I tried to ignore him. By using both hands and firmly wedging the end of it into a blackened, sugary-looking crack in our rock, I'd finally managed to set the rod still, yet I fared no better than he had. In fact, I was worse. There was nothing pulling except for the small, soft muscles in my shoulders and it wasn't long until Kyle was bowing right over the water, shaking his head.

"Shit," he said. "Would you look at that?"

He'd started to laugh again.

"What?" I said. "*What?* You're supposed to be quiet."

I couldn't see what he was pointing at; his quaking shoulders blocked my view of the end of the line. I lifted an elbow and shoved him aside.

I saw that there was a new shadow in the loch directly below us, beneath the cream of tiny bubbles that swirled across its surface and clung to the base of our rock. And I couldn't work out what that smear was at first. I wondered if we'd stirred up some underlying mud – but then the patch turned and expanded. Glistening holes appeared within it; it frayed and squirmed, and I saw that we were surrounded by a slithering mass of oil-coloured fish. *A hundred, at least*, and though our line was floating right there, in their midst, not a single one was biting.

"Shit," I echoed Kyle.

But he wasn't peering in anymore. He was already up again, back on his feet, tugging at his T-shirt and then raking it up over the shallow hollow of his stomach and his narrow shoulders. He snatched at his belt buckle and pushed down his jeans, his eyes as shiny as conkers. With his trousers caught around his bony knees, he hopped from one trainer to the other, grabbing for the grey tangle of his laces.

I found myself gasping and laughing, just as he was.

"What are you doing?" I shouted. "What's going on?"

"Going to catch us a fish!" he exclaimed. High-pitched and breathless, he finally managed to stamp off both trainers. He stood before me in just a pair of beige boy's pants, and raised his stick-man arms to the enormous sky.

"With . . . my . . . bare *hands!*" he cried.

And then he leapt from the rock.

With his sharp knees bent and his arms spread wide, he crashed explosively into the water. I was showered with stinging droplets, as shocking as hailstones. I shrieked, scrubbing at my face and inside my collar with my cuffed fists, while Kyle dipped and then resurfaced, his hair glittering, his eyes glittering. I couldn't imagine how freezing he must be. The loch's chill had already marked his wiry torso with ruddy patches, but although he looked so small and blotched, his smile was enormous.

"You're mad!" I shouted. "*Looney.*"

He nodded. Water scattered, sparkling, from his hair and dripping chin. The rack of his ribs stood out as if his bones were something separate from the rest of him, an awkward cage, and his throat fluttered, where his breath rushed in and out.

He plunged back under. His feet kicked up through the bubbles. The clouds had lifted further and in startling contrast to that new rash of livid splotches, his heels looked bleached and bloodless beneath the brighter sunlight breaking through.

Of course he was never going to catch a fish. Their tumbling darkness had already scattered; they were flitting away, as slippery and elusive as their own murky shadows. But it didn't matter in the least, Kyle looked so happy out there. He looked like a much younger kid. Years younger than me, even. I couldn't take my eyes off him. Carelessly, I pulled in the line and let the rod roll away a little, across the rock. I shielded my face and squinted, in order to watch him better.

Beside his usual physical confidence, I was surprised by what a clumsy, uncoordinated swimmer Kyle was. *Weak*, I thought. *Far weaker than me.* At school, in my almost imaginary other-life, I'd taken part in swimming galas; I'd won rosettes, a trophy. Not that Kyle's lack of grace, or basic skill even, appeared to faze him. Each time he emerged, cutting and pouring through that churning surface, he looked happier and sillier. *Actually more like an animal than a kid –* he moved with such puppyish bounds and lollops, with such simple pleasure. When he came paddling and stumbling towards me, his expression was totally unguarded, eager and expectant.

"Well?" he said and even that word was broken with his breathlessness.

Water streamed from his hair and nose as well as from his chin now, in brilliant twisting wires. His enflamed chest shone, scattered with sequins. So much about him flashed and sparkled.

"What?" I said, although of course I knew what he was asking me.

"Aren't you coming in then?"

While he panted, his hands swished back and forth, weaving patterns in the bobbing water. They looked distorted where they drifted under the surface, swollen out of all proportion to his delicate wrists, too white and almost fingerless.

"Come on," he urged. "What's the matter with you?" He beamed. "It's great in here. Bracing, my Granddad would call it. *B-r-r-r-racing.*"

133

"I'm sure it is," I said.

The loch winked at me. It crept up the sides of my rock, and then slipped back down, leaving some of its lace of froth behind.

"Oh, come *on*, Liberty!" Kyle urged, and then he wheeled one arm, lifting a great wave towards me in a dazzling gush. I glimpsed rainbows before I covered my face and squealed again, although this time his splash mostly missed me. What felt like a single chip of ice curled cautiously down my neck.

"Dare you," Kyle sang.

I stared at his flushed cheeks and at his sloping shoulders, at his tiny pink nipples that were hardly there. I gazed between the flushed watermarks to the pure, smooth alabaster of his skin. Although not quite as rawly boned, my own skinny body was very similar to Kyle's. I was shorter, naturally, and slightly softer, slightly browner, but that was all. I certainly had nothing to hide yet; I wouldn't do for at least another year. Nevertheless, I thought I'd keep my T-shirt on when I dived in.

I leant forward and began to pull apart my trainers' knotted laces. I rolled away each sock. But as I stood to unzip my jacket, I glanced out, and stopped.

It was the loch itself that stopped me, or at least its darkness. A darkness that I was abruptly and intensely aware of, that I could feel gathering beneath the copper-blue flickering of its surface. Something entirely aside from those glimmering fish. It seemed to collect around the pale blur of Kyle's narrow back as he waded awkwardly away from me. And before he plunged under again, I noticed something else about his body.

There were a series of tiny, circular marks, which curled from the knobs of his spine and around his side, and then rose to meet the dents and curves of his ribs, like the dot-dot-dots in a story. They were even whiter than the rest of him, a spattering of scars. But before I could wonder any further, I was once more distracted by that spreading dark. It appeared to condense around Kyle as he swam. Each time he ducked, it closed seamlessly over his head.

I stood there, dumbfounded. I wanted to call out to Kyle, but I was frozen and uncertain, unsure what I was seeing, or not seeing, and why exactly I felt so afraid. Surely that surging shadow was just an effect of some undercurrent, or my vision blurring? A trick of the light?

Disorientated, I sunk down to a crouch once more. I wanted the reassurance of solid rock. I screwed my eyes closed, hoping to clear my head – but instead I found myself transported back to a single moment from the night my parents died.

And what I remembered was the police car that they sent for me.

I remembered its open door and how patiently it had waited beyond Jemma's garden wall, on that quiet, curtained street. I remembered how there was no siren, and how ominous that silence was, how it seemed to make everything worse. I remembered the black pools that welled and vanished between those sweeping, blue-white lights –

And I felt those shadows reach me.

A hovering pressure as if that darkness was leaning right over my small, bowed head. The hair on the top of my scalp ruffled. I imagined cool breath, a wordless whisper.

I opened my eyes –

The sky was clean and clear and the shadows in the water were much less definite. And yet that helpless feeling remained. I didn't understand what was happening, and whether, whatever it was, was happening to the world, to the universe – or simply to me. All I knew for sure was that regardless of my certificates and rosettes, there was no way that I was going swimming in that loch. Even the idea of Kyle's challenge couldn't convince me, or the fear of how he'd tease me, mocking me for my uncharacteristic squeamishness, this apparent girly-ness, which was entirely new.

And although Kyle surfaced shortly afterwards and the dark had all but vanished, I remained hunched on our rock's edge, certain I could still sense *something*, a separate squirming underneath. As if I couldn't stop myself, I went on imagining it; I pictured that darkness billowing, eating into the horizon, rolling in thicker than any storm.

And it was uncannily like the gathering shadows of the loch house, I realised. The same dark that leaked from those old, damp walls into the chilly hall. That brushed too close, that waited.

But when Kyle dropped me back there later that morning, the house was just a house again, an ordinary, sunlit holiday-home once more. It appeared quaint even, *pretty,* nestled into the hillside, with its neat roof and creamy walls. After climbing from the boat, I stood shakily before it, wondering, and wincing with the shine. I wondered at myself mainly, at how ridiculously unnerved I'd been. I couldn't hold its blue glass eyes for long.

The beach shifted beneath my feet. I stared down at the pebbles, feeling ashamed now, feeling stupid. Absently, I traced a thin brownish-red trail running between the stones, a fractured line that curved in pieces towards the scrub. Then I turned back to where I thought Kyle's boat might still be bobbing, but he was already rowing determinedly away with his head bowed, his clothes sticking to his skin in wrinkles and grey patches. He didn't wave or even glance over – he was definitely disappointed in me, in my lack of daring. I couldn't blame him.

All around his little boat, the loch went on shimmering, pouring endlessly, as if it spilt somehow into forever, but that darkness had seeped away completely. Instead, in the far distance, back in the direction of our island where the water flattened, its shine only grew finer. It became a plate of battered bronze. It held no secrets; between its dazzle, the shadows were simply shadows and nothing more.

I watched Kyle grow smaller, in the heart of it; I traced the dip and lift of his shrinking shoulders, the slide and cut of his oars. I had no way of explaining my fear out there. No explanations at all.

I turned back to the stringy stain snaking past my feet and as I peered closer, it seemed to glint back at me, more red than brown. *Blood?* I thought, although perversely, even this notion couldn't frighten me now. This trail was something tangible, an ordinary mystery, and maybe an opportunity to prove myself after all?

And so with an odd sense of duty and detachment, I found myself following that rusty path as it wound and crept back on itself, sometimes seeming to vanish altogether. The stones clinked beneath my scrappy trainers before they gave way to the scorched heather and that tufty, tattered grass. Less than fifty feet away, the house huddled, its windows shining now in the soft, slow-blinking manner that Mr Whiskers' eyes would often gleam. There was no sign of Marie and the building went on looking empty and harmless, but the trail didn't lead me back there. It zigzagged deeper into the undergrowth, between the mossy logs and rocks and leaves.

I picked my way around a clump of purple wildflowers and an ancient, fallen branch, its bark battered and flayed to reveal a yellowed core like cartilage. A wasp, which surely wouldn't survive much later into the year, buzzed dangerously close to my tramping feet and then weaved on in its dull, deadheaded way as if bewildered by itself. I stumbled on too in my own dumb manner, while high above, gulls called and swirled. I could smell the loch in the wind, and the mulch underfoot. There was the thin, bitter odour of snapping bracken too, and the stones' cooler, clammier scent. I glanced back over my

136

shoulder, at the house. I saw that the door had opened. A figure wavered, just inside.

I made myself keep staring until Marie had emerged completely. She stood straight and tall in the sunshine on the step, facing the loch. Her hair dripped loose around her shoulders and her bump was startlingly distinct. There could be no mistaking her pregnancy now and I felt a strange, sharp pang as I gazed at her – but I refused to explore this. Instead I smirked and made myself wonder how she'd ever manage to cope once that cardigan no longer fitted. Perhaps it was growing alongside Marie? *How much more shapeless could it get?*

The wind picked at her hair, lifting tea-coloured strands, twisting them as she turned to look over at me. There was a flash of silver at her side and I recognised the blades of her gardening shears hanging from one green-gloved hand. She raised her other hand to me, waving as Kyle had not. I ducked my face away.

The trail had petered out. I kicked at the leaves and bent grass stalks and then hopped up on to a small cairn of chalk-white stones, speckled with lichen. In a hollow in the ground, I found skeletal ferns and more mushrooms nuzzling out of the black earth, but the marks had disappeared. For a moment, I was scared to look back in case the whole trail had gone and it had only been yet another trick of the house, or of my imagination.

Except then I spotted something matted amidst the crush of slicker grass and leaves directly below me. There was something curled into a gap at the base of the rocks, some kind of creature. When I dropped to my knees in order to get a better look, Marie's gaze tightened the skin on the back of my neck. I felt her speculation from the step. Wondering, alongside the house. I ignored them both.

It was difficult to gage exactly how big the animal was; it was huddled into itself, for comfort or protection, obviously hurt.

So the trail *had* been blood, I realised, after all. But any alarm I might have felt was overwhelmed by my concern and curiosity. I was still struggling to make out what it was. At first, I thought it might be a cat, and then a rabbit. Its deep, burnished coat was too chocolate-coloured to belong to a fox, although finely layered with bronze – a brighter russet where it caught the light.

I bent forward and parted the leaves to get a better look. I pushed aside the stones. As I did so, my fingertips inadvertently brushed across its breath-soft fur, and a shudder rippled across the entirety of its tightly hunched frame. It was alive still, as I had hoped. It was warm, and I could see no blood from this angle. Bracing myself for the nip of teeth or claws, I leant closer still and then tried to slide my hands beneath it. Stiffly, carefully, I scooped it up.

I gasped. I was a city girl, and I'd never seen an animal like this before, certainly not free like this, out in the wild. As I lifted it, the animal unfolded a little and I was able to see its small velvety ears, a creamy bib. Its bowed face was ridiculously sweet, with a round, brown, teddy-bear nose and in the gummy slits beneath its flickering lids, I glimpsed the gentle black of its eyes. However, I remained clueless; was it a stoat, some kind of weasel? Maybe a ferret? There had been an odd, shambling man who'd occasionally walked a ferret on a lead back in our local park in London...

But of course it didn't really matter what it was. It was hurt and needed help. I drew its little body into my own, resting it against my chest and supporting it with both hands, although it weighed next to nothing. It was like cradling feathers, and a memory came to me from years ago, of holding Mr Whiskers when he was just a kitten. I felt that same zipping flush of sheer delight – although I also noticed that my clothes were beginning to spot already. I felt its wetness on my skin.

There were several bloody patches stiffening the fur on its belly and more on one bent forepaw, but I had to peer closely to inspect the actual cuts. I wondered what had happened, whether this animal had been attacked, or perhaps become somehow snagged on barbed wire or farm machinery. I imagined a corroding, but razor-like edge – and then found myself picturing fishhooks. I rose hastily, unsteadily, to my feet.

With our first step, the animal's tail unravelled between my fingers, dropping with the grace of a magician's handkerchief, wafting and silky. I shivered, enchanted, and drew it closer still. I felt the quickening of its breath, and I could see its breathing too – a tiny jumping and uneven fluttering amidst the paler fur of its bib.

A rush of strange emotion engulfed me, powerful feelings that I couldn't clearly express. It was something to do with life, with *living* – with the exhilarating, irrepressible power of life, and with its terrifying fragility. But mostly, there was need. The need to save this one small thing –

I was hoping against hopelessness, even then.

I walked gingerly over the weeds and rocks and heather, with the animal clutched, warm and quivering, beside my heart. I walked back towards the loch house, to where Marie was waiting for us – already stepping forward, with a frowning question on her face, but her woollen arms outstretched.

Some things have never been forgotten. Some things *cannot* be forgotten – however hard I might have tried.

Twenty-five years have passed since the loch house, but lying here inside my grown-up skin, between these five-star, grown-up sheets, I can still feel the delicate weight and quiver of that tiny body. My hands go on yearning for that faint, but urgent warmth.

In fact, as the fitful minutes have ticked by, this particular memory has somehow become more vivid to me than *anything* else. It's more tangible than my overstuffed mattress or the scent of laundered cotton. Truer than my own body, my lukewarm flesh, still clutched a little desperately beneath these sheets. And now when my hands meet across my stomach, I find myself fighting back a whole fresh wave of sadness.

I want my present to be as real as that. As vital as that downy life, that feathery quickening –

Instead, I find myself recalling Kyle's fishing flies once more, those hooks.

Now, overwhelmingly, it is this that rushes back at me – the sudden brilliant island moment when Kyle's blood spilt – the sheer *life* that flashed between us then. And the metal bringing everything together, while simultaneously undoing it all, when I pressed it to my own skin. How alive that pain made me feel, how unexpectedly liberated, separated. Unleashed. I remember it so clearly – how I felt myself unspooling with the sunshine, flitting with our breath. Dissolving into such spinning, dizzying pieces, and yet at the same time, crystallising. Becoming a single icy well of perfect, gilded light.

I remember the relief that came in the seconds that followed, once the blood was running, once I'd dropped the fly. The surprising dip in sensation from all that giddy excitement, that high-pitched hysteria, to something far quieter, something somehow cleaner. An unexpected, pristine calm.

I could do it now, I think.

I could use a razor from the bathroom, or a letter knife, there's surely a letter knife, tucked inside the neat rack of chintzy stationary on the pointless desk beside the door –

139

But –

But: No.

No. Of course I won't do anything. I *can't.*

However tempting the idea of a blade might be, an opening, that instant of pure focus – I can't. Because I'm not alone now. At least that is what I go on telling myself. And telling myself. Who knows? It might be the only fact that's real.

With a renewed determination, I attempt to gather my head together. I slow my breathing. I touch myself. The wholeness of me.

I caress my shallow belly-flesh with concentration, with deliberate care. I draw circles with my thumbs and fingertips, creating heart-shapes and crosses (as if I am that young girl again regardless, still doodling lines through the clinking shingle, still playing with the stones). And I try to focus on feeling these movements through my stomach, instead of through my hands.

Because what I want to feel right now is something far more basic than my fumbling, stupid, chilly fingers, something essential. A sense of recognition. A fluttering acknowledgement.

I want you –

I am resolute. I push my fingers down more firmly. I want to prove myself worthy this time. To cradle you, to hold you safe. I pray it's not too much to ask for. *To have you finally, for keeps...*

But when sleep comes for me at last, it's dense with dreams. Such cloying, unsettling nightmares, of a kind I haven't experienced since childhood. Not since the loch house.

And at first, I dream of ghosts.

They're everywhere. I am surrounded. Holed in with them. They're featureless, repugnant, hot. I don't know where one ends and the next begins. They turn in great white swathes, an explosion of down, of tatters. They roll closer and then recede in churning waves. And I'm tiny amongst them. No more a person than they are. I see my mother's old pearl earrings, trapped inside their trinket box. Shreds and clouds of cotton wool.

And then I dream that I'm standing by an open door, but I can't see out.

There's something sticky covering the back of my head, gluing my hair in heavy, swinging clumps. I reach out to touch it, and feel nothing. My own emptiness. I draw my arm away and stare down at my black-tipped fingers and then further, to a loose bottom button and the fraying hem of my grey cardigan. To my tight-laced, mannish shoes.

I dream that I'm hovering on the threshold of Richard's youngest daughter's bedroom, a place I've never been.

The room is dimmed, lit only by a night-light. A mouse-face plugged into the wall. It takes a while for my eyes to adjust. I see an oval that is the main lampshade and another blacker, thinner shape beside it, like a boomerang, or a bat. I watch it turning slowly. A mobile, I think. I wait patiently for the crib to emerge from the other shadows. There is a pillow in my hands.

I dream of my headmistress's study at boarding school.

I remember fussy lamps and walls lined with books. I smell furniture polish and although she's hovering way over at the window, I can smell Mrs Philips too. Her perfume, Lily-of-the-Valley, stiff and white. I sit alone at her mahogany desk.

"Liberty, we genuinely wish you well," she says. "But this – your *condition*. I'm afraid we cannot have such things. There's no way we can explain this to our parents. Let alone the other girls…"

And I remember how after a while, I stopped hearing the actual words, but only their tone. A husky murmur that already invoked tyres on gravel. Cars turning on the tree-lined drive outside.

I dream that Kyle is calling for me.

Although I don't know if he is wanting me or warning me. It doesn't matter, since I don't care. As if it's a piece of paper, I fold his sound down, thinner and thinner. I throw it out, across the water.

Turn away.

On our third visit to his island, as if through some unconscious agreement, Kyle and I each brought along something we'd stolen in the village (less than a week earlier, although that was difficult to believe). Kyle had the cider bottle wedged beneath the wooden plank seat of the boat, while back in my night-steeped bedroom, I'd torn out that newspaper report with careful, pinching fingers and then pushed it impulsively into the pocket of my jeans.

But I wasn't intending to blab to Kyle about my parents. Nor was I planning to tell him more subtly, by showing him the article maybe, without explanation, in order to let him figure things out for himself. At least, I didn't think that I was; after all, it would have risked too much. While I might not have been able to express it, I understood nonetheless that one of the major reasons I treasured the hours I spent with Kyle was because they stood so apart from the rest of my life. They weren't simply separate from the accident, but from my old life too – from everything that had ever happened. When I was with Kyle, I could be just another normal kid, un-precocious, without money or glamour drifting even remotely close by. I was a stranger to myself.

Without knowing it, Kyle offered me respite, a kind of freedom. Perhaps, in his innocence, he was keeping me sane.

And so why did I bring along that balled-up scrap of newspaper, that morning? Why, when I was so (impossibly) determined not to think about it, was I so aware of it, pressing like a stone against my hip? There had to be another part of me that, although terrified, was also longing to explain. And thinking back on it now, thinking about the cider and the way that Kyle behaved that day, perhaps it was the same for him, too. Perhaps he wanted to tell me about his family, to share his own secrets? Except that we were both so clumsy, so fumbling.

But it wasn't our fault. Not any of it. *We were just kids.*

It was to be our last time together on the island. It was the very last warm day too – not that we knew that then. The sun was busy rising by the time Kyle rowed us towards the beach. The island's rocks and pebbles were bathed yellow and a little further in, the gaps between the

142

branches glowed, threaded through with mist. As if called, I climbed eagerly and unthinkingly too early from the boat and inadvertently plunged up to my knees in ice-bright water. At least I wasn't wearing my pyjamas that morning, but still, the cold closed like metal cuffs around my calves and while I stumbled, gasping and desperate, towards the dryer stones, I could hear Kyle laughing behind me as he hauled the boat in. Smug and superior in his grandfather's battered boots.

I narrowed my eyes and poked my tongue out at him, and then squatted on the cool shingle to peel back the sodden denim of my jeans and tug off my trainers. While I lifted each shoe, emptying out the water in glistening streams, Kyle's laughter continued to rattle on; it was beginning to sound faked. *Bloody boy*, I thought. He probably still hadn't forgiven me for refusing to swim. Admittedly, I remained frustrated with myself for that – but I was angrier with him.

He was still sniggering as he strode over, the cider bottle swinging from one hand, the metal fly box flashing in the other. His shadow bobbed across my knees and I felt him waiting for me to look up. But I wasn't glaring anymore; I was too busy wringing out my shrivelled socks. Too busy concentrating on my curling toes and the miniature roads that the dripping water wove between the pebbles. From the bushes behind me, there came the familiar ruffling of wings, and then those mocking, waking quacks. Kyle's shadow sloped away and then he sat down hard, planting his cider in the pebbles between us, though he continued to grip that metal box.

"Want to see what I've got?" he said.

I shrugged.

He set the box between us. For a few seconds, his skinny hand lay ceremoniously across its lid, but then with a swift, decisive gesture, he reached for the catch and flipped it open. The stench was immediate – unbelievably horrific. A sickeningly wet and heady combination of grease and urine, rust and rotting flesh. *Fish guts*.

Sure enough, in place of those fishing-flies, all those beautiful feathers, there was a dead fish packed into the bottom of the tin. Its fat glossy body had been coiled and bent in upon itself in order to fit, so that the delicate, scalloped layers of its silvery tail were almost curled into the wide, black hole of its mouth. Its eyes were black and gaping too; they gazed directly up at me, and that inner darkness was repeated in the opening, which ran the glimmering length of its swollen belly. I covered my lips with a shaky hand. It was as if the fish's eyes and that knife-slash and its wide, dried mouth were somehow, repulsively, interchangeable. I noticed how some of its spilt insides were drying, solidifying, in each separate corner of the box.

"I did it," Kyle told me. "I caught one."

But his tone wasn't right. His words clogged inside his throat and I suspected that, like me, he was suppressing the urge to gag. I knew too that he was lying. I'd seen his fishing attempts and besides, this was no freshly hooked fish. I was only twelve and a Londoner, certainly no expert, but judging from that stink and puffiness, and from both its gleam and rank, leaking darkness, even I could see that that fish had been dead for days. He must have found it, washed up or discarded, abandoned on some other empty beach.

"What? Catch it with your bare hands, did you?" I said.

For a while, Kyle didn't reply. He'd gone a little too pale and shiny himself. There was a silvery sheen beneath his eyes. *Fish-belly face*, I thought. I was probably far angrier than I should have been. But I couldn't stop myself from imagining him discovering it, perhaps wedged among some stones, as I had uncovered my own wounded creature – except that his fish would have been motionless and already festering, perhaps crawling with bugs.

I pictured Kyle snatching up a stick with which to poke it, and then his expression changing, calculating. Might he have really used his bare hands to scoop it up? I felt sick. What was he thinking, showing me this? I didn't understand boys – was this supposed to be *impressive?*

"I used the rod," he murmured.

"Liar," I hissed.

He didn't bother arguing. Instead he shrugged and turned away. The loch stretched before us, cold and wide and gold, and I felt myself sighing along with Kyle, although I felt so distant from him. I was conscious of my newspaper scrap; I hoped that it wasn't poking from my pocket. I didn't want Kyle to notice and start asking questions. I didn't even want to tell him about my animal now, about the strange, magical creature that *I* had saved ("A pine marten, I think" Marie had announced, after consulting one of the loch house's ancient, yellowed nature books). It was as if Kyle didn't deserve to know, not after this stupid dead fish stunt. He didn't understand *anything*, I thought.

But after we'd sat for a while side-by-side on the stones, huffing and brooding and pointedly not glancing at one another, Kyle jumped to his feet and slammed the tin lid closed with a decisive clang. Straight-backed and tall, he marched determinedly off with it, back across the pebbles, towards the loch. I saw how the stones from the beach had marked him, imprinting a fine chalky powder across the seat of his jeans. I wondered if I was similarly stained as I watched him climb the largest rock. It was the same rock that we'd sat on the morning before. Our fishing rock. With unease pinching queasily through my stomach, I pictured him ducking under, that darkness – but I pushed the image away before it could drag me any further, and concentrated instead on the stretch and bend of Kyle's crane-like legs.

When he straightened, his dust patches caught the sun, and for a moment, he sparkled as brightly as the water. He raised the box high above his head. It winked briefly from between his fingers, blazing-white, and then, with a little bouncing hop, Kyle hurled it, long-armed, out and out. The water that leapt up around it looked thick and opaque, as if he'd cast out a pail of milk. The splash appeared to hover for a second or two after the box had vanished, and like the softheaded fool that he secretly was, I saw that Kyle was waving manically after it, and hopping and skidding from foot to foot now too, without any grace at all. It would have been ridiculously easy for him to slip and fall in, but I knew he didn't care about that.

"Bye-bye little fishy!" I heard him calling. "Bye-bye. Bye-bye."

Jogging back, he kept glancing up and then hastily down at his borrowed wellies, sliding small, daft smiles in my direction. The stones clicked and sprayed with the flat thudding of his soles.

"What's that face for now?" he said, when he was almost beside me, raising his empty hands in exasperation. "Did you not want me to chuck it? Wanted it for your breakfast, did you?"

He rubbed a slow circle over his stomach.

"Ooh," he said. "Lovely. De-e-e-licious fish. Luscious fish. Mmmm. Yummy-yum."

I picked up a handful of cold pebbles and grit and threw them vaguely towards him. It was obvious that I was going to miss, but we watched their arc anyway, their pearly shower. Kyle sucked in his cheeks and raised his eyebrows.

"Get you!" he said, as if we both hadn't already started laughing. He pulled the cider bottle, with a crunch, out of the ground, and then screwed up his nose and grunted as he twisted off the cap.

"Pig," I said and he nodded, lifting the bottle and swigging extravagantly.

I watched him closely as he drank, studying the long, slow bulge at his pasty throat and then how he winced and swiped at his eyes as he set the bottle down again. He hadn't really downed very much at all, but he was practically panting. A cidery smear shone across his chin.

145

I didn't wait for him to dare me. I reached over and grabbed the bottle and swigged myself. The cider was exactly as foul as I'd imagined. I had never really drunk alcohol before – the odd sip of an indulgent grown-up's beer or champagne at one of my parents' parties, and my mother's gin once, when she wasn't looking, and I was unable to resist the seductive fizz of her frosted glass. I hadn't liked those drinks either. The gin in particular had left me retching, actually running for the bathroom, for my toothbrush and the spearmint paste, so that I could scrub its starchy, greenish flavour from my mouth. A flavour combining liquidised lettuce and something chemical, nail-varnish remover perhaps. *Toxic.* I was amazed that anyone would actually choose to drink the stuff – and this cider was equally repulsive. Warm, but acidic, it tasted like apple juice gone bad, and there was the colour to consider too, that murky yellow. But Kyle was watching me now and so I took another sticky swallow. It squeaked across my teeth.

"What do you reckon?" Kyle said.

"It's disgusting." I replied and then gulped down another mouthful.

He laughed when he had to tug the bottle forcibly away from me. I rubbed my fist across my wet lips and wondered if I was drunk yet; I wondered what it would feel like to be actually drunk. I thought about my parents' friends, the way in which some of them would sway as they loomed over me, flushed and grinning and smelling overly sweet. I remembered being patted clumsily on the head as if I were a puppy and their endless, fathomless jokes. I thought too about the clouds that sometimes drifted across my mother's eyes, and the contrasting quiet that would descend around her. A quiet that was almost physical. Something like snow.

Hastily, I pulled away from such thoughts. Really, I told myself, I had no idea. Drinking was yet another grown-up mystery.

A breeze ruffled fleecy threads across the water and the sun had grown wider. Although Kyle's box had been so resolutely banished, the dead fish odour lingered in the air, but it was fainter now; it mingled with the mossy earth and leaf smells and with the damp, weedy scent of the rocks, and it seemed more natural. I decided that I wasn't drunk at all yet, or even tipsy. That I simply felt as I usually did when I was with Kyle – only half-there, but almost happy, probably because of that. The bad parts mostly blanked. He passed me back the bottle. I drank some more.

"I can't believe it's going to be October next week," Kyle said. His long legs were stretched out now and he was slumped against the stones, resting on his pointed elbows and squinting at the sky. "It's like I've been living here forever."

I nodded and then set the cider down and lay back too. Several birds circled the blue overhead. They looked like a series of little black arrows, a cartoon flurry of tiny spears. I wondered if I could really hear them talking to each other in their fine, piping voices, and then imagined I could feel the whir of their wings too, rippling downwards with the wind.

I thought about the pine marten. I thought about him dozing, right now, in the loch house kitchen, in the warm spot near the oven. Marie had unearthed a wicker picnic hamper from somewhere. She'd cut away the lid and lined it with an ancient crocheted blanket before carefully placing the animal inside. When I'd sneaked out earlier, into the spreading dawn, he had appeared to be sleeping. I'd paused to check his breathing. Even in the half-light, that quivering, brown coat had shimmered from his new nest of faded colours. I thought about how the downy brush of his tail had flicked once, parting the wool, and how when I saw it, something small and precious had seemed to bump inside me too... And then I couldn't help myself; dismissing my earlier misgivings, I began to talk to Kyle about the pine marten, talking and talking as if compelled.

I told him about following the blood-trail and about not knowing what the animal was, and how it felt to lift him, to have him curled against my chest. I told Kyle about the fast, faint fluttering beneath his fur, that flickering breath or dancing pulse. And as best I could, I described how, when I'd carried him, everything had been momentarily transformed, the world briefly revealed as incredible and fragile, terrible and lovely.

I even told Kyle about Marie too – or at least, a little of what had happened with Marie, when we'd reached the house. I described the practicalities, how she had set out that makeshift bed and brought over a saucer of water and a saucer of milk, encouraging our new pet to eat by soaking a hunk of bread and then breaking it up into sodden squares. I told Kyle about deciding that the animal definitely looked like a boy, and after consulting her wildlife book, Marie had suggested naming him Marty, but I'd opted for 'Pie'. I thought about how Marie had laughed as she agreed. Our animal visitor had delighted us both, despite his stillness, despite his bleeding. His trembling hadn't filled us with foreboding, as it probably should have, but instead with stupid hope. I'd never seen Marie so animated. It was more apparent than ever just how young she was, even to me. She was as determined to rescue Pie as I was.

"She wanted to help," I admitted.

"Don't she usually then?" said Kyle.

"She…"

I stopped before I began. I'd been chattering so hurriedly, so unthinkingly, I found myself blushing. I felt wrong-footed, caught out; I was worried that Kyle might laugh at me, that I'd given too much of myself away. But I felt something else too, something far worse. My thoughts slid from Marie to that clipping in my pocket, to my mother's name in black and white, and my chest clenched so intensely that I gasped.

"She's got that baby in her, in't she?" said Kyle.

I went on struggling as I nodded. I didn't trust myself to answer him more fully and it was almost spooky that he'd even mentioned Marie's pregnancy, like he'd been rummaging through the secret places in my head.

As if casually, I rolled over on to my stomach and turned my gaze away from him and away from the brightness of the loch, towards the bushes and the rustling trees. The sunlight between the scrawny branches swayed in time with the lapping water and with the sweet, cider-thick rhythm of Kyle's breath. I tried to slow my own breathing to match his. I took several quavering drags of fusty, mushroom flavoured air, but I couldn't stop thinking about Marie.

I remembered how she'd messed about, tugging that crocheted wool into a hood around the animal's sleek head – daring to touch his black button nose, and then flinching and squealing when his whiskers twitched. But I couldn't talk about any of that, as I couldn't tell Kyle about how Marie's hand had dropped to her belly, as her grin grew even wider.

"The baby's kicking again, Libby!" she'd exclaimed. "He's definitely kicking."

And she'd reached for me. She had reached for me thoughtlessly, snatching at my fingers, and although I'd pulled away before I actually felt anything, any movement inside her, for an instant, I had almost wanted to. For an instant, it was close. We were too close.

I screwed my eyes tight against the truth of it.

Except that it was Dad's baby too –

But my mother…

And then, in my confusion, I found myself picturing Kyle's stupid dead fish once more. I visualised it so vividly that I had to battle

148

to cast the image off. *There* was that bloated flesh again, and *there,* that inner dark. I pressed the heels of my palms into my sockets. I realised how clammy my hands were. I was covered with guilt –

Everything shattered.

I felt my separate selves collide and I wanted my mother back so badly that I hardly knew where I was; I hardly knew *what* I was. In that moment, the wanting consumed me so utterly that it somehow became me. *There was nothing else.* I was only that longing, that searing ache.

Somewhere far away, in another realm, my breath caught and twisted, becoming a whimper.

"Hey," Kyle called. "Hey, Liberty…"

He leant close. He touched me. His hand was warm against my arm.

"Please, Liberty," he said. "Come back."

And I did. Or at least, a part of me did.

I turned and sat up gradually, in jolting stages, holding my head. I wasn't quite sure what had happened, exactly where I'd disappeared to. I blinked at the bottle Kyle offered and at all the sharp, broken shingle between us. There were bright kaleidoscope-patterns caught between my lashes, a dazzling mist, which parted and re-formed. I reached out slowly for the bottle. We both ignored the way it shook.

Kyle leant back once more against the pebbles and as I sipped, I noticed his frown and the stretch in his lips, and then a pale indentation in the flushed skin on the side of his neck. As if recalling a dream, I remembered him shirtless, his reddening torso rising and dipping through the freezing water. I remembered those other white marks speckling his body, and I thought about the weaving path that had led me to the pine marten. A trail of blood, a trail of scars.

"How did you get those marks?" I asked.

My voice was a thin whistle, far away and hardly human, still. It was more like the wind, where it was trapped in the highest branches. Yet perhaps it was only because I hadn't fully returned to myself that I dared to voice the question.

But Kyle didn't even have to ask me which marks; he knew.

"From a cigarette," he said.

I looked down at the bottle propped now between my knees, its label wilting. I began to pick at it. The sun grew hotter on the back of my neck. From the corner of my eye, I could see Kyle's newest mark, that hook-mark, where his sleeve had been pushed back. My own cut was already healing, disappearing, but as I stared at the curve of his

149

scab, I felt a fresh ache tingling towards my wrist, and I wondered how often he hurt himself, and what that might be like. Whether it helped.

"I didn't know you smoked," I said.

Kyle shrugged. "No," he said. "I don't. I've never even tried."

I didn't understand. I glanced back to that older scar, resting a centimetre or so above his collar. Its edges looked puckered. It was as if the flesh there was stiffly knotted underneath; I imagined that it would feel harder and tighter than Kyle's ordinary skin.

"My mum," he said.

He wasn't looking at me. He gazed out, eyes narrowed, towards the water. "But I'm not allowed to stay with her anymore."

Even though I still wasn't altogether whole, or completely present, I watched my hand rise. It was my turn to touch him now; perhaps I might bring him back? My fingertips trembled as they brushed his collar, and then his neck, as they skimmed across that burn-mark. To my surprise, it was as warm and soft as the rest of Kyle. It was a part of him. Except for the dip where it began and ended, I could hardly feel the change.

He took my hand in his, linking his fingers through my fingers. It was as if we were much younger kids, I thought, playing a game, choosing a partner, the way that we used to, back in Infants.

Like Kyle, I stared out towards the water. I watched his boat rock. I saw how warped it was, the peeling paint greyed to almost the same shade as its weatherworn, bent wood. But I liked looking at it. There was a sense of calm in the sunshine that fell across the seat and balanced oars, the same lapping gold that welled and winked across the water. I imagined the ancient, ragged rope coming loose and the boat bobbing free, floating lazily, hazily away. Taking with it that little pool of light.

From the small, ragged copse behind us came the peeping and chirruping of hidden birds, their chatter far more frivolous than the ducks' lower, wryer conversations.

"I wish we could stay here forever," I said.

Kyle shifted beside me, but he didn't take his hand away. It wasn't like my hand; it was larger and thinner and much warmer, but it was odd how easily it fitted into mine. The stones clicked beneath us, and then something clicked inside Kyle's throat.

"But I won't be coming here again," he said.

I looked at him sharply, before I could stop myself. He seemed to be gazing down at our fingers, to the place where we were connected, but it was difficult to tell because he'd started blinking. He blinked too rapidly and between each blink his eyes seemed to grow a little browner. A little shinier. Perhaps I'd misheard.

"What?" I said.

"I found my Dad's address," Kyle told me. "In a cupboard at Granddad's. I didn't mean to find it; it was just there. But I think I've got to go. I've got to try. I can't be here anymore."

"What are you talking about?" I said. "You can't leave."

He went on, as if I hadn't spoken: "My Dad will let me stay with him. At least, I think he'll let me stay."

Although my fingers continued to hang coolly, passively, inside his, I could no longer look at Kyle. My gaze crept across the ground between us, picking out the palest stones. As I stared, their whiteness blazed and I felt the cold beneath.

"I'll come to see you at the loch house though," Kyle continued. "I won't go without saying goodbye."

I could hardly hear him. I was too pre-occupied. I'd found myself thinking about the whiteness inside us. About bones and scar tissue, with all our softness and surface stripped away. And I realised that Kyle's hand only felt warm because mine was so chilled, even with the day's heat and the thrumming in my flesh.

I squeezed his palm then, as hard as I could. I squeezed it as if I might wrench the warmth right out of him. I squeezed until I felt his knuckles grinding, until he gasped and tried to twist away.

"*Liberty,*" he said.

For a few more seconds, I went on clinging. I dug my nails in too as if I might reach right inside him, right through his warmth and blood, to his brittle chalky frame –

But then as rapidly as it had risen, that whiteness cleared and I threw Kyle's hand away from me.

I would have cast off the whole of him if I could. As desperately as I'd held on, I now wanted to be apart. My disgust was all encompassing; every part of my small body felt brutally betrayed.

And finally, my dreams turn to Richard.

We're immersed in the never-ending twilight of 'our' restaurant, a cellar-place a few streets from his studio, where the candles don't ever quite die out and each intimate booth fits snugly into an alcove of brushed stone. I can smell coffee from a nearby table, coffee and perhaps quality chocolate. A rich, sweet scent, with a bitter edge. We've finished eating, but only just opened the second bottle of Merlot. The wine looks lacquered, black and seductive in my glass, but I don't reach for it. Richard's hands twine mine on the embroidered cloth.

"I've been turning it over," he explains. "And I think it might well be our final chance."

Bemused, I draw back from his insistent gaze. The entire dimmed restaurant is rustling with hushed conversations, each booth twitching quietly with secrets, but for once, I don't want to talk seriously. I don't really want to talk at all.

The candle putters. The shadows tremble and I imagine the light tickling across my shoulder blades too, playing down my spine and with the silky outline of my backless dress. And when Richard leans close, and then closer still, it's far too easy to picture myself pressed up against those cavernous walls, his mouth hot against my throat.

I slip one hand out from beneath his. I trail two fingers from his solid wrist to his shirt cuff. I ease them inside.

"I don't understand," I say. I rub gently. But his arm feels rigid, unyielding, and –

"We have to get away," he says. "Finally make a decision. Or at the very least, lay things to rest." He blinks down at his glass. "It's now, or never. You do understand that, don't you Liberty?"

I feel my mouth open wider. Heat flits along my arms in quivering threads.

"Richard, what do you mean? I'm not sure... What are you saying?"

I think I'm calm still, but when my voice emerges, it's a child's, high and catching. Where my fingertips meet his wrist, they tingle.

Is he genuinely suggesting that he'll leave Amanda and the children? That he's finally willing to tell the whole world, to give us a chance? In all our years 'together', it is more than he has ever openly suggested, even when I first thought I'd have his baby. He's never wanted to mislead me and now I hardly dare to hope. But my pulse flickers and there's that fizz and crackle, that igniting, to our touching, and I'm hoping, nonetheless.

Yes Richard. Please Richard. It will work out – I promise you. We'll make our own family. And it will be different this time. It will be right.

"I think that, at first, we should go away," he says. He's nodding slowly, his weighted gaze resting on my collarbone, my jaw.

"It seems like forever since we've had a holiday. And I think it might help, to begin with. A bit of space, away from here. Away from everything and everyone."

I nod absently along with him. I picture Greece, that garden, and as he clears his throat, I suspect I'm smiling inanely. Surely I ought to be holding myself more steadily for this? I should be stiller, and quieter. More in control. *Like a good little girl*, I think. Not like I'd ever been, of course, but like some other child, sitting cross-legged on the story mat at school.

"After all that we've been through together," Richard explains, "we have to give it one last try." He unhooks my fingers, reaches for his glass.

"After all the deception. The kids – I owe my marriage that much, at least."

I sit up with a groan. Slump awkwardly against the bedstead. My head's stuffy, overfilled. Obviously, none of this was just a dream.

The restaurant is real. And it's exactly how Richard left me, how he left me for his wife. Although he did return to my flat, for one last time.

And was that the night when it happened? I wonder, and draw my knees up, covering my stomach. Or might I have been pregnant already, as I sat there, listening to him? Nursing my wine in that enigmatic light?

It's not difficult to imagine, yet another restaurant secret bristling beneath the gloaming... Though I can't pretend Richard's decision would have altered even if he had known. Underlying the effort I'd made that evening was my awareness of the strange bitterness that had begun to seep into our relationship. The way the sadness between us had caught and twisted, and was starting to turn in.

Straining for comfort, I stretch until my taut back cracks, then twist to bash the swollen pillow at my side, only to toss it out a moment later. Despite everything, I miss him.

Although I know I shouldn't. I mustn't. I can't afford to, not on top of everything else. And I'm more than aware of how depressingly predictable our situation is, a ridiculous cliché. Yet that missing, it doesn't go away.

Sometimes it astonishes me how stupid it all is. When I look back over the life that I've spent 'with' Richard, what do I actually see, especially during these last few years? Nothing but endless meals, often finished off with tears. And even the sex, which had once been so languorous, so life-affirming, has become increasingly grasping. A strange, angry rush towards orgasm. We snatch at that obliteration – I clench his seed inside – and then cling grimly to the shallow validation of still coming together once that brief peace has worn off.

And then there is the waiting.

I have spent so much of this relationship waiting. Innumerable hours gazing through windows or simply into space, in bars and other restaurants, in his studio or on set somewhere. In my empty, echoing flat. All that clock-watching and determinedly *not* clock-watching, hovering over telephones and fantasising... I seem to have made a kind of career out of it, especially since losing the acting work, giving up the voiceovers and the bumbling, short-run pub-theatre productions, the few odd days of extra-work. Now, aside from the occasional random adult education class (in life drawing or beginners' yoga, an ill-thought-through 'Introduction to Psychology'), what I mostly do is drink, and wait.

Of course I know how pathetic I am. His *'Mistress'*. Except –
I love him.

That's the ancient battle cry. The relentless justification. It's also true.

No matter how we hurt and who we hurt, that love remains. And despite Venice, despite Amanda, I'm sure Richard still loves me too. Because haven't there been occasions, even during those terrible months after the hospital, when Richard went on looking at me in the old way, the best way? As if he couldn't quite believe in me, or in his own shocking luck, his mouth bent into a lopsided smile as he reached over to brush back my hair, or to cup my chin in his large warm fingers.

"Let me look at you, Angel. Let me just look..."

And my body would respond to that sliding glance exactly as it used to, my skin stiffening and goose-bumping, even before his knowing fingers had crept close. Times when my whole self rippled beneath the appreciation of his gaze, and I shivered with his laughter. His rich and gloriously filthy laugh.

Because there is that boyishness in Richard that I'll always cherish, but there are the quieter times too. Lapping awake to find his breath against my neck, his broad arms crooked about my waist. Holding me tight.

I have loved him more deeply than I've loved anyone, except my parents. And it isn't even about having a baby; although the baby is everything, it's an entirely separate need. I have sacrificed so much for this relationship; I don't have any choice.

But isn't that the secret belief that mistresses everywhere share? Surely Marie would have made the very same claims about my father. In her ignorance. In *her* stupidity.

But I love him.

Poor, stupid Marie.

Except I don't want to understand her. Even now I'm grown, I hold on to my hatred. I need it –

And besides you weren't even a mistress, the 'Other Woman', by the end. You'd already stolen my father. Married him. You had him all to yourself for those last precious weeks. I am not like you at all.

But these are my three-in-the-morning thoughts and the relentless way in which they roll over me is as predictable as their content. They're almost as bad as the nightmares. And I'm bored with them. As I'm more than bored with myself, and yet there's no escaping any of it (*"You can never escape yourself"* - thank *you*, Dr Gilchrist), especially at this night hour. The stillest hour, the blackest hour, when the sleepless and the good of the world are so clearly divided.

But I mustn't do this anymore. *I'm not Marie.*

And yet I am her. I cannot help myself. I can't change a single thing.

I kick impatiently at my covers, feeling a small, petulant satisfaction when my duvet slithers off to join its pillow on the floor.

There's no point, I think, *in anything.* In this not-sleeping, this self-pitying. I wonder if the bar's still open. Nevermind my resolutions, I'm wondering. Not that I have to drink anything, that's what I tell myself. Not anything alcoholic. But there might be other people. Distractions. I think of Tim –

What's wrong with me?

155

I scrape the sticky hair out of my face, and then catch the green alarm clock digits through the dark.

7:04 a.m.

And with a jolt, I realise that it's day again, way too late for my three-in-the-morning fears, or way too early. And the bar, I realise, would have shut hours ago. I must have slept longer than I thought, though I'm exhausted. Bruised with dreams.

I climb from the bed and go to the window, lift aside one heavy curtain. The thick, bunched fabric is chilly in my hand. Sure enough, a dingy morning spills into the room. Out there, the night has almost washed away completely; it lingers only in the dense knit of shadowed corners and in the blank, black windows of the building opposite.

The street below looks more like something from a fairytale than ever, some winding, wanderer's path. Even the presence of a refuse sack, overflowing with glinting cans, doesn't spoil the illusion. I raise my fingertips to touch the cold pane and all too clearly, recall those dawns at the loch house when I watched for Kyle's small boat. I remember how I could smell the new day back then, even through the glass. I shiver.

A new day, I think.

Today, I think.

I'm going back.

Of course the pine marten died.

I knew it before I saw him. Before I stepped into the kitchen or pushed open the loch house's weatherworn red door. Perhaps when Kyle dropped me off for the final time at my beach and the wind picked up, chipping at the day's pale warmth. I seemed to understand even before I heard Marie keening, when there was only that whispering grass and the swirling water, the empty ticking of the stones.

I remained ill prepared, however, for the mess that I found in our pallid kitchen, for Marie's hanging, shaking head and bowed shoulders. For how she rocked, crouched on the grit-flecked floor beside his basket.

She held a corner of that crocheted blanket in one clenched fist, while with her other hand, she stroked him, those movements tentative as if she was afraid of hurting our new pet, of breaking him. As if anything she might have done could have made any difference then.

And there was nothing in the least sensitive about the noise coming out of her; her cries were harsh and relentless and hardly human. The pained rhythm of some ancient machine, they sawed back and forth between the faded cupboards and the cluttered sink –

I wanted to turn around and run straight out again before they could work their way through me. Yet somehow, I didn't give in to the pull of the snowy shoreline, to that clean, flashing water. I held myself together; I made myself stay. Although it wasn't for Marie, but for Pie that I walked over.

I hovered for a few seconds behind my stepmother's hunched, racked body and then, focusing only on the pattern in the wicker basket, I sunk to my knees. Slowly, I reached out.

But unlike Marie, I couldn't bring myself to touch Pie, though I was close enough to smell his coat and his dense, musky odour seemed unchanged. He still carried the scents of soil and heather and muddy woods, and there was that same gritty undertone too. A deeper, sweeter odour, which was like the night somehow. The lull and mystery of a rainy night...

Except Marie's weeping kept on at me. Her wails were everywhere so that I couldn't even escape within myself. I turned and stared. Through her sticky hair, I made out her blotched cheeks and her mouth, hanging open. A raw, pink hole, strung with spit.

"Stop crying," I told her. "Stop it."

But she didn't even stop rocking and if anything, her sobs hitched louder. *Like nails on a blackboard*, I thought. Rusted nails inside my head.

I gazed back at the open door and then up to the wide, smeared window. It wasn't long after midday and the sun was too high for me to see from where I crouched, but the sky itself pressed hard against the glass, bare and brilliant, a square of radiant white. Dust danced amidst the glare and I noticed how it layered every surface too, a carpet of spilt flour. In contrast, the stains pooling the cooker-top were very dark, burnt in. It hit me how completely we'd been neglecting the house. As we hadn't done enough to rescue Pie.

But Marie's fingers went on sliding through his rich brown fur and they were more distracting than the kitchen's disrepair, more mesmerising even than her rocking or those cranking sobs.

I realised I was becoming rooted too, trapped beside her, stuck with the crumbs to the tiled floor. Dust-motes spun, a snow-globe overhead, and it wasn't hard to imagine the dust coating us in the same wintry way that it had covered everything else.

We might stay like this for hours, I thought. *Forever* –

I stumbled to my feet.

"Get up," I said. "Come on, Marie. Get up now."

But still her shoulders went on heaving, the blanket twisted in her fist. I touched her shuddering back with the toe of my trainer.

"That's enough," I told her. "We need to get him out of the house. We need to bury him."

Outside, the bleached daylight was rimmed with gold once more. The loch shone, although the temperature was definitely dropping. Wind rippled the scrub – and Marie had managed to regain a little control. She was no longer wailing, just sniffing and swallowing, and while she carried the basket with exaggerated care, attempting to hold it steady between her splayed hands and her woolly breasts, I could tell that she was refusing now to look inside.

I walked determinedly ahead, deliberately keeping her going, leading her on, although the spade was far heavier than I'd thought it would be. Its pull ran from my wrist to my shoulder, the blade dragging an uneven furrow in the earth. Every now and then, I swung it too haphazardly and flinched at the flat, tinny clang as it ricocheted against a loch house wall, or hit one of the garden's large, half-buried stones.

"Here?" I suggested.

After going all the way around the house once, I'd finally stopped between two rose bushes, only a few feet from where we'd started, at the door.

Marie shrugged. "Ok."

She couldn't manage much more than a murmur and her features had shrunk against her swollen face. Yet with more of her juddering, over-cautious movements and her eyes still averted, she managed, finally, to set the basket down. And when she straightened, she opened her wide, rough hand to me.

"I'll dig," she said.

I passed her the spade without argument and once she'd begun, with a series of grim stabs and careless grunts, I allowed my eyes to shut. I leant back against the whitewashed wall. The loch's pervasive green scent, I realised, was almost overwhelmed, obliterated, by the bolder fragrance of the roses.

It was an affront, that smell. Too rich and ripe, when it was practically October. Too blatant even for a funeral. Sweet and cheery, and overly familiar, it was like peeling back the lid of a brand new ice-cream tub, 'Neapolitan', with its strawberry and vanilla. But when I blinked, I saw how the roses' silky heads were actually curling and browning. Their petals wrenched and quivering, desperate to tear free.

And below us, all about us, the water spread and spiralled. Gusts puckered gold from black, knitted white through blue. The loch looked self-contained and vast and very empty and I thought about Kyle's boat. I thought about how he wouldn't be coming back anymore, not unless he kept his promise and returned to say goodbye. And I wondered at the way that everything had seemed so different when I was with him, how he'd let me be a different kid, a safer kid, without loss. Without *this*.

The spade's scrape nagged at my ears and after a while, I turned; I couldn't help it. There was a strange fascination in its broken rhythm, in the way the blade caught repeatedly in the stiff, clinging earth. The soil turning in strings and clumps and puffing powder, and Marie's hair jittering with the wind. She worked relentlessly, panting. As if this was no more than another gardening job she'd single-mindedly complete.

Except suddenly, she stopped.

"I don't think I can do anymore," she said.

I stared into the grey. Gradually, my gaze crept back up, tracing past the hacked roots and teetering stones. I nodded.

"It's big enough." I agreed, but when I turned to face Marie I saw what she really meant. Her face was slick again, freshly broken. Her eyes weeping slits, the light in them crushed. She couldn't do this anymore.

It was up to me.

I wouldn't think about it, I decided; I'd just do it. There was no other way. I bent over Pie's basket. I blinked past the shine of his fur, ignoring how the sun offered a whole extra tawny layer to his coat. I folded the blanket across him. As I covered his simple face, I tried not to notice the way that his chin rested on his paws as if he was just sleeping, or the new gum sealing his eyes.

I gathered up the bunched crocheted corners and I lifted him. He seemed to weigh no more than when I'd carried him only yesterday, when I'd borne him so carefully towards the house. When he'd filled my arms with warmth and treacherous hope – but I wouldn't think about any of that, *I wouldn't*.

I had to do this.

I had to ignore the burnished down fanning through the gaps in the wool. I had to suppress the ache that I suddenly felt for Mr Whiskers too. A hot longing, and then a new horror, as I caught myself wondering what they might do with *him*, down at the cattery, if we never made it back.

I dropped the blanket and its contents into the hole. I snatched up the spade from beneath the largest rose bush, where Marie had left it. The handle was still clammy with her, but I didn't care. I didn't care about anything anymore. I grasped it tighter so that I wouldn't slip and plunged it into the cobwebby pile of newly turned soil. I began piling the earth back in.

And although Marie's gaze burnt into me, I kept going. I didn't pause to acknowledge her, not her hurt or her shame, or the squeaking mouse-words that came scratching out of her.

"I'm sorry, Libby," she kept saying. "I'm so, so sorry."

But I didn't answer; I wouldn't even look at her. As I refused to listen to the soft, heartbeat-thump the earth made each time it hit that bundled blanket. As I refused to think about everything that I had lost.

"We can't leave," Marie told me. "We're not going back."

We sat opposite each other in the living room, with only the rickety coffee table standing between us. Marie perched on the sofa,

160

her face concentrated behind her steaming cup. Gently, she blew and as I watched the steam fragment, the loch house felt quieter than it ever had before. The wind had died down and the beams and floorboards seemed to be at rest. For once, the entire house was sleeping, and when Marie spoke, I didn't have to strain to hear her, although her voice remained husky. Perhaps for the first time, she had my full attention. My thoughts were with her and nowhere else.

She'd led me here once we'd finished outside, or at least as finished as we were ever going to be. As soon as the hole was filled, we'd abandoned it. A clumsy mound between the flowerbeds. We hadn't marked it in any way; we didn't even have the heart to tamp it down. The spade and Pie's emptied basket lay where I'd thrown them, beyond the garden. Left to rust and rot for all I cared, among the heather and the bracken.

I'd followed Marie back into the house as unthinkingly as a beaten dog. There was no fight left in me. I sat where she told me to sit. I sipped her scalding tea. In contrast, though her voice remained frail, she seemed to have discovered a new determination.

"There's too much to deal with in London," she said. "Too many people and too many questions. Too much to face. I don't know how we – how you, especially, would cope with it all. I understand that this might be difficult to take on board. You're so young. But that's *why* you're far better off up here, away from everything... And don't you think that there's something about this house, as well? A kind of protection? I've always felt safe here. Never mind the stories."

Her lips jumped into a small, sad smile, which she covered with her blue-flecked cup, but the heat made her wince and she set her tea down. The table trembled with the clink and when she moved to steady it, I saw dirt, circling patterns of soil, engrained into her palm.

"And of course there's the baby," she said. "There's my blood pressure, my general health, to consider."

A wave of exhaustion flooded through me with her words. I found myself longing to curl up on the ancient velour, to rest my head on a threadbare arm and sleep. But each time Marie's flitting gaze returned to me, I felt the small, tight energy inside her. A bright, secret snapping, perhaps exaggerated by the shadows.

It was much darker in the living room than it had been in the kitchen. The day was growing older and the window in here was smaller, and divided by its frame into twelve poky panes. In the grubby light, my wrinkled socks were grey, and the skin on my knee, where it peered through a ragged hole in my jeans, was also grey. And my tea

161

was grey too. My thoughts wandered to the greyness of the earth outside, but once more, Marie pulled me back.

"Y'know, Libby," she said. "I do understand something of what you're going through. More than you'd imagine. And not just because of what your father meant to me."

She leant forward and lifted her cup again. I watched her grey tea rock. A solitary splash leapt at her fingers.

"I wasn't much older than you when I lost my brother," she said. "That was a car accident too, although not the same thing of course. Nothing's ever the same... He ran out into the road."

She paused to make a laughing sound that wasn't anywhere close to a genuine laugh.

"All his fault, apparently. He was fourteen. Old enough to know better."

She stopped again and shrugged. Then looked straight at me, waiting.

After a moment, I nodded. I couldn't think what else to do. I could hardly take in what she was saying, or why she might be saying it. *More death*, how could she be talking to me about *more?*

And I was itchy with exhaustion now. The buttoned padding of my overstuffed chair gathered itself around my shoulders as if urging me to nestle deeper, to disappear. My vision was grainy – *grey-knee*, I thought, already drifting. Where the living room door stood ajar, I could see that the hallway was beginning to turn black.

"For years afterwards, I wanted to come back here," Marie said. "It seemed like our summer holidays were the only times when my family had been happy – *properly* happy, you know? But they wouldn't do it. They wouldn't even try. Not without Jamie. I suppose they thought it would be too painful. But I knew that it would help! And it is helping, isn't it, Libby? A little bit, at least?"

I found myself nodding again, nodding even before she'd finished framing her question. A thin draught unfurled from the cramped windowpanes, crossing the thread of stagnant water, which ran along the sill.

"But it was your dad who really helped me. Did you know that Libby?"

Marie had taken up her cup again and she was leaning forward, closing the gap between us, even as her voice grew louder.

"I know what some people said about us. What people wondered. And not only your mother's friends, either. But none of it was true. They had no idea. He *loved* me, he honestly did. And he helped me.

162

What we had together, it was real. He said I was the most real woman he'd ever met."

Even with the dimming light, I saw her flush. I pictured the tears rising inside her, pressing against her features with that spreading rush of blood. Her words slid into one another, growing thicker and faster as she went on.

"And he understood about my camera! About what pictures meant to me. How it wasn't just about representing the world, but recreating it. Re-inventing it and keeping it, the way you wanted. He understood that – and I didn't have anyone else. My parents hadn't felt like parents, not for *years*. Our family, after Jamie, it wasn't the same. I had no one. Until your Dad."

The light in her eyes condensed; it was opaque, so that when her tears began to spill, I was surprised at how thin and clear they were, as if I'd expected her to weep milk.

"And then, when I told him we were going to have a baby," she said. "*A baby* – I so wanted everything to be right."

Her sobs took over as they were always going to, and I was propelled back to all the other times I'd heard her cry. Once more, I was hovering beside Pie's basket in the kitchen. I was turning slowly from the weeping that slipped beneath her bedroom door and standing, mesmerised, in the dark at the top of the loch house stairs, too late at night. I was back in my own separate, watching, listening place. My tearless place. But this time, I didn't feel resentful. I was only cold. Too aware of the chill approaching with the creeping shadows. I was only tired. I longed for sleep.

But then Marie's head jerked and she was sucking down her sobs once more, attempting to smile.

"Libby, I just remembered!" she said. "I found some photographs last night. Photos of your Dad. I hadn't even meant to. I was looking for my camera. I wasn't going to shoot anything serious. Some snaps of Pie, that's all – though it would have been the first time I'd picked up my camera. The first time, since."

She shook her head, flicking away stray hairs and tears, rapidly regrouping before gabbling on.

"Oh, but they're such lovely prints. I'll fetch them now, shall I? Would you like to see them, Libby? Would you?"

I grew fearful then that I was still nodding, or about to nod. Forced brutally back to her, I felt how the cold of the loch house had concentrated. It flooded right into me, into the core of me. A stinging ice.

163

"No," I said.

I didn't want to see those pictures. The very last thing that I wanted was to have to look at those pictures, with her. "I can't. I'm sorry."

But Marie wasn't listening. Her head and shoulders were shaking with laughter instead of tears, except that this laughter kept snagging. My head rang with it. She set her cup down with a crack against the cheap wood and in the next moment, she was on her feet, striding unstoppably towards the living room door.

"I don't want to see them. I don't want to –"

I threw my words like pebbles against her woollen back, but I knew that it was useless. I could run away; I could lock myself inside the bathroom or barricade my bedroom, but I knew that it was futile, that wherever I went, she'd find me. And as she moved through the shadows in the doorway, I watched her arm rise in an all too familiar gesture. I watched her hand rub and then close across her stomach and somehow, insanely, I felt trapped inside her too.

I went through the motions. I showered and dressed and drew my 'face' on before the bathroom mirror, eyeliner and concealer. A dab of lip-gloss, just enough. I gathered together my wet towels and nightdress, zipped closed my suitcase. I checked out.

Of course, I hadn't dismissed what was due to happen, that today was the day of my return. In fact, I was more aware than ever of the loch house. I kept seeing it in primary flashes, blue windows, red door, yellow sunlight bouncing between the waves. At the same time, I felt disconnected from it all.

Waiting at the reception desk for my payment to be processed, I blinked numbly back at the keys strung in rows across the wall. They seemed to flicker, a dull fairy-light pulse. I set my hands, palms flat, on the buffed wood, but still couldn't quite steady myself, embody myself. Everything was off-kilter. The hotel, with its gilded surfaces and rich rugs and paintings remained less vibrant than my dreams. It was only when the receptionist returned my credit card that I briefly woke.

"Are you sure you have to go just yet?" she said.

Her manicured fingers brushed mine, and then lingered – and for an awkward moment, I thought she was about to seize my hands in hers. But in the next instant, she was withdrawing her pearly nails, her clinking rings. And when I looked into her face, her smile seemed wholly professional.

She was a woman about my age, but built more solidly. Well dressed and generally well kept, although unlike me, she'd allowed the first few strands of silver to glimmer in her carefully pinned hair. She wore discrete gold earrings and a tailored blouse. Beneath a patent belt, her uniform black skirt clung only a little too tightly to her hips. She looked as polished as her desk, and sensible; she was a proper grown-up – which made the wet emotion of her gaze all the more startling.

"Won't you sit awhile?" she said. "Won't you wait?"

Bewildered, I glanced at the clock ticking slowly behind her. It was after eight, but I had a whole hour to make my way to the station, more than enough time.

"I've a train to catch," I told her.

She nodded and folded her arms over her ample breasts as if she was done. But her damp eyes stayed with me.

"I'm sorry," she said. "I know I shouldn't keep you. Only. You don't look completely right this morning, if you don't mind me saying. Quite well, I mean."

In the desktop, my reflection was nothing more than smudges, and I recalled instead my en-suite mirror, registering, as I hadn't at the time, my true face before the make-up. I thought about the purplish circles below my eyes and the small, chewed patch on my bottom lip. My sallow, porous skin.

"I need more sleep," I said.

I tried to sound firm, curt even, but I nearly laughed, briefly flooded by a sudden mad urge to explain *everything*. I wanted to tell her about my parents and about the loch house; I wanted to tell her about Marie, and Richard. And about the baby too.

So badly did I want to tell her about the possibility of a baby, a real, live baby inside me, the words seemed to gush into my mouth. I sucked back a rush of sweet, cold water. It was all too easy to imagine her response, how she'd come right to me. Enveloping me with her sturdy arms, pulling my head to her shoulder. For a second, I actually felt the sigh of those ridiculously maternal breasts.

"There now, there. It'll be all right. You're not on your own. There, there..."

But of course such comfort was pure fantasy. I wouldn't say a word.

There was pride and there was privacy and apart from anything else, wasn't this impulse to speak, to 'offload', perhaps even *weep*, far too close to the way in which Marie had talked to the village shopkeeper about her pregnancy all those years ago? *Spilling her guts*, as if she couldn't help it. Even now, I flinched, reliving that profound, twelve-year-old's disgust.

I lifted my hands from the desk and pulled back my shoulders. I stood taller and thinner. There was no way anyone could guess my condition from my shape, not yet, but then, like an echo of that young mother back in St Pancras, I realised that the receptionist was also urging me to eat.

"But you haven't had your breakfast yet, have you?" she said. "It's included. And it might do you a world of good. Surely you've time for a quick bite?"

166

And what was this, this desire to feed? Something instinctive, something peculiarly female? Even without a confession or the slightest physical evidence, could these women, these strangers, somehow have *felt* my pregnancy? Sniffed it out? I imagined our hormones stirring and colliding in the air, as intent and relentless as those old midge clouds – unknown women had certainly never stopped to worry about me before. And hardly thinking, utterly passive, I'd already turned towards the dining room.

Between wide double doors, I glimpsed a pattern of tables, each one dressed in crisply cornered white. I stared at the shining silverware and a row of jugs containing very orange juice, waiting to be poured. But along with the persuasive order of that room, so the pink, bubbling smell of bacon fat hit me. My stomach recoiled.

"No," I heard myself say. "I need to go."

I wouldn't tell her anything; I wouldn't give her anything. *I would not give in.*

I pocketed my credit card, resolutely turning from the temptation to share my troubles. I had to unravel my own secrets – unless I simply wasn't ready yet, to confess. Either way, I found myself eagerly reclaiming that muffling detachment as I walked through the hotel's grand, scrolled Edwardian doors, my case grinding on the sloping steps.

And although my spine felt stiff and I had to concentrate on each uncoordinated, jerking footstep, I trundled down those picturesque streets without once looking back. The case wheels clacked against the cobbles and I told myself that I was a machine again. Functioning, but no more.

It was what I needed. That mood, or lack of mood, carried me through the trial of another bustling station. Despite the early hour, the concourse was packed with festival tourists already leaving. Heading home. I easily negotiated their clamour and swinging backpacks, though the station smells claimed me. Thick, singed coffee mingled with an underlying odour of oily metal, and here and there, the stink of hangovers. A combination of old cigarettes and last night's beer unfolding between mumbling strangers. But soon those scents also slipped past me, rising to disintegrate before the criss-crossed ceiling. And I felt protected, almost invisible, as I located the correct platform, as I waited for my train.

And now that I've boarded, I have left them all behind. There aren't many passengers for this obscure little line, so few in fact that it seems odd for such a train to be running during peak travelling times, for it to

167

be running at all. But then, there isn't much to it, just two ancient shaking carriages. There's no first class and no buffet car – no guard either, it seems. The windows are grimy, speckled with dirt, and the seats, where they're not actually torn or pockmarked, are loose and faded. Dustily upholstered in a geometric seventies-style pattern of mustard-coloured triangles and squares. *A train from the past*, I think. It even smells vaguely of stale tobacco, the way trains used to.

Although the tobacco smell is probably coming from the only other passenger in my carriage. An old woman, buried in a mound of fabric. A fraying headscarf shadows her face, while her body is indecipherable inside a stained overcoat. She's walled in further by a bulging canvas bag, gathered to her lap. Another bag obscures her feet, spilling what looks like more smeared rags on to the floor.

I try not to stare and I try not to judge as I move past with my case, except it strikes me that she seems like something from another era too – although aren't such people timeless?

Her odour, I realise, is both denser and sharper than old cigarettes. She smells distinctly overripe; there's the unmistakable cling of urine, combined with the rotting-softening-fruit flavour of cheap alcohol. And though we've only just left the station, she looks as though she's been asleep for hours. For days. Where it shows, her drawn, sealed face is deeply lined, wispily whiskered. Her eyelids a startling mauve.

She could be dead for all I know –

But it's a nonsense-thought and I scold myself for it as I scurry on, choosing a seat as far from her, well, as far from anyone, as I possibly can.

It isn't until several minutes later, when I'm finally settled, with my jacket folded beneath me and my case placed gingerly on the rack, that I notice a spidery trail of graffiti on the wall beneath my window. The lettering is jagged and uneven, childish, although not necessarily penned by any child. A demented scrawl in purple Magic Marker. Even considering the probable hate behind it, it makes me smile, or almost smile.

Go home, it tells me. *Go home. Go home.*

And I wonder when the truth of this return will finally hit me? Maybe when I disembark? Or perhaps a little later, when I arrive back at that tiny village, which is such a surprisingly short walk, only ten minutes, from the station. Perhaps the sight of that pub will do it, '*The Plough*' I remember. Or maybe the church? Those graves…

Once again, I picture those crowded, lopsided headstones. I remember the steeped leaves and the way their damp, streaked surfaces sparkled, as if dusted with greenish sugar.

But although I can conjure up such images in great detail, none of it feels completely mine this morning. I've created some extra barrier. But surely that's natural, considering what happened later? "Self-protection," Dr Gilchrist would have said. "Denial."

Through the window, I see that the morning sky has whitened. The day is bird-less, blanked out with thick clouds, and more cool than warm. The buildings rapidly give way to open country. Striped fields and rustling trees, fences. My head rocks gently with the carriage. I can feel sleep hovering close by and I wonder why it's so much easier for me to doze, to disappear, on jolting public trains than in the privacy of an hotel room. I think of the old lady lolling a few seat-rows ahead and wonder if train-travel doesn't perhaps induce some mild form of hypnosis? Except that the changes in my sleep patterns, these irresistible waves of exhaustion, could possibly be down to the baby too.

It's all because of you, I think as my eyelids flicker. As I begin to give up, to give in and drift. *Your fault*, I think. I hope...

My fingers relax, loosening across my lap. For now, I let them rest there. I like them there. Through my lashes, I see a fine silver dimpling rain dash and disappear and then dance again across the humming glass. And as I half-watch those rising-shrinking trees and fences, I feel I could be anywhere. *Or nowhere*. It's unbelievable that I only left London yesterday. It's as if I've been travelling, riding trains specifically, forever. Yet at the same time, I know I've barely started –

Outside, hovering on the scraggy verge, a figure catches my eye.

I force myself to sit up, to look back, even as she's already vanishing with the train's onward lurch. I'm confused, blinking. My cold hand on the cold glass.

A child? *A little girl?*

A girl just standing there, on the flattened scrub beside the tracks. Leaning through the drizzle towards the spin and spark of our rushing wheels. Watching for my window maybe, for *my* smudged face.

And clutching a bundle –

No.

I crane my neck, attempting to see. But all the while telling myself: No. No. *No.*

There is absolutely no way I could have recognised her. And what she'd held, surely it wasn't large enough? It couldn't have been a baby.

And besides, yesterday's children belong to yesterday. To a whole different train. She can't have followed me. It's impossible, and yet –

That tangled angel-hair.

I sink back against the lumpy seat. My fingertips squeak like rubber down the pane. The rain leaps against them, close. Tearing and pattering and outside, everything blurs. Sways. Scant bushes, stunted trees...

There aren't any kids out there. There's no one. Nothing. I'm simply over-tired again, overwrought. Half-dreaming already. And anyway, we're rattling on – she's gone now. Long gone.

She was never there.

I close my eyes and refuse to allow the bumping carriage to jostle them open. I need to sleep; it's no more than that. I won't look up again, as I won't keep thinking, wondering – not even as the old woman, in her separate row, begins to growl.

Even as: "It was you," she says. Or I think she says.

"It's what you done. *What you done –*"

I will *not* listen.

Like snatching at a weighted curtain, a blackout blind, I draw down sleep.

With each new photograph Marie showed me, I felt myself thinning.

She'd forced me to sit beside her on the sofa with a firm pat of her great, flat hand and where the cushions dipped beneath her widening hips, I couldn't stop myself from sinking towards her. I was so small and light that I rocked when she reached across to snap on the table lamps. Against the settling twilight, their glow was gaudy and unrelenting. I was wincing even before Marie started flipping through her prints.

The whole room sighed as if resigned. The slow, drawn-out flick between each image soon grew louder and more aching than the clock's never-ending tick and the scent of earth, of digging, went on rising from Marie. I imagined it matted into the wool of her cardigan, woven through her flesh. This close, there wasn't any escape. It took all my remaining strength to hold my shrinking, flimsy body clenched and rigid, to maintain an essential inch of lukewarm air between us.

But at first, I tried to focus on this, and not the pictures. I was determined that although they lay right there before me in an almost-book-sized-pile, I wouldn't truly see them. I'd somehow remain remote. At the same time, another part of me was well aware that there was no way I'd be able to stop looking once I'd started.

And there were so many of them. So many. There was Dad – and Dad – and Dad – and –

Dad bent over his favourite camera, adjusting the tripod. Dad close up and grinning, with two day's worth of patchy beard. Dad in a dinner jacket. Dad wearing a baggy blue jumper, with frayed cuffs and moth-holes, which I'd never seen before. There was Dad with his friend Pete, clinking tankards in a room filled with deep shadows and gleaming wood. Dad and Marie in some brighter, airier cafe. Dad and Marie at his studio, rearranging lights. Dad, tawny-chested in an unbuttoned white shirt. Dad with a group of very young-looking people who I did not know at all. Dad in a park, where the trees billowed with blossom. Dad, bent over someone's pink-tongued, black Labrador, wielding a stick...

And as I stared and stared, staring until my eyes ached, I found myself remembering one of my mother's phrases: "It's beyond endurance." I remembered how she'd hiss the words, spitting them out and then biting down on them, her teeth gritting. Grinding. "It's simply *beyond*."

Briefly, her image overlaid my father. Helplessly, I pictured her standing beside the telephone table at home with her thin back arched, her silhouetted elbows knife-sharp against a timorous light. She held the receiver in one hand and pressed her clinking glass to her forehead with the other. I was probably watching from my quiet place, in the turning on the stairs. Gazing, mesmerised, as if there was no choice.

As if, like now, I owed my parents. I was their witness –

Except, if that was the case, why wasn't I shouting as Marie went on dealing out her pictures? Why wasn't I screaming?

After all, wasn't there something contemptible about those photographs of my father (something entirely aside from the fact of Marie's presence in so many)? It may just have been that Dad appeared so vital and handsome in them, so rigorously healthy, ridiculously alive. They mocked everything that had happened. And they hurt my head. *They hurt.*

Marie, however, remained utterly engaged.

"Look at him here!" she kept saying. "Look at him *laughing*."

And she wept and grinned simultaneously throughout the whole ordeal. Her tears were silent now, yet they kept on, running constant, steady paths down through the creases around her smile. Looking over those pictures, Marie unravelled as she so often did. Along with those tears, there was the drip-drip-drip of her inane comments, and there was her trickling hair. Again and again, long brown strands fell into her face. They stuck to her cheeks and lashes, though she scraped them back repeatedly. She tugged and picked and even snapped at them, rubbing them impatiently behind her ears. Her silvery eyes crumpled, and her sniffing nose grew increasingly clown-like, turning by degrees a shiny red. But it was her mouth that was the worst. Her mouth that would not stop talking. Shuffling, like her hands, on and on.

Beyond endurance.

Yet I went on sitting there as if trapped, while at the window, the evening gave way to the true, steady blue of the descending night. The windowpanes quaked when the wind lifted once more. The room grew chillier. There was finally a feeling of sharpening autumn to the creeping draughts. I shuddered.

But I'm not here, I kept thinking; I was determined. *I'm not really looking at these photographs. I'm not tucked up beside Marie.*

172

See how far I am from her, I told my mother. *How distant, how tiny.*

It was true; I felt smaller than a button now, smaller than a penny. *Smaller than smaller than small.* And I would have disappeared altogether, if I'd been able. I imagined my inner-self somehow separating, shrinking further as it burrowed deeper, away from Marie. I pictured some eyeless creature curled tight inside its shell.

Not even a tadpole, I told myself, *but a thing without features, a thing without feelings. A thing that barely exists –*

Except then I became aware of Marie's body. Of Marie's belly in particular, which was spread beneath those photographs, providing a cushion for them and for her fumbling hands. As if it had never struck me before, it occurred to me that that stretching flesh wasn't entirely her – and for the first time, I truly wondered about what *she* had hidden underneath.

I was twelve years old, but I knew very little about pregnancy, about the way that babies formed. I realised I had no idea what that growing thing was supposed to look like at this stage (*five months*, I remembered, unless it was now actually closer to six?). I didn't know whether it was meant to have hair yet, or hands, or a small, sucking mouth – or whether it was actually still a kind of tadpole-thing itself? Or perhaps, I wondered, it was a different kind of basic? A fleshy bag, like the featherless baby-birds that Mr Whiskers had brought home repeatedly last spring. I could visualise *them* clearly enough; they were unforgettable. Blind and veined and repulsive, with their spindly necks and lolling heads and only the tiniest bumps where their wings should have been...

But then I remembered Marie talking about kicking. So the baby must have a foot at least, I thought. A doll-sized leg?

And somehow, with all this wondering, I had achieved what I'd wanted; I wasn't looking at those photographs any longer – I wasn't seeing Dad. Instead I was thinking, with a new crisp clarity, about how there was a baby inside Marie, and how none of this, how none of what had happened, was actually that baby's fault.

It doesn't know anything, I realised, and although I experienced a flicker of jealousy alongside this revelation, my envy was rapidly engulfed by a rush of pity. A simple, dawning sorrow.

Poor Thing, I thought. *Poor Baby, having to be born.*

Afterwards – after Marie had made me wash my face and drink a mug of sweetened, heated milk, and the photographs had been hastily hidden out of sight once more, I took myself quietly, obediently, up to my room. I changed into my nightdress, steadfastly ignoring the way that my fingers trembled with the tiny, pearly buttons at my throat. I turned off the light and half-lay, half-sat, propped up by pillows, on top of my cold, high mattress. I breathed carefully, almost silently, and watched the dark.

The room was so thick with night that I couldn't see the wardrobe from my bed or even the edges of my window, although I'd left the curtains gaping. Within the press of shadows, I felt fragile, husk-like, and still too close to crumbling. I couldn't quite believe what had happened. What I had *allowed* to happen. How I had given in – suddenly weeping, *sobbing*, before Marie.

Of course she had thought it was because of the pictures, because of the "pent-up emotion" that they'd unleashed. She'd worried that she might have pushed me too hard, too early, but then in the next minute, pondered aloud about my tears' *value* – their "therapeutic worth". She'd gabbled incessantly the whole time I cried, a high-pitched tumble of banal platitudes and pop-psychology. She had put her big hands around my shoulders and on my face and on the back of my head. She'd cupped my neck and drawn me into the seedy softness of her body until I'd felt close to smothering. But I had let her.

Despite her endless squealing and her choking wool, even despite that dank, clinging scent of upturned soil – *I'd let her*.

And yet what choice really, had I had? My crying and shuddering had been such that I could hardly move. I couldn't swing away from her or find the breath to argue, regardless of the thin triumph that I sensed now and then, beneath her chatter. I let her hold me, despite what my mother would have felt were she to see me there, because I was trapped; I was *frozen*. That's what I told myself, at least.

But it wasn't my fault –

Wrapped in Marie's heavy arms, sobbing into the dense folds of her inevitable cardigan, I remained mesmerised, hooked, by the proximity of her swollen belly. I couldn't take my eyes from it. I couldn't pull away, even though Marie continued to soothe and coo all around me. Thankfully, I did manage to resist the urge to reach out, to reach closer, to touch that bump with my small, curious hand, although my fingers had been itching. Nor did I tell Marie the truth about why I was finally weeping. Even if I'd been tempted (which I certainly was not), I had no way of explaining that it wasn't simply the weight of my grief that had sent me reeling, but somehow the innocence inside *her*.

174

That it was the absurd, precarious hope of a new, waiting life that had undone me – and the way in which that hope would have to end.

I hardly understood such thoughts myself. I'd imagined my head might clear once I was away from Marie and her unborn child (*my half-brother or half-sister*, I thought now, numb with wonder), and yet in the black sanctuary of my bedroom, I had to brace myself against disintegrating afresh.

I bent my shaky legs. I drew my knees up to my chin and hugged my narrow ankles. I closed myself as neatly and completely as I could, resting my swollen eyelids and then my lips on my bony kneecaps. Absently, I sucked at the skin there and pressed it gently with my teeth, but I could only taste tears. A mouthful of brine.

Gently, I began to rock. I didn't want the bed to creak; I didn't want Marie to come. And as I rocked and the night deepened, rain came tapping at my invisible window. The sound of it stood out in pinpricks against the darkness. A scattering and padding, as if a small, evicted animal was scrabbling soft, clawed paws against the glass.

But to my surprise, I actually found sleep. A deadening, merciful sleep, as far as I knew without dreams, and when I woke I felt oddly better, although I shouldn't have. My sheets were soaked again, and not yet cold. The skin on my thighs was clammy, raw and sore, and I knew that when I clicked on the light, I'd see the beginnings of a rash beneath that shameful shine. And yet, for a little while, I continued to simply lie there, almost uncaring, engulfed by my mess and ugliness, that familiar stink.

But even with my 'accident', there was a strange comfort in those slippery moments before completely waking. The long, draping shadows appeared to turn in time with the rain's rhythm. Such a deep and velvety drumming that I imagined the walls vibrating, the feathers in my pillow quivering beneath my head.

Goosebumps ruffled my sticky flesh, but I wasn't afraid. And I wasn't hurting anymore either, although bit-by-bit, as my eyes adjusted, I became convinced that I was no longer alone.

My small hand lay, half-open and seemingly empty on the damp covers at my side. As the shadows cleared, I was able to see it with an increasing clarity, and it looked just as it always did. There were my stubby fingers and my bent thumb; there was the paler patch of palm inside. There was nothing else to see, nothing unusual, and yet –

There.

Right there –

I felt the lotioned press of my mother's skin. Her smooth, clean, unforgettable hand was curled about my own.

I couldn't see her and yet I was sure, almost certain, that she was with me. Through the fluttering dark, I caught the expensive musk of her perfume and when I concentrated, there was even the sharper citrus scent of her clinking glass –

Her cool, smooth fingers folded gently over mine.

I remembered the dream I'd had of a man in my room back on that strange, cold night when I'd first glimpsed Kyle outside the window. But it wasn't Kyle who I thought of now; it was the way in which, that same dreaming night, I'd briefly allowed myself to believe in my father's return. How desperately I had wanted that, to see my Dad again, beside my bed…

And then I found myself recalling Marie's story of a lost fisherman and of a woman left behind, left waiting forever for his return, and I was flooded with hope. With wonder.

Because what if they truly can come back? What if tonight –

Focusing sharply on my own eager fingers, I opened my eyes wide into the swirling shadows; I opened them as wide as I possibly could.

Oh please, let this be real.

I needed this; I needed her, so badly.

And once more, it struck me how completely different my mother was from Marie – Marie, with her clumsy weight and musty flesh and fraying wool. In comparison, my mother's touch was silk. So delicate, meticulous. So light.

My fingers tensed against the mattress. I was terrified of breaking the spell. I tried my very best not to grasp or snatch or strain too urgently, too obviously. Yet at the same time, every nerve ending in my body was vibrant, alert; my whole *self* reached out.

But no matter how desperately I concentrated, the sensation of my mother's touch was already beginning to lift away. Diluting with the dark.

"I'm sorry," I whispered. "I'm sorry that I cried. And I'm sorry that I let Marie put her arms around me."

But perhaps it was too late, or simply unforgivable; my mother was fading. She was leaving me –

All over again, she was gone.

My empty fingers dug into the sheet.

176

Yet I continued to lie there, waiting and hoping, praying to feel her. I didn't need much, the faintest brush, the slightest sigh. *Just once more...* I waited.

And I kept on waiting, in the way of ghosts.

Eventually, the windowpanes emerged in patchwork squares. As the night dissolved further, I strained and squinted, but there was nothing to interrupt their pattern. No figure stood before them, obscuring my view.

However, I went on staring. I stared until those grey squares peeled away from their black frame and seemed to float before me. There was nothing to contain them and after a while, the whole room began to feel wall-less, as if the emptiness inside me had loosened and then started to leak out, bleaching the shadows and clinging to the scraps of furniture, stifling everything. Even the rain, I realised, had dripped to a stop. And it was beyond endurance.

"*Simply beyond...*"

I sat up fast, suddenly aware of how disgusted my mother would be to see me lying there, drifting so passively, surrounded by my own dampness, my stink. I pushed the duvet away. I wasn't going to loll in my filth for a second longer. And I wasn't about to collapse either; *I would not cry again.* I sprang out into the chilly draughts and swept through the shadows, across the room. I reached for the light-switch by the door.

In the blaze of white, my room was abruptly boxlike, crowded with my ordinary clutter and an ordinary cold. I glanced quickly, appraisingly, from one pale wall to another. I took in my sprawl of clothes and my Misty annuals, my drawing pad. The dust already gathered across a heap of neglected books. I blinked past the wrinkled mound of soiled bedding, and then I turned my back on everything.

I reached for the pegs on my bedroom door, which held my dressing gown and jacket and a small blue rucksack. It was time to leave.

I am, I thought, *your daughter after all.*

I wouldn't stay there, with Marie, for another day. Another hour, another minute, seemed too much. I'd run away with Kyle. If he actually kept his promise and returned to say goodbye, I'd make him take me with him. If he refused or simply didn't show, then I'd just have to leave by myself. I could do it. I wasn't some little kid anymore. And I didn't much care where I went. I could probably return to London, although not to my old house; I couldn't go back *there*. But perhaps Jemma's family might take me in, or maybe I could find Alice's new address? Not that it mattered. It was the getting-away that mattered. I pictured my mother again, standing silhouetted by the phone.

I swerved about the room as swiftly and quietly as I could, tugging off my wilting nightdress, hopping and bending as I rolled on clean socks and a clean-ish vest while at the same time, I tried to gather up my things. I stuffed spare knickers and a notebook and a couple of felt-tip pens into my rucksack, and while I dressed and packed, the wind picked up again. It hummed through the walls, and my window began to rattle once more, the loch house chattering its old, loose teeth.

But it took less than five minutes to get ready. I only paused at the end, when I picked up a pair of very rumpled, muddy jeans to reclaim their belt and my newspaper clipping glided from a pocket. For a heartbeat, two heartbeats, I stared.

'DEATHS OF LONDON FASHION COUPLE – INQUEST CONTINUES'

And although I had the article practically memorised, I crouched to read it one last time.

Skimming over the speculation about my mother's alcohol levels, I concentrated instead on the coroner's insistence that pending the mechanic's report, 'even basic car faults cannot be ruled out' – and I clung to this idea; I stretched it. Until I found myself wondering about Marie.

I wondered exactly how deeply she must have hated my mother. And where she might have been on the evening of my show? It occurred to me that Marie would have had no way of knowing that my mother would offer Dad a lift in her car that night, or that he'd accept...

I began to concoct a story, a series of cartoon-strip images in which Marie, consumed by envy, had somehow done something to my mother's car – perhaps even while my parents applauded in that dimly-lit auditorium, while I took my bow? *What if*, I wondered, *she had tampered with the brakes?*

But even as the notion grew, a part of me dismissed it. Despite my hatred for Marie, that part knew that it wasn't plausible, that such ideas had nothing to do with real life, or pain, or loss. It was probably a plotline stolen not so much from 'Misty', but from one of the detective shows I occasionally used to watch. 'Hart-to-Hart' or 'Quincy'... Nevertheless, I let those thoughts fuel me in their way.

I decided to confront Marie before I left. There would be no sneaking off, no cowardice. I thought about how I'd allowed her to

178

hold me. And about the contrast of my mother's feathery touch. How smoothly that touch had slipped away.

And I wanted to hurt Marie, to accuse her of *something*. Because while I could hardly pretend, even to myself, that she was in any real way responsible for my parents' deaths, I also suspected that if my mother had been alone in her car that night – alone, or perhaps even with *me*, Marie wouldn't just have been pleased. She would have been *grateful*.

I barged through the mothy shadows on the landing, bracing myself to slam into her bedroom – only to find that her door was already standing open. I snapped on the light, but her room was empty. Emptier than I'd have ever imagined.

I realised that I'd never actually stepped foot in there before. And I was shocked. *There was nothing there.* No dumped clothes or papers or abandoned coffee cups, and only the most basic of furniture. Alongside the single bed with its twisted rumple of covers, there was only a rickety, lamp-less table and a chest of drawers. The drawers were tightly closed and every surface was empty, clear of clutter. Even the floor was a barren space, uncarpeted and rug-less – only bare, untreated boards. The whole room reminded me of pictures that I'd seen in books and on television of prison cells. Freshly gutted, patiently waiting.

Marie's window was far narrower than mine, but like me, she'd left her curtains wide. A dingy pink flowered in the highest panes. It was dawn, I supposed. Dawn already.

I took a step, a single step. Although I was still determined to leave and just as eager to confront Marie before I did so, there was something intriguing about the room's blankness. Something that both tugged at and repelled me, as if the loch house was playing another game, daring me onwards. And while I hovered, uncertain, I became aware of the room's odour. A strange, fleshy scent, vaguely female, but different from Marie's ordinary smells of young, grubby skin and sour wool. It was something richer than that, denser and meatier, not dissimilar to the odour of damp sawdust at a butchers –

Blood.

The thought struck me slowly, as if I was stupid, but I didn't believe it. *Surely, it couldn't truly be the scent of blood?*

Where Marie had left her sheets, almost as I had, pooled in the centre of her bed, I found myself staring now at an exposed patch of mattress. At the deepening pink there –

179

I turned away quickly, pulling myself together. That stain was surely nothing more than an effect of the seeping light from the window. It was simply the new day, growing rosier by the minute, as that smell was only the house again, with its age and damp and childish tricks. Even so, I stumbled as I backed over the threshold and a new idea rocked into me. *What if Marie had left me first?*

But in another moment, I was outside the bathroom, surrounded by the rush and gurgle of running water. The sound managed to penetrate the door's thick wood and there was even the softer clank of an ancient pipe. I had found Marie, I realised; I'd found my *stepmother*, and she was simply filling a bath, as if she was perfectly all right, as if everything was fine. Getting on as usual with her mundane, day-to-day tasks, as if nothing in the universe was wrong.

Welcoming my anger once more, I took a few deep, shadowy breaths and then reached for the bathroom door.

The handle turned easily; it wasn't locked. I felt a blast of wet heat and I almost pulled back, disorientated by the thick mesh of steam curling before me. I couldn't see straight. For a moment, Marie's shape was distorted, as if she'd been deliberately hidden. Obscured and protected behind her own damp white wall of ghosts.

"No Libby. Please, Libby -"

The bath is close to overflowing. Silvery torrents gush from the taps, while the rocking water in the tub itself is tinged red, filled with that early morning light. The sound of splashing and roaring rebounds against the tiles, but Marie's voice manages to cut straight through it.

"Libby – no."

But it's too late, far too late. I've entered the bathroom. The mists have parted and I have found Marie. I've seen her gauzy pile of clothes, all that discarded fabric on the floor. I have seen her. Her naked shape.

Nonetheless, she goes on bending and twisting – stupidly bowing her body away from me as she tries, pathetically, to hide. I watch her shrink with my eyes narrowed. I've never felt so focused.

And yet although she's cowering, Marie attempts to stare right back. Her eyes are as dark and slippery as oil and I know what she is trying to do with them. She's trying to hold on to me, to keep us locked together so that I don't glance away from her face again – and of course I can't have that. Slowly and deliberately, I drop my gaze once more.

I take in the fine line of shadow running along Marie's collarbone, and then her hanging breasts. I look past her puckered nipples and the raised barrier of one defensive arm to the wrinkling flesh at her waist. I gaze all the way down to the wiry frizz of her pubic hair.

Of course I stare at her empty stomach for longer than anything else. I absorb the pale, slight sag of her skin, the tiny, winking belly button. I stare especially at what isn't there. At the unimaginable space where a bump, her baby, is meant to be.

181

I jerk awake.

I'm heaved back into consciousness as if lifted and thrown by well-practised hands, only to realise that these images are just a dream, *another dream –*

The back of my head bumps hard against the musty seat and my teeth click together as my mouth snaps gracelessly shut. Initially, the waking world's fragmented, returning in snapshots. I glimpse my suitcase's handle and its twinkling zip, my own bony, stockinged knee swaying with the motion of the carriage. I see a crumpled can caught with the dust beneath the seat opposite. At the window, dense, rain-stained trees unfurl.

The trees nod their darkened leaves and wave like a crowd at a parade as we judder past and it's difficult to know which reality is more uncertain, this moment or the pictures lingering in my head.

Just a dream – I keep telling myself.

Except isn't it a dream I've dreamt before?

A dream that in the past, I've tried desperately to hang on to – only this morning, it remains vividly with me. The heat and water. Marie's empty body, most of all.

And could it be true? Is this the truth I've kept buried for all these years? Was it this revelation that sent me reeling out on to the black loch that morning, this that propelled Marie so recklessly after me?

I picture it again, her body, cringing through the steam, stripped of that extra flesh, that new life. *As if there was no baby.* I can still feel the pleading pressure of her gaze.

The whole notion is madness surely, and yet –

And yet.

Could it be true, Marie?

Could it be true that in your grief and instability, you put on a disguise? Like a little girl yourself, playing dress-up? Did you miss my father so much that you invented a child for him (*another* child, who wasn't any part of my mother, who wasn't me) or was it the hook that you used to drag him into marriage in the first place? And once he was gone, what then? Is that why we had to run away?

182

I know what it's like to be seen as a sick woman.

I know the panic attacks. I know the fear, that sense of being trapped, so trapped, inside yourself. *How sick were you, Marie?*

And yet how deeply you must have loved my father.

After all these years, I finally concede this, at least. I'm able to imagine how the longing might have grown inside you – growing until even your large, ruddy body couldn't contain it. Until it split you at the seams.

And perhaps there was genuinely a baby in the beginning, and something happened –

Or perhaps there was, simply, a baby.

There *was* a baby. Of course there was.

It was just a dream.

The train slows. On the other side of the smeared window, beyond the sheen of rain, the rocking trees take a small step back. They're heavy headed, seaweed green, the sky beyond them battered with clouds. I glimpse the blackened tracks and then the grey slope of a platform appears as if from nowhere.

I almost turn away; I don't want distractions now. There are too many memories to be recovered, unless they should be sharply discarded – except then, without meaning to, I read the platform's sign and discover with a single heart-knocking jolt, that this station is actually *my* station.

Already, I've arrived.

The trouble with my memory of the loch house bathroom on that final morning isn't that it's so distant. In fact it's the opposite, Marie, and the bathroom, that suffocating heat, it's all so close, *too close*.

Even at the time, it was hard to see, a struggle to think. The creeping dawn-light added its flesh to the swirling steam and I knew that Marie was crouched somewhere amidst those clouds, possibly backed up against the cold toilet bowl, but I couldn't truly see her, no matter what I've dreamt. And yet somehow, I can remember that bath overflowing with a crystalline clarity. I can still see the water rolling down its side in a trembling panel. A rosy puddle on the tiles.

For certain, I recall leaning into the denser mist directly above the tub. I remember how my reflection bobbed and broke there. I can even remember considering plunging my hand in to release the plug, but then changing my mind. The steam itself was scalding, and beneath the rushing taps, bubbles went on expanding and bursting with the thick fury of boiling milk. Eventually, I reached over to twist them off. The thrumming metal stuck to my palm, but I managed it. The torrent slowed. It became a dribble and then nothing, but for what seemed like a long while afterwards, too long perhaps, the water went on dripping.

Finally, as if reluctantly, it stopped.

I think it was then that I felt Marie shift behind me, perhaps uncurling a little. But I glimpsed her only in smudges. I couldn't see her body clearly – I'm certain. What did emerge briefly was her face, only her face, raw and staring through those tropical clouds.

She must have scraped her hair back into a bun in preparation for her bath, but it was already slithering free in its looping strands. *Rat-tails*, I reminded myself. *Nothing-coloured strings*.

However, behind that hair, her gaze was truly black and irrepressible. Her eyes were undeniable, except that they weren't brimming with any dreamy shame or worry, but with something far worse. Something like anger, or hunger. A terrible longing.

She lifted her hands. I remember this much.

She lifted her hands to me.

And as Marie clawed her way towards me, the steam slipped its own sticky, pinkish fingers into my head, confusing everything further.

184

In all honesty, I didn't understand what was happening, what I was seeing. Or what either one of us was trying to do.

I didn't understand – I was not responsible.

But I am remembering. In pieces.

There was an unnerving floppiness to Marie's movements. When she reached through the steam, her head lolled forward as if it were heavier than she'd expected. A giant rag-doll, trailing stuffing.

And yet she wasn't as weak as she appeared. I felt her hatred rolling over me in another sweaty wave, soaking into me with the reddening light. And I smelt that butcher's stink once more. It hit me even more powerfully than previously, an upsurge of newly cut meat; I couldn't stop myself from breathing it in. My head swam with it and yet it was in that reeling, dizzying moment that I somehow found my feet again, *myself* again. I'd never been so terrified in my whole life. I turned from Marie. I ran.

"Libby! Libby, *please!*"

The tide of her voice spilt after me. She called out repeatedly and between her cries, there came a sharp ceramic crash. I pictured the old cracked mug, kept beside the bathroom sink, teetering and falling. A jangle of toothbrushes and shattered china. But still I refused to look back, although as I fled, it wasn't the shadows, or even Marie, but the house itself that drew closer. I was no longer aware of the blood smell – instead I found myself gasping down the loch house's familiar graveyard-scent. Damp wood, old stone. And now, perhaps more than anything else, I didn't want *that* inside me, but there was no escaping it. *No escaping anything at all.*

I felt so loaded down; I was already struggling to keep going.

From somewhere in the house below, a door slammed and then another. The wind had barged its way inside somehow and was gusting gleefully from room to room, downstairs. I thought of it rifling through the curtains, trembling through cupboards. It swept and moaned up the twisting steps and when it burst onto the landing, I had to push, facedown, against it, with my eyes squinted and my small jaw gritted, my shoulders braced. At the same time, the ceiling seemed to lower; it almost brushed my scalp, a great, black cloth just overhead.

"*Libby!* Libby, come back!"

But even Marie was growing fainter, drowned out by the new rush of noises. The floorboards whined and creaked. The windowpanes rattled as if there were invisible hands at every casement –

I could not stop.

The house willed me on.

I headed straight for the staircase, at the same time trying to block out the building's moaning and shuddering, its childish ways. But even in its animation, the house was not as frightening as that last distorted image of Marie, rising towards me through the steam –

I couldn't shake free of her.

Each uneven, splintered step smacked back hollowly beneath my feet so that I half-fell, half-staggered towards the ground floor. I threw myself through the muttering hallway, the whole time clinging to the idea of the door swinging open. The promise of escape.

But even as I grappled clumsily with the latch and bolt, I remained almost certain that I wouldn't make it. That she would not let me. I heaved –

And shuddered involuntarily before the swell of new, cold light.

The sky wasn't shrouded anymore, or even flushed. The day had truly begun. Beneath the clouds, the grass dipped and lifted with the wind. The loch flickered, its surface choppy. I'd never seen it like that before. It was opaque in places, rolling white between the silver.

But there, *right there*, in the middle of it, small and clumsy and rubber booted, dragging his little battered rowing boat through the bumping shallows, was Kyle – as I hadn't dared to fully hope.

My ragged breath concentrated. I felt each gasp break sharply in my chest. In the spreading daylight, beside the landscape's fluttering majesty and emerging colour, that red bracken and bruised heather, the weight of that bleached sky, Kyle looked tiny. So insubstantial he might wisp away at any moment.

But he had come for me, as he had said he would – he'd surely wait.

And despite everything, I felt my heart opening, my spirits lifting. I raised one hand before realising he wouldn't be able to see me, not yet, not while I remained within the doorway's darkness. But just as I was about to run out to him, the house clattered loudly, deeply, at my back and I knew, before I turned and before she spoke, that Marie had caught us.

"Libby," she said. "Come back."

The hall shadows fell away from her in clumps, and in that chilly light, I saw her finally, I thought, for what she was.

She'd become monstrous, I realised. *A monster.*

186

Her face shone, her black eyes bulged. And although she'd pulled some garment on, a grey and shapeless nightdress, her repellent, unspeakable body was all too present. It pressed great wet patches through the flimsy fabric. And as she stepped towards me, I saw that her outstretched hands were red. They were sticky and dripping, and there was more redness collecting beneath her. A trail of scarlet footprints padded in her wake.

She reached out to me.

"*Liberty -*"

And I thought of my mother.

I thought of my mother's cool, soft fingers wrapped in mine, and I thought of my poor father too – and there was no way I could let Marie touch me with those red hands. She wouldn't take another single thing away from me.

So when she rushed forward, her gleaming face in mine, I swung back at her awkwardly. I pushed her. I pushed her with all my strength and all my fear and all my hate –

I pushed her with my sadness.

And she fell.

And when she fell, there was a crack, such a small, neat cracking sound, as the back of her head hit the loch house wall.

But I didn't pause to check on her. Instead, I turned around. I ran.

I need a drink.

And this need is what I try to focus on as I follow the road from the station to the village. *A dry white wine to blanch the tender spots, something cool and soothing on my tongue...*

The shaggy trees close in, the highest branches meshing overhead. Everything is green and gently dripping, although beyond the trees, the rain has thinned. It mutters quietly against the lace of leaves and pine needles, and I suppose I ought to take comfort in the hush. But instead I'm craving noise and other people (*a drink*), but there's no one about. The road looks abandoned, at least by cars, and there isn't even the murmur of an engine in the distance. There's nothing to distract me, and no wine to numb me. My thoughts go on clamouring –

And when I blink, I see her hands.

I see Marie's red hands reaching for me, her palms red, her fingertips red. The whorls and cross-hatching of her prints and all her fortune-telling lines are startlingly defined. There is so much detail. Too much detail.

Surely, this can't be right? These images seem more aligned with nightmares than with any kind of truth and yet uncontrollably, relentlessly, they keep coming. I picture a red puddle spreading across the worn tiles between Marie's feet. I watch the puddle jump as more blood falls –

But how can such 'memories' be trustworthy? *They found her in the water*; it's undeniable.

Nonetheless, I see her eyes.

Somehow I manage to keep going, stumbling through that tunnel of leaves, my case dragging at my arm, juddering through the potholes and at last, the road widens. The creeping roots and weighted branches slink back and there, abruptly, is the village.

Through the trees, I see the whitewashed houses, although today, beneath this glowering sky, their walls are soaked a deeper cream. But I glimpse the church too and it looks exactly as I remembered, with its modest spire and mossy wall. Beyond the wall, a gravestone peers. A granite face between the shrubs.

It's all strikingly close to how I remembered it, and yet in my desperation, I barely pause to draw it in. I make a beeline for the pub.

And I'm almost overtaken by a moment of renewed dread during those last quickened steps as I imagine the building empty, derelict. The whole village feels as deserted as it did when I was young and I strain to see in through a thick windowpane, envisioning curtains of cobwebs and upset tables, abandoned ashtrays brimming with dust.

Instead I see a bright and breezy looking room, decorated in bland lilac and blond pine, with a chalkboard running above a long, glass bar, offering a whole world of wine and Speciality Beers. I turn gratefully to the door, only to find it padlocked closed.

The lock's chain is beaded with old rain. In the air, the drops are finer, a frail skin, skimming my own. The chain is icy in my hand. I tug at it hard, twice, and then hear my own frustrated groan rise irrepressibly behind my teeth.

"Are you right there, Chick?"

The voice is deep and heavily accented, and so close that I literally jump. I bob, ridiculously, up on to my toes and collide with my case as I swing round.

The man hovering behind me is about my age, perhaps a little older, and around the same height as me too, at least, while I'm in heels. He's dressed in jeans and a short-sleeved shirt and there's a gingery sheen to his collar-length hair. His skin looks sun-worn, although it isn't reddened or ruddy, but evenly browned, *baked-*looking. In fact, there is something oddly, but reassuringly doughy in the solidity of his general shape. Although as his gaze drops from my face to my shoulders, and then inevitably lower, I see that his assessing eyes, in contrast, are a piercing green.

As cool and sharp as loch water.

The padlock knocks shamefully, too loudly, on the bolted door. The man dips his head.

"Always shut on a Monday," he explains. And then he clears his throat, repeats his question. "Are you? All right?"

I unearth my smile. I nod. Once again, I think of that girl, that young mother, in the station at the start of this mad journey, and of the hotel receptionist. All these anxious strangers... Except there was Tim of course too, whose interest offered a whole different kind of comfort, and now my grin aches as I wonder about this new man's motives.

189

"I've come a long way," I explain, a little curtly. "I haven't eaten, that's all. And I need to eat," I shift. Swallow back a mouthful of warm saliva. "In my condition."

To eat. For a second, my selfishness threatens to overwhelm me, but the man's eyes dart once more down to my hips, and then skip back up, over my breasts.

"Early days?" he says, and I nod. He continues to smile though; that kindness remains.

"Are you staying in the village?" he asks.

I glance with him, towards the houses. Of course there are people here still, and probably more tourists than ever. I think of that glimmering bar and wonder if that strange little shop has survived. If it's still hiding here, and then for several absurd, appalling seconds, I find myself focusing on the memory of Kyle's pilfered cider, recalling that plastic bottle far more vividly than anything else.

Almost defeated by a fresh wave of self-disgust, I gabble together a reply, and I'm actually blushing as I falter.

"No, no, I'm not staying here. I've only just arrived. This minute, almost. I walked up from the station. I've been travelling since yesterday. I was staying in Edinburgh – well, for last night. Not for the Festival though. I'm here for the loch. For the loch house – do you know it? I don't know if you know it? Or whether it's even still here. It's a little way away, actually. A car journey, I think. I need a cab. Maybe a bus? I don't drive myself. I've never driven... But is there something, a restaurant maybe, around here, that might be open? I'm – I'm starving."

The man doesn't interrupt or try to hurry me along. While I ramble, his green gaze laps at my flapping mouth. But I don't detect any judgement about him, just a curious blankness. At last, he nods. His smile twitches.

"Wait here," he murmurs, and as he turns on his heel and starts walking, he throws more words, gruffly, softly, back over his shoulder.

"It's your lucky day," I think he says.

As I watch him wander off, the whole village (the pale houses and the trees, the church with its narrow, shadowed windows) shimmers. The effect is dreamlike, as if the picture-postcard scene has been contorted by a wave of heat, although the day remains overcast, weighted. I wonder if my hormones are to blame, or my empty stomach, or my thirst. But I don't feel truly dizzy or nauseous; it's probably simply the quivering haze of rain. As he recedes, the man blurs too, briefly

190

separating into watercolour blotches of brown and amber, a wash of denim-blue.

And suspended there, passively waiting for him to come back to me, I wonder afresh whether I should trust him. But on this journey, ordinary rules of safety and common sense no longer apply. *And it's me*, I think, *who's stranger*.

The bad pun brings a thin laughter to the thick of my throat, but it's the idea that this very normal, gingerbread-type man might be dangerous in any way that propels the giggles from my lips. How stupid it would be to have come all this way only to be randomly murdered by some villager serial killer – and while I'm fully aware that this idea isn't remotely funny, I find myself suddenly doubled over, snorting. A certain layer of tension falls away and by the time I've managed to pull myself together, hastily swiping at my eyes and pushing flat my hair, the shaky, dream-like houses have stabilised once more.

When the man returns, he arrives not by foot, but behind the wheel of a cab. The car is a hulking, battered blue range rover. It seems to chug and rev its way out of nowhere, although it must have been parked simply further down the road, between the houses. Mud scrolls between its giant wheels, while the proud declaration 'F & L CABS' has been painstakingly hand-painted in hot-pink letters across the bonnet. After quaking to a halt, the man reaches across the passenger seat and swings open a heavy, rust-specked door.

"In you get," he says and obediently, if somewhat awkwardly, I lift my case and clamber in.

The car's interior smells musty, the trapped air textured with dense scents. Damp boots and old biscuits. There's more than enough room for me to manoeuvre, yet I still manage to knock the top of my head on the rear-view mirror and then have to withdraw carefully, having snagged my hair on the collection of decorations that have been strung there. I glance over these ornaments as I slide cautiously into the passenger seat. A swinging St Christopher, a rabbit's paw.

Reaching for my belt, I'm aware of crumbs grinding beneath me and I notice more yellow fragments, dropped crisps, in the foot-well between my shoes and wedged-in case. There are several curled dead leaves down there too and a couple of coloured pencils, orange and mauve. I think how different this cab is from the one in which I left my London flat, with its resentful seat-covers, its driver's disdain.

My new driver goes on smiling his easy smile.

"Sorry about the mess," he says and shrugs resignedly. "Kids," he explains, and his grin grows as he lifts his wide hips, reaching into his jeans pocket for his wallet. He flips it open, revealing a picture.

"Here they are," he says. "The Gruesome Twosome."

I peer closer, readying myself to make the appropriate appreciative noises – except then my breath catches. My hands grow heavy on my lap.

Behind that smeared plastic, a thin blond girl lifts a baby towards the camera. She's wielding the infant, her baby brother, as if he's a fairground prize, some trophy. *A giant, garish doll*. She's beaming proudly, although she seems so overwhelmed, dwarfed, by the younger child. She's elfin-featured, her wrists tiny; they don't appear capable of supporting such a weight. It's as if she's possessed of some kind of fairy-strength – an idea reinforced by her shining eyes, which are the same haunting green as her father's.

The baby, in comparison, looks all too human. Solid and fleshy, he's sucking on something, a rusk, or some kind of teething toy. His eyes slitted in earnest greed above enormous rosy cheeks.

An icy wave creeps over me. The skin on my shoulders tightens, but I do my best to suppress the shudder, telling myself firmly that there is no way that these are the same kids who found me on my Edinburgh train. *And that half-glimpse beside the tracks...* Their similar appearance must be coincidental, my tired mind playing tricks again. But despite my self-assurances, the shiver passes right through me and leaves a small, pooled draught low down, in my belly.

And I'm suddenly filled with longing. I don't want to be alone doing this, I realise. *I shouldn't be alone.*

Richard. All over again, I'm wanting Richard.

Although he'd never understand. Although he doesn't want me.

The pang is overwhelming.

I want his warm, broad chest and his hands and his scent of musk-and-cotton. I want his voice too, his laughter – and without thinking it through any further, careless of the time and our supposed rules, I lean over my case and start clawing through the side-pocket. I grab my mobile and dial.

"Hey," the driver says. "Hey there."

I turn to him, blinking, as the phone begins to bleat against my ear. I'd forgotten him, almost.

"I'm sorry," I tell him. "I ..."

But he's already shrugging again, dismissing my apologies; he's truly a good man. *A considerate man*, I think, even before I see that he's set down his wallet and is holding out a cellophaned wad of sandwiches. He waves them towards me, doorsteps of white bread, lined with ham.

"You can have these, if you want," he says. "The Mrs always makes them in case I get caught out somewhere. I get stuck at the airport sometimes. Waiting."

His voice is quick and quiet, no doubt lowered in deference to the phone clamped so rudely to my head. I feel abruptly shy. His green eyes tug at me.

"Go on," he urges.

The sandwiches float between us. They're perspiring in patches through the plastic and although the idea of eating them is repellent, I take them. I can't think what else to do. His kindness threatens to unravel me. For an instant, the cold inside me vanishes. I'm flushed with warmth, and almost with tears.

"Thank you," I say. "I'll have them in a bit."

"Good," he murmurs. "It's important. You're eating for two now, remember."

And then, as if it's a completely natural gesture, he reaches out and touches my stomach. And I don't gasp or flinch. In my left hand, I'm holding his sandwiches and my mobile's grasped tight inside my right, still ringing a world away, but I don't set anything down in order to push him aside; I don't even shift. I simply stare at his stubby fingers spread-eagled on my belly, though all the while, I'm also aware of his children. His wallet is right there, lying open on the dashboard. And they're watching him touch me. My passive response.

But he doesn't mean any harm; I'm sure that he doesn't, and as unusual as this gesture might appear, particularly coming from a man, a stranger, I realise that what he's offering me is a kind of comfort. Recognition. *He's acknowledging my baby.*

And I sit very still beneath his fingers as a second, deeper warmth takes hold of me. I'm grateful. Almost at peace.

"So – out to the loch then?" the man says.

He returns his hand to the wheel, but I can't look back at him, not directly, not yet. I feel too fragile. I keep my lids lowered. My whole face feels taut with the effort of keeping back the tears, of keeping everything in.

Her red hands. That crack –

It's all still there, I'm brimming. I just about manage to nod.

193

The catch of the engine is halting, distracting, and it takes several seconds for me to realise that the distant sound of ringing has stopped. That my call has been answered –

"Hello? Hello?"

It's a small, bright voice. A little girl's voice.

"Who is this?" she says, before I cut her off –

"Is anybody there?"

Beneath the fragmenting sky, the loch looked larger than ever and deathly cold. Its surface was a scratched and polished grey, hard and unforgiving. I knew it didn't want me coming any closer, but I kept going. Kyle waited, standing thigh-deep amidst that dense expanse as if he was trapped. He clung grimly to his rowing boat with one spindly arm. Wood and flesh reeled together.

I couldn't reach him fast enough, although my feet were a blur beneath me and now and then, I leapt – I almost flew – across the larger rocks and shivering heather. Again and again, I landed heavily, gracelessly, scuffing up puffing clouds of earth and tiny seeds. I left a trail of trampled wildflowers in my wake, their thin necks bent, their faces wet and broken.

I was clumsy and blundering, but I didn't worry that I'd slip or turn my ankle, that the rocks would jump up, like teeth, to close around me if I fell. I couldn't permit such doubts to make me stumble. I remained single-minded, wholly focused on Kyle's boat. I ran without thinking any further than the ground tumbling beneath me, and the loch, ahead. Perhaps I was already beginning to slip beyond thoughts, beyond everything. And I trusted my body, back then. I held on tight.

It wasn't until I reached the chalky curve of the beach that the idea of Marie struck me with such force that I had to stop. For a moment, everything faded beside the black shine of her eyes. Those stigmata hands. It took a huge effort of will to bring myself back.

The shattered stones returned first, in luminous fragments. I blinked past them and out across the choppy waves to the fragile disc of Kyle's face, and then up, helplessly, to where the clouds were rolling in, a ghost-ocean building overhead.

But Kyle was calling, although the wind kept whipping his words away so that I caught only the small and fraying tail-end of his voice. And it was such a sad, torn sound – except then it struck me he might be crying out a warning.

I swung around, scattering pebbles, fully expecting to find Marie coming after me. I pictured her, head hooded or bowed against the elements, her arms outstretched. Almost, I heard *her* voice:

"*Libby, come back!*"

But there was only the wind whining as it shuddered through the grass and heather. Nothing but scrub and shining stones. That sky, brooding closer. And of course, there was the loch house too. Most of all, there was the loch house.

With its pale walls and square windows and neat roof, it looked as unreal as when I'd first set eyes on it. *A storybook house*, only the flowerbeds were ashen now, the rosebushes had withered. It looked stripped back, laid bare, and there was something of the loch's iciness about it too.

That same secretive hostility, that waiting –

But maybe that was just an effect of the light, or the lack of light, the glare and press of those gathering clouds? While the walls went on radiating their sallow glow, the darkness at the house's windows appeared swollen, solid, and the doorway was the blackest thing of all.

A punctured hole in the weathered stone. A gaping mouth, where in my panic, I'd left the door wide open. I couldn't see anything of the hall inside. I couldn't see Marie, but as I stood there, momentarily mesmerised, I glimpsed, or thought I glimpsed, a movement there. I might have imagined it, a drawn-out shifting, an unravelling. The slow tongue-flick of a single shadow uncurling from the rest.

Real or not, it was enough for me. I darted between the rocks. I plunged into the loch. The shock of the water helped. The cold shot right through me, bursting in my head like snow, a scouring blizzard, almost thick enough to block out those nightmare images –

Of Marie reaching, Marie falling.

That smell too, of a butcher's shop, a chopping block –

Seized by a wave of revulsion, I realised that her stink was clinging to me still. I pushed onwards, into the darker waves, that cutting cold. The water surged against my calves and I welcomed the growing numbness in my legs at first, that general loss of sensation. But when the loch covered my knees, I became terrified, as I hadn't been before, that I would fall as Marie had fallen. That I'd let go –

But then Kyle was there, *right there, beside me.* He'd wrestled his boat over. And he would help us; he would save us, I was sure of it, although his face was whiter than ever, as pale as pressed linen, while his mouth looked huge and bruised.

"What the fuck?" he said, and then, although he was standing so close to me now that the wind couldn't interfere, he said those words again, practically straightaway, and this time his voice was louder. Straining.

"Liberty – *what the fuck?*"

196

He stared at my grasping hands as if it were only my fingers that were covered in blood, but I shook my head. There was no way I could explain. I hardly understood myself what had happened, *what was still happening* –

"We have to get out of here," I blurted and he nodded, as if understanding anyway.

"Need help," he muttered, and then grabbed my elbow and together, with much grunting and manoeuvring, we finally managed to heave ourselves into the boat. I fell in first, and lay for a moment, blinking up at the sky.

Although engorged, the clouds moved endlessly. The wind dragged them, raked at them. A frail, white sunlight seeped through in vein-like fissures. I found myself seeking out and hanging on to those glacial threads, but the fear remained. *I hadn't done enough.*

And while Kyle had stared at them, I couldn't even glance down at my own hands, at my sticky fingers. *Everything* was lost.

I forced myself to sit upright when Kyle came tumbling into the boat beside me, but I couldn't take an oar from him. I couldn't help. As he began to row, he stared doggedly past me, back towards the loch house. I didn't need to turn to see what he was seeing – that black doorway, the windows' bulging dark. I had no idea what he imagined I might have left behind.

But while his face retained a glazed expression, as un-giving as a mask, Kyle's young, rangy body worked powerfully, rhythmically. Despite the waves, there was nothing unwieldy about his movements; the oars' sweep and rise was strong and measured. I'd never seen him row with such confidence. The flimsy boat rose and plummeted, moving rapidly away from the shore, away from the loch house, as if everything, the whole churning universe, was being pulled helplessly along by the same dim hooks and ropes.

We seemed to reach the deepest part of the loch in barely any time at all. The pines on the far shore merged into a rippling blue block, while the islands materialized ahead. The water tugged and smacked at the boat's shallow sides, showering us with spray and creamy froth. My stomach jolted with each sickening bump, and I realised that I was overflowing too, my face ragged with tears.

I had no idea how long I'd been weeping for. I bowed my head over my cradling hands. I wondered if I'd ever stop.

But then Kyle gasped and for the first time since we'd set out, he ceased rowing. One oar hit the wood with a hollow clang. I looked up to find him sitting forward, craning past me.

"Your stepmother," he said at last, and beside the sloshing water, even with a brief dip in the wind, his voice was surprisingly quiet. "At least, I think it's your stepmother... Marie?"

Louder than the loch, my heartbeat filled me. I couldn't turn around. I couldn't follow his gaze. Once more, I pictured Marie falling, her expression contorting –

"She's in trouble," Kyle said, and then before I knew what I was doing, I had twisted around; I was straining to see. But because I was expecting to catch the rough shape of her on land (silhouetted just outside the loch house maybe, dragging herself down the crumbling path, or perhaps hovering, watching, from the beach), I couldn't see her. I started to wonder if Kyle had imagined her, or seen her ghost – except that then I found her.

She was in the water.

And she wasn't standing in the shallows either. She was about halfway between our boat and the shore she'd left behind. Her head looked seal-like from this distance, her hair glued to her skull. But although she appeared to be struggling now – raising one arm as if grasping for the sky and then rapidly bobbing under, vanishing altogether before re-emerging in an eruption of froth, I couldn't begin to guess how ferociously driven she must have been to have swum so far so fast.

It didn't seem possible. The loch was so rough today, and so very cold, and Marie must have been so weak. Perhaps I'd been right and this swimmer wasn't my stepmother at all, but some spirit? A part of the loch house itself, pouring vengefully after us.

From another place, another world, I heard my own voice, small and rasping.

"Keep going, Kyle," I begged. "Please keep going. *Row.*"

But with a single, powerful heave, Kyle drew both oars out of the water and threw them awkwardly onto the boards. The whole boat clattered with the impact, but undeterred, Kyle clambered to his feet. We rocked with more violence as he straightened, but instead of crouching back down, he braced his boots against the wood.

"What are you doing?"

I wanted to scream at him, but my words were barely audible over the strain of the boards, the swilling water.

"I think," Kyle began. He caught his bottom lip beneath his teeth.

"I think," he said, "that she's drowning."

198

Across the loch, but not far enough for me, I watched as a wave covered Marie's sleek head, sealing her within. I studied the metallic surface, wondering if she'd make it back up this time.

I didn't want her drowned; I didn't want her dead – I was almost sure of that, and yet at the same time, I prayed that she'd somehow vanish. I wanted her to stop or be stopped; with all my being, I longed for that.

Go back to the loch house. Go back. Go back.

Kyle's shadow passed over me and I looked up in time to glimpse the anaemic gleam of his narrow chest. He'd already yanked off his T-shirt and without even pausing to glance back at me, he took one step, out of the boat.

He vanished and the boat tipped so extremely that I came nearly face-to-face with my own twisted reflection.

"Kyle!" I cried. "*Please.*"

Further out, there was still no sign of Marie, but Kyle broke rapidly through the foil surface, hardly a foot away. He shook his head like a dog, lighting the air with whirling droplets. The skin on his throat and collarbone blazed.

"She needs help," he panted. He clung to the wood between us while he scanned the loch. I bowed over the side, as far as I dared.

"You can't," I said. "You don't understand. There are secrets – she isn't *right*."

I was babbling, pleading, becoming confused. I remembered my stolen newspaper, that ripped-out article. "There was a report," I gabbled. I wrapped myself tighter. "She might have killed my parents. She hates me. She *truly* hates me. She'll want me dead…"

But Kyle wasn't listening. He'd seen her. Marie was back, and she was closer; I had to do something to prevent Kyle from swimming out to her.

With some difficulty, I lifted one arm. For a moment, my slick fingers brushed his bony shoulder, and then his throat. His flesh felt clammy, but he was beating, quivering, with life. His skin glittered.

"Please, Kyle," I said. "Don't go to her. Don't go. What about us?"

He finally turned. He stared at my right arm, still clasped protectively across my chest, and his eyes contained their own damp sparkle. Soft with melting light.

"There's no helping you," he said.

Then he slipped away. He plunged out, half-crawling, half-doggy-paddling, towards Marie.

And I think I knew then that he wouldn't make it, as Marie wouldn't make it.

Yet I didn't pick up the oars. I didn't go after them. But how could I? *It wasn't my fault –*

My hands were full.

I turned away from Kyle to what I carried, and when the clouds finally broke open, the icy rain found me huddled over, although at first, I hardly felt it. As I was scarcely aware of the heaving loch, or of the loch house.

There was only the weight that I'd carried all that way, the love I had stolen –

Only you, inside my arms.

A tiny, silent baby. My half-brother, born too soon.

"Stop." I say. "That's far enough."

"Just stop the car. Right here. Right now. *Please stop.*"

Despite my urgency, the driver does not pull over. He simply looks at me and his green eyes have paled, capturing some of the vast blankness of the sky through my window. Now that the drizzle has petered out, a dome of cloud surrounds us. A great glass jar of smoke.

At last, he nods, and yet for several seconds, he goes on driving, taking me back.

"Please," I try again. "*Please.* Stop the car."

I'd glimpsed the loch house as soon as the road began to dip, and now I can't stop seeing it. I strain against my seatbelt, squinting through the leftover rain sheening the windscreen. Less than a mile away, those white walls flutter between the smudged green of damp fields and trees, the bluish rocks. I think of flags, of surrendering. I brace myself as the car slows at last and before my driver's cut the engine, I've swung the door open. I leap out – only to find that once more, the house has vanished.

As if deliberately, we're parked in a place where the road twists and begins to climb and the building is obscured once more within the protective folds of the land. If I walked back ten paces I'd see it still, but I don't walk back. There is the loch to deal with first, and the breeze, which is exactly as I remember, flavoured with pine needles and mulch, although mostly it tastes of the water. Of tangled weeds and winter stones.

The loch has accompanied us for much of the drive. Through my wound-tight window, it shimmered in pockets between the rippling leaves and then with an increasing frequency, broke cover, managing to float above the highest branches as well as through them, pressing up against that hanging sky. I gaze out at it now, following a gap in the trees. It's as huge and cold as I knew it would be, as patiently waiting.

"Steady, there, Chick."

I turn in a daze to find my driver behind me. I had no idea that he'd climbed out of the car, and there is his soft hand again too, but on my elbow now, cupping my arm.

He probably wants his fare, I think, and although it's madness, I almost laugh again to see him standing there, looking so red-faced and human. Even his searching eyes have lost their otherworldly veneer and his ordinariness jars. It's as if he's yet more debris from my dreams, another slippery illusion.

"You can go now," I tell him. "I don't need you."

He has my case beside him and I bend over it in an absurdly business-like manner, searching for my purse. But within the fabric pocket, I fumble, my fingers stiff and numb.

"But there's nothing here," he says.

I unearth a crumpled ten-pound note; I hold it out.

"I'm going to walk the rest," I explain. "It isn't far."

I point towards the top of the hill, but since the loch house is back in hiding, there's only more blemished tarmac to see, and a few loose stones. A little further on, barbed wire binds a surge of trees. A single crow cries out from them, as if to emphasise the emptiness.

"It *is* there. It's not far... Just around the corner," I insist, as if we're dealing with the city, with blocks and streets. "The loch house," I remind him.

"Oh," he murmurs. "The Ghost House, you mean."

Something hardens at the back of my throat. An icy pebble.

"What did you say?"

He blinks and I think he's about to launch into an explanation. Some long-winded tourist speech, repeating stories, as Marie did on our way here, so long ago.

"Sightings of shadowy figures and sudden lights. Strange noises in the night ..."

Instead, he glances down at his shoes, a pair of soiled trainers. He shakes his head and mumbles "nothing" as if he's a child and I wonder if I misheard, if I'm making things up again. I push my money into his round, brown fist and snatch at my suitcase handle. I can't cope with his kindness any longer. I walk away.

"You'll be all right?" he calls after me. "You've got keys? Or is there someone waiting? Someone expecting you?"

I nod, but I don't turn to see whether he's caught this gesture. I concentrate on moving, on the scuff of my shoes and my whirring case. I keep going, only glancing back once I've caught the growl of his engine. Over my shoulder, I watch the cab's mud-caked tyres grind into the road. The whole vehicle appears to rock as it swerves away, but I don't allow myself to stop walking until it has picked up speed and skittering stones. Until it has taken the bend beneath a weighted evergreen, and then disappeared completely.

As I stand there, panting into the quiet, the sun breaks unexpectedly through the cloud cast, making something lovely, briefly, of the deserted road. And alongside the brilliance, I feel the tug of the loch just as I used to. Hardly thinking, I turn and then involuntarily lift one cold hand to my mouth. The grey surface burns silver beneath the gold, brought suddenly to life and I feel the flush of a new heat as I stare. I want to close my watering eyes, but I don't; I can't. I can't drag my gaze away. I am alone now, and the loch is way too full of beauty. So full, it's painful.

Although of course it remains hard, practically impossible, to believe that this is the very same body of water that stole over us that night. Almost as difficult to comprehend as the truth that I began it, with that first deplorable act of theft.

It was my mother who guided me.

This is what I believed, at the time. Or what I told myself, at least. While the last of the night gave way at the window and the bath dripped pink, my mother returned to me. Together, we pushed through the steam to where Marie had crumpled. We went to her, hand-in-hand.

It was true that Marie was naked when we found her. She was curled on her side, her head propped awkwardly against the cold toilet. She looked huge. Beached. She wasn't conscious, not at first. Her skin was covered in a fine, glistening dew, but beneath this, her flesh was sack-like and discoloured. She looked as if she'd been beaten to that tiled floor. Her clothes lay bunched nearby in their own separate gauzy heap. I imagined her ripping them away in her distress.

As I took a step closer, I felt my mother's eyes through mine. I felt her wonder – she wouldn't have been frightened the way I was, and so I held on to her more tightly. I stared at Marie's engorged breasts, fascinated by her brown, stretched nipples and the heavy rise and fall of her unconscious breathing, the heave and shudder within that flesh. But my mother wanted more.

Our gaze searched on, to Marie's large, loose hands, lolling open at her side. And then to the doll that lay between them, just out of reach.

I gasped, pushed forward. I sank down to my knees.

The baby was tiny, and much darker than I'd ever have imagined, his fine, new skin suffused with the fine, fresh blood inside him. Marie, it seemed, had begun to wrap him clumsily in a towel, perhaps seconds before she passed out, and I was awestruck by how delicate he appeared beside the towel's thick folds. His little mauve feet lay among them as lightly as clumped leaves; his toes were the tiniest of berries. His curled limbs looked so full and soft that at first I was frightened to touch him. I was scared that he'd burst, or fragment. That I might break him.

But my mother was with me. *Guiding me.*

For a moment, the bathroom's soiled odour dissolved beneath her perfume. Light musk and lemons... And the whole time, her smooth, cool fingers remained entwined with mine. I watched my hands reach out.

And I gathered that tiny body into my awkward arms. Carefully, I repositioned him and once we were settled, I allowed my gaze to unfold shyly across my newborn brother's face.

Such gentle curves, such exquisite detail, I could never have guessed that he'd be so beautiful. It didn't seem possible, especially born as he was, months early. Marie had managed to wipe most of her muck away, although here and there, his skin remained streaked and floured, but even that made no difference. He was perfect. I stroked the towel back from his forehead to study him better. I traced the fullness of his lips, the flow of chin and cheek and nose.

He didn't look back at me. His eyes were closed. But that didn't matter either. Like her scent, my mother's cool, clean love cut through the heat and steam, and she surrounded us. She made us right.

Because of course my mother would have understood my emptiness. No one knew me better. She understood that this was more than just wanting. After all that I had been stripped of, this was what I deserved.

And besides wasn't this child, my father's child, also mine too, in a way? Wasn't he a part of me? I held him closer, sharing my warmth.

When finally I glanced back, towards Marie, I was enveloped by a wave of revulsion. She hadn't stirred. Her naked body remained slumped beside us, *right there, beside us*, baggy and lumpen – and leaking too, I realised.

Recoiling, I understood how truly torn apart she'd been. She was gashed right open. There was blood coming out of her. A long pool spread out from the back of her, from beneath her thighs. And blinking through the steam, I noticed several other smaller splashes on the tiles, red pathways in the grouting. The more I looked, the more blood there was. A pair of scissors lay open in its own crimson puddle. The scissors were the orange-plastic-handled pair from the kitchen. I'd used them myself to cut out different shapes. Absentmindedly creating paper snowflakes. A whole quivering string of tiny girls.

It took me a moment to understand why the scissors were there, that Marie must have used them to cut the cord. Remembering the fact of a cord, a fresh surge of nausea wobbled over me. It all seemed so animal-like, so inhuman. *Monstrous.*

I dipped my head protectively. I brushed my lips against my brother's cheek.

And Marie opened her black eyes to me.

"Libby?" she said.

Her voice rasped. I rose to my feet and then took a step away from her. I held the baby against my chest so that his forehead nestled into the hollow of my throat. His skin against my skin.

I thought about finding the pine martin. About how carefully I'd carried him back to the house, stepping nimbly over nettles and heather and jagged, waiting rocks. And then I thought of him in his basket, in the kitchen, lying there dead beneath Marie's hands.

My hatred lifted between us. Even in that moment, it remained harder than my stepmothers; it was cold and metallic and utterly ungiving.

"It's all your fault," I told her.

Through the steam, her black eyes flickered. Her slack mouth opened further and her pink tongue touched her lips, but she hardly seemed to have heard. She was too busy trying to focus, gazing into my arms. Straight into the heart of me.

At her stolen son.

"Libby, *please.*"

Her voice was as broken as the rest of her; it was pathetic, *wheedling.* And it was too late by then anyway. Far too late. We were already backing away from her. I was already preparing to run.

*　　　*　　　*

But despite what I'd stolen, I remained as alone as Marie. More alone even.

This was the truth that finally hit me when I was out on Kyle's boat, when the waves grew so angry that I was forced to look away from my beautiful brother. When, dazed, I turned at last to that falling sky, the blistered water.

I hadn't been able to see far. With the thickening storm, the loch rose to meet the hissing rain, forming a glimmering cage – and yet I could see enough to know that Marie was gone, that we'd escaped her. But that Kyle had been taken from me too.

The boat had rocked with more violence and I'd turned hastily back to the baby. I cowered over him, attempting to shelter him, but I couldn't even keep him dry. Water dripped from my hair and sodden shoulders and with the damp cuff of my sleeve I wiped his face from chin to forehead. Again and again, I pushed the rain from his sticky lids and his parted lips and all the while, I tried not to think about how light he felt against me, how husk-like, or about the clotted black inside his mouth.

But I couldn't stroke away his shiny pallor any more than I could dismiss the fear that I had no one.

Because out there, on the loch, even my mother had left me. I could no longer sense her beside me, although more than ever, I wanted her. *I needed her*, with all my heart and soul.

As the boat reeled, I cried out, but the only response was the spit and roar of rain and waves. The whole world had turned to wind and water, and there was nothing else.

And it struck me then that I might have been wrong about her, as I was wrong about my newborn brother. My mother wasn't with me; she wasn't even waiting. Perhaps she'd never been there, and Marie's baby –

Marie's baby was cold against my hands.

Maybe that was why when the boat finally rose too steeply – when it teetered and then flipped right over, pushing me under – I made no attempt to fight the loch, but let it come. I let it enter me. And it was surprisingly simple. A moment of piercing ice when even my ragged gasps vanished, and then just darkness. A black hood, which slipped so easily over my head that I didn't even try to struggle. I opened my arms. And I let go.

I took Marie's baby, and then I lost him.

When I was found, I was alone.

Later, I was told that the fisherman who discovered me had been out on one of the islands, but decided to head home at the first sign of a let-up in the storm. He'd spotted Kyle's boat first, capsized, but unbroken, still floating – as I was, not far away. Initially, the fisherman had thought me dead, but I was only unconscious. Pushed and thrown by that heaving water, I must have resurfaced at some point, only to smack my head on the upturned wood. I was drifting on my back when he saw me.

Lucky, some people said.

It's one of my few memories from that time in the hospital, in the weeks afterwards. Drugged and drifting, circling gradually towards consciousness, I overheard the nurses talking.

"A lucky girl," they said.

"A miracle," they said.

They were unaware I might be waking. They were chatting, sharing a newspaper, during their rounds. Marie and Kyle had only just been discovered. Almost a month had passed before they'd finally washed up, practically together, along a stretch of shore three miles from where I'd been found.

"Barely identifiable," one nurse read.

And in my half-dreaming state, I saw them.

I saw their battered, bloated bodies. Limbs knotted with old netting. Torsos stripped and strangely bloodless beneath streaks of weed and mud. And Marie's eyes –

So clearly I saw her eyes, and they weren't closed as a corpse's eyes should be, but rinsed wide-open, frozen open in a look of dazzling sadness. There was no darkness, no hatred to them anymore; instead, they gleamed. Her longing, fish-scale bright.

But as I floated towards waking, beneath the rise and fall of the nurses' murmurs, it wasn't Marie, or even Kyle I truly mourned. When I finally managed to lift my heavy lashes, what throbbed into focus first, were my hands. My own young hands, looking so very small and pink and harmless against the sheet.

208

For a long time, I couldn't do anything but stare at them. I couldn't make them move. I could only gaze, on and on, at my clean, trimmed nails and my open palms. While their emptiness flooded through me.

Decades on, sitting with Richard in another hospital, that exact cold emptiness had returned.

While the doctor talked and Richard's fingers loosened around mine, my awareness of the vacuum within me had grown increasingly acute. That's why I'd found myself so angry, and then struggling for breath. Struggling to remember how to breathe around the edges of that gap.

All that time, I was still twelve years old, inside. Like Marie, I was still longing.

For a moment, the truth had threatened to rise like a rush of silver bubbles against the dark, like the distraction of static on a blank, blank screen. I'd hurried to suppress it then, but of course it couldn't be discarded. The truth remains.

As you have remained with me, inside me.
As if I'd never let you go.

I turn over this new knowledge as I stand on that quiet road, gazing out past trees and fields, out towards the shimmering water.

The very water that filled you, that claimed you. That keeps you, still.

I have no idea how long I've been there, staring. But when the clouds begin to knit together once more and the sunlight fades, I move on before the loch's shadows can rise and spread. And as I walk, I allow one hand to rest deliberately across my stomach. There's no longer any hesitation about my touch. I press the cotton gently, reaching towards my softest flesh.

And – *please* I think, as Marie once begged me.

Please, this time, despite what I deserve.

Despite the fact that I took your baby, and that I lost him.

Despite the way I've contorted the memory, burying it in wrappings and padding, stripping your child from you completely in my dreams as if he'd never existed, when in fact, it has always been my body that has been empty.

Please let this pregnancy be real, I think.

Let it be real, at last.

A thin wind flutters through the heather. I glimpse the place where the road vanishes at the top of the peak, and it comes back to me in snippets, that first time I was possessed, when I was only seventeen, at boarding school. I remember how my periods stopped and my stomach swelled. My breasts even became larger and tender, and I threw up. It was insanity from the start. Nobody believed me when I protested my virginity – particularly when alongside those protestations, I nonetheless maintained an absolute faith in that unborn child, so much so that when the doctors finally uncovered the truth of it, the trick of it, it was I who called them liars. I was utterly bewildered, and as innocent as I could be.

That year my life was turned inside out, but I was hastily propelled away from it, pushed onwards, ever on. The school never officially expelled me, but simply rushed me early through exams, keeping me separate from the other girls, as if I might be in some way contagious. And before I knew it, I'd been given a different kind of doctor, my very own Dr Gilchrist, and then there was my place at drama school. It was all so easily arranged, as I had wished.

Blinking back tears, I focus on my cool palm, pressed against my stomach. Of course I'm more than aware that I should know better by now, and yet I go on seeking out that secret stirring, even as I reach the road's summit and the land unfolds in a dizzying rush –

And it's all still there; *it's just the same.* The thick brush of the fields and the curving drive. The stunning pallor of the beach, and of the loch house.

The loch house remains as neat as a little kid's drawing, with its red front door and shining windows *(though not like any drawing I'd have ever made...).* And beside everything I've misremembered, I feel a quiet shock at how well I've recalled this building. It's clear, even to me, how deeply and preciously I've hoarded it, wrapping it in more careful layers, like a picture made of glass.

I scan the scraggy grass and splintered rocks. Somewhere down there, I know there is a cattle-grid smothered in dead leaves, and beneath the overgrown flowerbeds, a clumsy, unmarked grave...

But the loch house waits, brighter and darker than anything else. I can feel its waiting, although it's patient, perhaps even as patient as the ancient loch. I picture the spaces behind its glowing walls. A cluttered kitchen, a mildewed bathroom. Rooms muffled with dust and memories, creaking softly through countless days.

I wipe my eyes. I'm still too frail and human to hold the house's gaze for long. I drop my case. I give it up so that I can wrap both hands now, around my stomach.

I took Marie's baby.
I lost Marie's baby.

Surely, there can be no end to the punishment for such a crime, and yet –

I have to keep praying that finally, it might be over. After all, I've come back; I'm facing the past. I'm accepting my part in it.

And I hope with every fibre that that will be enough to break the loch house's spell. That at last, I'll be able to hold on tight enough for long enough, and instead of my body being haunted, this time my pregnancy will be true. *This baby will be real.*

Please, I think, although I have no right to.

Please. *No more ghosts inside.*

211

And now I find myself striding, ever faster, down the cratered drive towards the loch house, towards the faintest, finest possibility of forgiveness. And as I start to run, the sun breaks through the clouds once more, although the light is softer now. The water glitters and the house's weather-beaten walls flicker with a delicate, smouldering gold. The sunlight urges me on so that I keep going even when my head starts pounding, even though I'm awkward and ungainly, clasping my body as I run. Cradling, treasuring, that nervous flesh.

And my heart actually lifts as I draw closer.

Pebbles skit and fly beneath my scudding feet and I realise that I'm excited in these final moments. The white walls loom and I can already smell the old, familiar scent of chilly stone; I picture the dark corners in the hall.

Of course Marie will be a part of those gathering shadows now. I imagine her watching for me along with those windows, along with the rest of them –

Exhilarated, I think I have understood, finally, why I needed to return.

And so I don't stop; I *can't* stop. Not even when that red front door swings open. Eager to know what my stepmother will determine, I push on. I rush over the step, into the house's darkness.

"Marie," I call. "I'm home."

Acknowledgements

For my Ghosts, I'd firstly like to thank Ian Collinson, for his ongoing encouragement and faith, for his insight and general loveliness.

Thank you to the tutors and students at Manchester Metropolitan University, who were there at the very beginning of this book and thank you Cove Park for offering space and reminding me about the beauty.

Thank you to everyone at Nottingham Writers' Studio too, for being so brilliant, especially the talented writers in my fiction group – Ni Smith, Marsali MacDonald, Giselle Leeb, Ian Douglas, Arthur Piper, Jane Kirtley, Jayne Pigford and Richard Madeley.

For their continuing support, I would also like to thank, among many other friends, and family, Catherine and Dad, and Dan, and Fred and Lola (of course!). Thank you as well to Caroline Smailes, for so much.

Mostly though, my deepest thanks continue to be for Nigel, who this book is dedicated to. A fine man and fabulous friend, an excellent writer and editor, who gave my words so much time and care, amidst everything else.

'The Lives of Ghosts' is Megan Taylor's third novel.

Her second, 'The Dawning' was also published by Weathervane in 2010 and was widely acclaimed in the press and on radio.

Megan's first novel 'How We Were Lost' was published by Flame Books in 2007 after placing second in the Yeovil Prize.

Megan lives and works in Nottingham. She is, of course, currently working on her fourth novel.

THE DAWNING

A dark and mysterious thriller set in the Peak District; the stunning second novel by Weathervane's

MEGAN TAYLOR

It is New Year's Eve, a time for fresh beginnings – but for each member of the fragmenting Haywood family, this night could mark the end.

Set against a backdrop of wintry beauty on the edge of a Peak District town, 'The Dawning' explores the danger that can arise, even at the heart of a family, over the course of one dark night.

Paperback ISBN 978 0 9562193 4 3
Also on Kindle.

'A beautifully written, tightly controlled and intricately constructed novel – extremely rich and evocative' - Nicholas Royle (author of 'Antwerp')

'Compelling, enthralling, ensnaring. Megan Taylor spins each character into life and then she makes us wait, breath held, as they unravel, as they twirl and twist before our eyes. This writing is fearless, is full of heart, is very very good.' -
Caroline Smailes ('In Search of Adam', 'Black Boxes' and 'Like Bees to Honey')

'a dizzy, poetic, brutal, page-turning novel about a family in trouble one New Year's Eve'-
Annie Clarkson, Bookmunch

'brilliantly accomplished' -
Shanta Everington, The View From Here

'a deliciously realistic atmosphere plus some clever plot devices' -
Nottingham Evening Post

'rich and stirring poetic prose' -
Anne Brooke, Vulpes Libris

'I was so riveted by this book that I read it in one sitting' -
Pam McIlroy, guide2nottingham

Lightning Source UK Ltd.
Milton Keynes UK
UKOW042159200313

207957UK00004B/380/P